Cruiser Tank Warfare

John Plant

Published by New Generation Publishing in 2014

First Edition

www.newgeneration-publishing.com

 New Generation Publishing

Dedicated to the memory of
the 13th/18th Royal Hussars

Contents

Introduction

At the start of the Second World War all the major armies, with the arguable exception of the German army, were mistaken in their basic expectations for tanks. The result of this was that armoured units were badly organised and, in most cases, their vehicles were badly designed.

During the course of the war these problems were largely overcome.

In the British army this mistaken process began around 1930 with the theoretical development of a form of armoured operations which will be termed 'Cruiser Tank Warfare'. With the pure wisdom of hindsight it can be seen that this vision was basically flawed, but at the time it steadily gained ground until the early desert campaigns seemed to confirm that it was true.

However actual experience of warfare in Europe forced changes on British armoured tactics, until the British armoured divisions were starting to take on a modern look. The war ended before this process could reach its conclusion, and British armoured divisions never developed their full potential. This represented a substantial wasted opportunity.

In general, over the years, the British Army has proceeded on commonsense lines and has not, as have some continental armies, been prone to fads created via the overheated imaginations of officers during peacetime. Its approach to tank warfare in the late 1930s was a case when this commonsense failed.

Chapter 1

TACTICAL IDEALS

The operations of conventional warfare can take an infinite number of forms, it is this fact that makes the course of conventional operations difficult to predict. However for the sake of analysis it can be seen that there are two extreme cases of types of conventional operations. These are ideals and cannot exist in reality, in the real world the form operations take is on a sliding scale between the two extremes.

One extreme can be termed 'Attrition Warfare', the other 'Mobile Warfare'. Neither of these expressions is really appropriate, but they have been adopted for want of anything better.

In Attrition Warfare, operations can be expected to be infantry-based and their aim will be the destruction by battle of the enemy's forces. The forces may move a great deal but the purpose of that movement is purely to gain advantages for the next battle. Attrition Warfare operations, being infantry-based, can be expected to be slow in coming to a decision. It is one of their characteristics that, with the arms involved, like will fight against like, that is infantry will fight infantry, tanks against tanks, and the same with artillery.

In Mobile Warfare, operations will usually be AFV-based, their aim will be to manoeuvre against an enemy's critical point, when a 'critical point' is normally defined as a geographic location the loss of which will be disastrous for the enemy's fighting capacity. Capturing this critical point will throw the enemy's forces off balance, and once off balance they can be assaulted in such a way as to destroy their coherence.

It is possible, if unlikely, that the enemy is so badly deployed, and so weak, that there is no need to attack a critical point but dislocation attacks on his troops can start immediately. In either case attacks should be directed as much as possible against the enemy's logistic and command systems. This should result in mass surrenders, and enemy units that keep fighting will become immobile and either fall apart, or wait to be surrounded. This state was to be termed 'Strategic Paralysis'.

Speed is naturally a characteristic of Mobile Warfare. Another is that similar arms will not fight against each other. Tanks will not oppose tanks, but engage soft targets, and artillery will not pursue counter-battery duels.

Of course Mobile Warfare in its pure, ideal state cannot exist. Some fighting will always be necessary and fighting, even on a small scale, is a matter of attrition. The more the enemy fights, the less vulnerable is the critical point, and the more operations will bog down. Also critical points tend not to be that vulnerable. If the enemy is expecting his command structure to be attacked then his troops will be fully briefed as to what procedures to follow if the command structure fails. Similarly units will stockpile ammunition and other supplies in case the logistic system is destroyed. Such factors will tend to force Attrition Warfare on the attacker. However, even making every allowance for 'real world' considerations it can be seen that there are two basic types of conventional operations.

It is but a small step from defining the two types of operations to defining the types of tanks best required to carry them out. Ideally there would be only one type capable of doing everything, but the resulting vehicle would be expensive and very probably only averagely good at what it did. Whereas vehicles designed specifically for one of the two types of operations may very well be cheaper and much better at their defined, and limited, role. Inevitably this kind of specialisation would be very tempting.

There was a further type of tank much seen before 1939, the light tank. This was not really a fighting vehicle and soon faded away. It will not be covered as a vehicle type, but will be occasionally mentioned in the text.

Basic thinking about the two different types of operations tanks may be involved in may be illustrated by a quote from the Field Service Regulations of 1935:

'Tanks are designed either to take part in mobile operations, for which speed and a wide circuit of action are essential at some sacrifice of armoured protection; or for close co-operation with infantry in the attack, for which armour is of more importance than speed or a wide circuit......Tanks of the former type are classified either as light or medium, are equipped with wireless for purposes of control and communication, and are organised into mixed and light tank battalions; those of the latter are called infantry tanks, and are organised into army tank battalions.'

The following study will consider the role of tanks in mobile warfare. Their role in attrition warfare may be mentioned, but only by way of comparison.

Chapter 2

Theory

During the later stages of the Great War a consideration of the two tactical ideals in the light of tactical opportunities created by the imminent introduction of a new tank resulted in a Tank Corps officer, Colonel (at the time) JFC Fuller producing a paper that was to have a long term effect on Tank Corps thinking.

This paper in its final form [1] was known as 'Plan 1919'. It is important to note that it was in no way a practical recommendation for operations to be carried out in 1919, the tanks would not be available, and the crews could not be trained, in time. It was more a futuristic view of warfare, its author called it a 'novelette'.

The essence of Plan 1919 was that fleets of medium tanks would, with no warning, burst through the German front line and attack their army and divisional HQs. They would be supported in this by the Royal Flying Corps. Once these HQs had been reduced to chaos an infantry assault, supported by heavy tanks, would be mounted on a wide front. The Germans, now without HQs, should find this hard to defend against. Once their units started to break up a pursuing force of tanks and lorry-borne infantry would be unleashed, and victory would be absolute. It can be seen that this plan involves three separate echelons of tanks. This would assume a material superiority so large that pretty-well any tactics must be victorious.

The crux of Fuller's thinking was that if the German command structure could be destroyed their fighting units would initially be paralysed, then they would disintegrate. In fact Colonel Fuller declared that the 'Strategic Paralysis' of the enemy was the real aim of operations not, as hitherto, his destruction. The idea of being able to fight the war without having to fight the enemy was very tempting.

The Strategic Paralysis concept was eagerly seized on by many soldiers looking for a way round the attrition of the western front, and it must be emphasised that there is nothing wrong with trying to destroy the enemy's command structure. In fact it is remarkable how few times it has been attempted by European armies before 1918. Attacking HQs could have had a very destructive effect in the Great War era when communications depended on land lines and dispatch riders, but after that as commanders came to rely more on radios so the importance of this kind of attack decreased. The long-term problem with Strategic Paralysis was that it seemed to be victory without fighting, and this would have an unfortunate effect of tank design. The Second World War was to show that the concept of attacking HQs was no panacea.

Following the Great War and the great, if inevitable, reduction of the British army the Royal Tank Corps was reduced to four battalions, which, though small was no smaller in proportion to the rest of the army than it was in 1918. Despite this reduction the RTC attracted a number of serious-minded and forward-looking officers who soon formed something of a clique and found a spokesman in Captain Liddell Hart who was the defence correspondent for the Daily Telegraph and later for The Times, and who, having fallen under Colonel Fuller's spell was a devout tank enthusiast.

Throughout the inter-war period this clique and Liddell Hart were to push endlessly, and probably irritatingly, for the adoption of a policy for conventional war based on the use of large units of tanks operating independently of infantry divisions. The army, it must be emphasised, was in no way hostile to the concept of light tanks and armoured cars for reconnaissance, or for heavy tanks for infantry support. It was, though, unconvinced about tanks in the independent role.

It was of great significance that the concept of independent tank units was pushed in conjunction with the complementary concept of 'Limited Liability'. This would have meant that, in the case of a major war, Britain would not deploy a mass army, as had been the case in the Great War, but only a few armoured units. Had the 'Limited Liability' concept been considered and rebuffed at the highest political level, then perhaps discussions about tanks might have followed different courses.

The lobbying of the tank clique, which was carried out in the full glare of publicity aided by Liddell Hart's journalism, was against a background of financial stringency, a ten year rule which decreed that there would be no major war for that period, and a foreign policy that was uncertain against which enemy the country should arm.

Despite the financial limitations some light and medium tanks were issued and small scale exercises were held with them attached to infantry units. Then, in 1927, the Experimental Mechanized Force was formed. This included a battalion of medium tanks, one of armoured cars and 'tankettes', a machine gun battalion, heavy and light artillery, and some Royal Engineers. 'Tankettes' were open-topped tracked vehicles from which the vehicles that were to be commonly known as 'Bren gun carriers' were developed. The title of the force was soon changed to the 'Experimental Armoured Force'.

The Experimental Armoured Force existed for two years and carried out a wide range of schemes, all of which were complicated by the wide variety of vehicles involved. At the end of the two years the tank clique could reasonably be pleased with the progress made. The experience showed two obvious trends relative to Tank Warfare. One related to the design of tanks, the other to their employment.

The problem with tank design was, of course, expense. It is easy to design the perfect tank, but if it cannot be afforded then compromises will have to be made.

The Medium tanks, Mk I and II, of the 1920s had worked well for their day but were obsolescent. The Mk III, their replacement, was too costly and only a small number was made, production being halted in 1931. Rather wastefully development was not halted but struggled on until mid 1939.

This halt in the production of what might be called the 'Universal Tank' resulted in production being concentrated on light tanks, and the Tank Corps having the time, and obligation, to consider its requirements. The first step in this process was the production of the manual 'Mechanised and Armoured Formations' in 1929. Its final version was 'Modern Formations' produced in 1931. This is the manual that will be considered below [2].

Although both of these were official manuals, published 'By command of the Army Council', they were titled as 'Provisional', and can be taken as really discussion documents based on the thinking of the tank clique, led by Colonel (at the time) CNF Broad. Significantly, in 1966, this officer admitted that he had misread the future for tanks and his manuals were based on the use of tanks in forays, raids into enemy territory, in the way that cavalry had been used in the American Civil War. Which is to say that the basis of British tank training for armoured warfare was fundamentally flawed.

Although 'Modern Formations' does not provide detailed technical specifications for AFVs, the employment envisaged for tanks makes certain requirements obvious. Because the Medium Mk III was too expensive for production the 'Cruiser Tank' was specified. It would be different from the Mk III in being smaller, more thinly armoured, armed with only machine guns and a light dedicated anti-tank gun, but quite a bit faster.

Warfare based on the mass deployment of such tanks is termed, in this study, 'Cruiser Tank Warfare'.

Such a vehicle was obviously not appropriate for infantry support so a separate class of AFV, the Infantry Tank, slow but thickly armoured, was born.

The Cruiser Tank Mk I, which even looked like a cheap version of the Medium Mk III, went into production in 1937, initially only in limited numbers. This was so close to the start of the war that there was little time for schemes and discussion to consider the usefulness of 'Modern Formations'.

'Modern Formations'

In this manual it is made plain early on that AFVs are distinct from *'infantry machines'*, and these machines are rather looked down upon. *'Armour will naturally have its place since it can be carried in any mechanical vehicle, but the machines to be provided for infantry will be different from those assigned to the tank arm. Infantry machines need not be fast, and they must be small so as to be capable of easy concealment. In the enclosed types of country in which alone infantry will normally operate offensively, concealment of such machines will be available....*

...Armoured fighting vehicles, as distinguished from these infantry machines, will not operate in enclosed or infantry country. Their action will be mainly confined to open ground which is suitable to their characteristics......In this way their mobility will find its chief opportunity, for their main strength lies in surprise. These machines will therefore require speed, with a good cross-country capacity.'

The specifications given for AFVs are those for the light and medium tanks in service in the late 1920s.

Having broadly decided on the required AFVs, the general context of operations is considered. *'For reasons economic, industrial and military, armies will be small, and they will seek for decisions more by generalship than by brute force...... Material will be valuable and not easily replaceable; blows will, therefore, be struck only when corresponding advantages are obtainable......Hence more frequent demands will be made on mobility, i.e. power to manoeuvre, than on the actual act of battle.'*

This being the case the temptation to make raids should be resisted. '*Increased mobility will render raiding easier than in the past, but the power of armoured formations should not be expended on raids unless these are likely to be definitely effective in producing superiority of force at the decisive time and place.*' This was true, but it is difficult to square this comment with Colonel Broad's belief in forays, noted above. It was also true that raids provided the scenarios for many of the exercises held in the 1930s. This could have resulted in an unrealistic appreciation of the potential of armoured units. Colonel Broad was, according to Liddell Hart, unofficially known as 'The Brain'.

The fixation on the small size of future armies was common between the World Wars. There can be little doubt that it was based on an emotional reaction against the attrition of the Great War and certainly not on hard reason. One result of the 'small armies' fallacy was the expectation that the enemy would always have an open flank to attack.

The basic armoured unit was to be the battalion, which could be of two types. The light battalion was to consist of 53 light tanks, with two mediums and five close support (CS) tanks. These latter were medium tanks with smoke-laying mortars as their main armament. The mixed battalions were to consist of 20 medium tanks, 22 light tanks and five CS tanks.

These battalions were to be grouped into two different types of armoured brigades:

Light brigades were to contain three light tank battalions, Medium brigades were to contain one light tank battalion and three mixed.

Divisions were to be made up of either or both types of armoured brigade, and infantry, as was appropriate for the theatre they were to be deployed in.

It was appreciated that infantry brigades were necessary, they '*will be used for offensive action in localities favourable to their action......They will further be required for defensive tasks; these brigades will at rest form the screen behind which mobile troops will from time to time retire for purposes of re-fitting.*'

There is, though, no doubt in the potential of the AFVs for decisive action. '*The armoured fighting vehicle acts by fire and movement with the immediate object of creating an opportunity for decisive action and the ultimate one of securing a concentration of superior force at the decisive point.*'

However it was appreciated that AFVs had to be used with care. '*The moral and material effect of armoured fighting vehicles on the other arms is great. They can, in fact, render immobile, by threat alone, such infantry formations as are unsuitably equipped......Since, however, guns will always outclass armour, and the accuracy of stationary guns will always be greater than that of those in movement, direct frontal assault on prepared positions will be costly unless supported by adequate covering fire.*'

The manual several times dwells on the requirement for '*skilful manoeuvres, intelligently conceived and rapidly executed*' which '*may well confuse the hostile commander and cause uncertainty in his mind; opportunities for producing superiority of force at the decisive time and place will thus be created. This result may be attained by a numerically inferior force which enjoys the advantages of superior mobility......A hostile commander will be embarrassed by the fact that any point within 100 miles of a mobile formation is liable to attack by it. Provided the mobile troops can escape the observation of hostile aircraft, the exact scale and objective of the attack will not be known to the defender in time to enable appropriate defensive arrangements to be made......Factors such as inclement weather, darkness, wooded country, combined with the power rapidly to concentrate scattered columns, will all assist in maintaining secrecy.'*

Skilful manoeuvres are to be made possible by speed, and commanders should bear in mind that *'speed of movement combined with fire in movement is their main protection, and therefore the attack should be kept moving and put through at speed.'*

Skill and speed should result in surprise. *'Furthermore, surprise should result from freedom of manoeuvre, since the time as well as the place of attack should be at the choice of the attacker. Tactical surprise must, to a certain extent, be foregone owing to the noise of the approach, but speed of manoeuvre on the battlefield, combined with the use of smoke, may prevent anti-tank weapons being moved to the correct locality until it is too late......If surprise has been achieved and the enemy has been caught at a disadvantage, success will be obtained by a bold assault delivered without loss of time......If the conditions are not favourable for immediate attack, concealment of one's strength, combined with suitable manoeuvres by light machines, may induce the enemy to act in such a way as to create a more favourable opportunity for attack......If the enemy succeeds in escaping into unsuitable ground, he should be surrounded and held until other troops arrive......Under certain conditions it will be sounder to cut the enemy off from all supplies, meanwhile subjecting him to fire, rather than to attempt a quick decision by attacks, the success of which is doubtful.'*

A conclusion repeated as '*attacks should not be pushed home unless success has been assured by the above measures. If this is not the case, it is better to manoeuvre for a more favourable opportunity.*'

Remarkably, for all this talk of skilful manoeuvre, surprise, etc, the clash of armoured formations is dismissed in two short paragraphs:
'*The presence of considerable bodies of tanks on both sides in a suitable theatre of war is likely to have a considerable effect upon the character of operations generally......Such formations do not, however, exist at the moment, and as the subject is therefore purely theoretical, it will not be further discussed in these pages.*'

However, after that omission the three phases of Cruiser Tank Warfare were spelt out. The first was the breakthrough. '*The object of the initial attacks is to make a breach of such a width in the defence as will enable their supplies to reach the exploiting troops. This will not be satisfactorily done unless this avenue is free from fire from the flanks.*' This phase, of course, is not unique to Cruiser Tank Warfare, and may very well not involve the use of Cruisers.

The second phase comes when, after the bold manoeuvres have succeeded and the enemy's front has been breached, then '*exploitation should be begun. Mobile divisions are suitable for this task. Troops detailed for exploitation should be distinct from those taking part in the initial battle.*' The use of the word 'exploitation' here is a little misleading. In the Cruiser Tank Warfare context it describes the use of tanks directly on the flank and rear of the enemy's troops in order to lever them out of their position.

The manual continues: '*The main object of exploitation will be to cause a general collapse of the whole front by attacks on the rear of the defensive positions, by interruption of the means of supply and by prevention of the issue of orders by the enemy except by wireless.'* A comment similar to Colonel Fuller's about the 'Strategic Paralysis' of 'Plan 1919'.

After the exploitation phase the Cruisers are out in the open, and can drive deep into the enemy's territory to achieve the aims of the campaign. They can now be said to be in the third phase, the 'pursuit'. *'The resultant chaos should create opportunities for decisive operations under the conditions of mobile warfare...... Tanks and armoured cars will be used with boldness, as the efficiency of the hostile anti-tank defence will have been shaken by preceding operations.'*

And finally a hint of caution. *'During the progress of operations, tank brigades may find themselves separated from the rest of the army, in which case they will become solely responsible for their own safety.'* A paragraph that will be referred to in the account of the 'Crusader' battle of 1941.

Although the manual assumes that once the enemy's front line has been reduced to chaos, the campaign was won, it is realistic about the difficulties of night operations. The manual's initial approach was to an extent optimistic. *'Tank brigades can operate at night in country suitable to their characteristics to the same degree as other troops.'* However *'the dangers and uncertainties of night attacks are, however, such as not to encourage the use of tank brigades in them except in special circumstances......At night, tank brigades should usually go into one or more "laagers"......A laager is arranged on the perimeter camp system. The armoured fighting vehicles are placed round the outside, with the transport and an inlying piquet of armoured fighting vehicles in the centre.'* The limitation that the difficulty of moving at night placed on the pursuit stage was not commented on.

As can be seen the validity of Cruiser Tank Warfare depended on the success with which the exploitation and pursuit phases could be carried out. This will be assessed by considering some of the tank actions of the Second World War.

In the year Modern Formations was published a tank brigade was set up, consisting of three tank battalions and a skeleton reconnaissance battalion, giving a total of 85 medium and 95 light tanks. The great step forward was the issue of rather primitive radios sets, so that the whole brigade could be easily manoeuvred by the brigadier over the air. This was a significant achievement and reinforced the futuristic message of 'Modern Formations', at least in the RTC. This innovation did not attract much attention from the rest of the army.

There can be no doubt that 'Modern Formations' was, in its day, a remarkable document, but like everything else, it was not perfect. One fault was its gross underestimation of the difficulties of moving regiments of tanks across country. Presumably exercises were run over unrealistically good going. The result was an underestimation of the engineering resources required.

A second fault was that the emphasis placed on manoeuvre resulted in the capacity for fighting being downgraded, and this in its turn resulted in the adoption of 'Cruiser Tanks'. These tanks had as their main armament a dedicated AT gun when the real requirement was for a dual purpose gun capable of firing high explosive ammunition as well as anti-tank. The main armament chosen, the 2-pdr, being of small calibre, 40-mm, had small rounds and large numbers of them could be carried which was in keeping with the RTC's expected deployment in forays.

Thirdly there was the lack of understanding of the absolute necessity for artillery support. The first version of the manual did specify the use of self-propelled artillery, presumably thinking in terms of Birch Guns which were self-propelled 18-pdrs. In

'Modern Formations' they were ignored, no doubt the close support tanks were expected to provide the required support.

Fourthly, although the difficulty of supply was noticed, particularly as the distance between the tanks and the railhead increased, the vulnerability of the lines of communication to enemy action, including that of by-passed troops, was not.

Finally the manual called for the organisation of two entirely different types of division, infantry and armoured and more importantly, two different types of brigades. Armoured brigades came to consist of three regiments of tanks and a 'motor battalion' of infantry travelling in lorries. There were to be occasions when this organisation was appropriate, but not often. There was a real requirement for infantry mounted in tracked armoured vehicles capable of keeping up with, and co-operating with, the tanks. These brigades should have been backed up by self-propelled artillery and have aircraft dedicated to their support. Because of the financial limitations of the time such a force could not be built, but the requirements should have been identified.

The rigid breakdown of divisions into either armoured or infantry was to cause problems, but even so it can be seen that, at the start of the Second World War, in terms of Cruiser Tank Warfare, everything seemed to fit together in a satisfying, if rather academic, way. The Great War had shown that any field defences could be broken through, but in that war the means of exploiting the breakthrough were not available; the defenders could always bring up reserves by rail, whereas the attackers must advance on foot. But now there were divisions, based on armoured brigades of fast cruiser tanks, which would form the Mass of Manoeuvre. They would surge through any gap in the enemy's defences made by infantry supported by artillery and infantry tanks. Once through, by bold and skilful manoeuvring they would hound and finally destroy the enemy before he had time to organise a new defensive front.

Probably the most remarkable aspect of Cruiser Tank Warfare is the speed with which it became the orthodox. As Captain Liddell Hart wrote at the time in his book 'The British Way in Warfare': *'The historically minded find it difficult to believe that the mere addition of an official imprint to a book, compiled by a temporarily prevailing group of officers, makes it the absolute truth – until the next edition comes out.'*[3]

It is known that the Captain made a significant contribution to the thinking expressed in 'Modern Formations', so 'The British Way in Warfare' should show what that contribution was. Unfortunately his major strategic theme, against the deployment of major British forces on the continent, has been blown out of the (blue) water. However, apart from his enthusiasm for light tanks, he wrote sensibly about the possibilities for the armoured warfare of the day.

'Thus the army, as a whole now strategically mobile, will group itself into two fighting parts with separate tactical functions: one a close-fighting part, composed of semi-mechanized infantry, and the other a mobile fighting part, composed entirely of armoured fighting vehicles. The close-fighting units would be employed to clear hilly and wooded country, to gain river-crossings, to evict the enemy from villages or trench systems, to occupy strategic points, and to act as general handymen. The mobile fighting units would manoeuvre widely to turn the enemy's flanks and attack his lines of supply. If they encounter an enemy in a well-prepared position bristling with anti-tank guns, their tactics will probably be to harass the inert foe by fire while they cut off his supplies of food and ammunition, until he is driven either to surrender or to expose himself in an attempt to get away. When acting in direct combination, the close-fighting part of an army would be used to pin and paralyse the opponent while the mobile fighting part would carry out a decisive manoeuvre against his rear.'

And again, when discussing exercises: *'The mobile arms – and hence the real strategic arms – cannot obtain full value through attacking their proper objectives, which do not exist in peace exercises, and so are used improperly: aircraft and tanks should both aim at the enemy's transport and communications, whereas their customary attacks on the fighting troops are merely spectacular illusions, mirages in the peace-time military desert.'*

He certainly showed a fine appreciation of the need for armoured infantry, which he referred to as 'land marines'. *'The 'light infantry' required for mobile operations need special transport and training. I foresee such units being made up of a proportion of motor machine-gunners in little armoured carriers, a larger proportion of skirmishers in 'baby' cars and a reserve in six-wheeled lorries or buses.'*[3]

These contemporary excerpts from the work of the most well known military pundit of the time should show how forward-thinking soldiers could believe so whole-heartedly in the Cruiser Tank Warfare concept

The Cruiser Tank Warfare concept of achieving its effect by manoeuvre can be contrasted with the German concept of mobile operations. This was spelt out by Lt Col (at the time) Nehring in the Year Book of the German Army in 1936 [4]. The Colonel was an expert on tanks and mobile warfare and ended the war commanding the 1st Panzer Army.

'The task of military motorisation is to strive for maximum tactical and operational mobility and speed, so that the army may be able in the shortest possible time to develop a maximum fighting strength at the fulcrum of the battle, in order that it may thus prove superior at the decisive point, even if inferior as a whole. This definition more or less covers the duties devolving upon the German motorised army.'

As this quote shows the Germans expected to fight, and mobility was to allow them to fight better. It is also of interest to note that, again in contrast with the British concept, the Germans regarded all their motorised troops, tanks, infantry, AT units and artillery, as coming under the general designation of 'fast troops' (*Schnellen Truppen*), subject to their own inspectorate. This was an aspect of the German commitment to combined arms warfare (*Gefecht der verbundenen-Waffen*).

To what extent these concepts described the real world will be considered in subsequent chapters.

Note 1,
The initial version of this paper was produced on 24th May 1918, it was titled: 'The Tactics of the Attack as Affected by the Speed and Circuit of the Medium 'D' Tank'.

This was soon changed to: 'Strategic Paralysis as the Object of the Decisive Attack'.

Then finally: 'Plan 1919'.

Note 2,
This manual is now rare but can be read at the Imperial War Museum.

Note 3,
'The British Way in Warfare', Captain Liddell Hart, London, 1932.

The strategic argument of this book was comprehensively countered by Michael Howard in the 1974 Neale Lecture in English History, 'The British Way in Warfare'.

It should be noted that since 1988, when 'Liddell Hart and the Weight of History' by JJ Mearsheimer was published, there has been much discussion about just how good Liddell Hart actually was. His reputation has been rescued to a large degree by Azar Gat in his article 'Liddell Hart's Theory of Armoured Warfare: Revising the Revisionists', Journal of Strategic Studies, Vol 19, No 1 (March 1996). However doubts remain.

Note 4,
Quoted in 'Hitler's War Machine', by Wilhelm Necker, no date, probably 1943.

As a result of the discussions observed in Note 3, there has been some doubt expressed as to how much influence Capt Liddell Hart and Gen JFC Fuller actually had on German development of armoured warfare. So it is worth noting that Herr Necker mentions neither of the English authors, but does mention General de Gaulle's book 'The Army of the Future'.

Chapter 3

THE TANKS

There are many books about tanks therefore this chapter will be restricted to providing a brief summary of tank development, relevant to Cruiser tanks during the period in question, to support the rest of the text.

The bulk of the tanks employed in the Great War were of the heavy type, vast, slow, thinly armoured and nearly blind. It would seem that this type was nearing the end of its development. Fortunately another type was emerging, the Medium.

Although medium tanks were involved in some colourful episodes during the last months of the war their actual achievement was minimal, but great things were expected of them in 1919. Colonel Fuller and his novelette 'Plan 1919' have been mentioned in the last chapter and even if Plan 1919 was not a serious practical design there is no doubt that the thinking he expressed in it had a profound effect on opinion about tanks.

As has been seen Plan 1919 required two types of tanks: medium tanks to surge through breaches in the German front and heavy tanks to support the infantry attack. Fortunately the war ended in 1918, but this left the situation with tank design and production in disarray. The requirement for fast medium tanks had been planned to be met by the Medium D which, in theory, could run at 20mph.These tanks were just entering production when production was halted on cost grounds. The Tank Corps argued against this and finally a small number was built for experimental purposes.

Financial stringency, lack of clear thinking and, in all probability, a degree of confusion about departmental responsibilities, made progress in tank design minimal until 1923 when the General

Staff called for two types of tank: a fast 'Cavalry' tank and a slower 'Infantry' tank. Colonel Fuller had identified the need for a small Infantry tank in 1919.

This specification was vague but enough. There was money available but if not quickly spent it would be returned to the Treasury. The result was remarkable. Without detailed specification, without comparative testing, and without extensive troop trials, emerged the 'Vickers' Medium Mk I, as the fast Cavalry tank. It was immediately issued to a RTC battalion. Although it was produced by Vickers and usually referred to by that name, it was never its official title. It weighed approximately 12 tons and was originally classified as light but this was soon altered, and the light/medium threshold was set, rather arbitrarily, at 10 tons. The Mk I was soon followed by the Mk II which was similar.

To modern eyes these tanks may seem a little quaint, but in their day they were revolutionary. They were the first British tanks with fully traversing turrets all of which carried a significant main armament. Most had the 3-pdr anti-tank gun, some had a 3.7-inch howitzer designed to fire smoke shells. This represented a total break from the Great War designs with guns in fixed sponsons or turrets and 'male' and 'female' versions.

The turrets showed features that were to become standard in tank design. They were manned by a commander, gunner and loader. Most marks had a machine gun, usually a Vickers, mounted coaxially with the main armament, (ie a 'co-ax'), although, contrary to modern practice these MGs could be, if required, elevated and depressed independently of the 3-pdr. This idea was considered again for the Centurion prototype, but rejected. The main armament fired both armour piercing, AP, shot and high explosive, HE, shell, even if there would not have been much explosive in such a small, 47-mm, round.

The best way to defeat armour was, and is, to fire solid shot at it at high velocity. To engage dug-in troops, high explosive shells are required, and the exigencies of the battlefield will require smoke rounds. Tanks must have a multi-purpose gun capable of firing these different natures. The Vickers Mediums had such a gun, but for a large period of the Second World War British tanks did not.

As with other tanks mentioned in the text the Vickers Medium's vital statistics are given at the end of this chapter. Here it is enough to say that they were fast, achieving a road speed of between 15 and 25 mph depending on tank and crew, but cross-country speeds were much slower. They were high and hence difficult to hide, and thinly armoured.

The total Vickers Medium production was 160 tanks, one survives, it is at Bovington. These tanks became almost symbolic of the RTC between the wars and cannot help but have made a significant impression on Tank Corps officers. The tanks came to be looked on as general purpose Main Battle Tanks – to use the modern expression – and the requirement for a heavy infantry tank faded away.

The remarkable thing about the 1920s is that the General Staff seems to have made hardly any effort to control the pace and direction of tank development. This is illustrated by the progress of heavy and light tanks.

In 1922 Vickers was asked to design a heavy tank, not it seems an infantry tank. It was specified to have no turret and be similar to the tanks in service during the Great War. Vickers came up with a design for a tank with no less than five turrets! Remarkably this design was accepted. A prototype was built in 1927 and was trialled until 1935. Vast quantities of money were spent on it and possibly some useful engineering knowledge gained. Otherwise it was a waste of time. It too can be seen at Bovington.

With the light tank it is difficult to pin down the original General Staff requirement for such a type. The specification seems to have resulted from a private initiative on the part of Major Martel, at that time a Royal Engineers officer, who made a start by building a one-man tank. Then the firm of Carden and Loyd built a range of light vehicles. This firm was taken over by Vickers Armstrong in 1928, which built the Light Tank Mk I was taken into service in 1930. It looked like a scaled down Medium, the power pack being in front of the fighting compartment. The turret mounted one Vickers MMG.

It may be suspected that the popularity of light tanks with the War Office was based on their cheapness, particularly as the development of the Mediums was becoming problematic. They were certainly much more fun on exercises than were the lumbering Mediums. Over 1,000 were built and they saw extensive service during the first two years of the war. By 1941 they were obsolete on the battlefield but still to be found in training units. They were replaced in reconnaissance units mostly by armoured cars, but some by Honeys, the American light tanks.

By the end of the 1920s it was plain that a successor to the Mediums should be designed, and Vickers produced the A6. The 'A' number, which was first used at this time, referred to the War Office specification. 'A' was for tanks.

Vickers produced two in 1928, and another one next year. They looked like a great step forward from the existing Mediums. They conformed to the basic modern lay-out of driver in front of the fighting compartment (turret) and power pack behind. As a kind of hang over from the Independent there were two small MG turrets on each side of the driver. These tanks showed significant improvements in terms of engine and suspension, but none in terms of fighting power. Its main armament and thickness of armour were the same as for the Medium Mk III. These tanks were called '16 Tonners'.

After trials a further three were ordered and they were designated Medium Mk IV's. After that there were no further orders. They had become too expensive, which was a pity. In the long run not proceeding with this type caused a much greater expense with little to show for it. None of the A6/Medium Mk IV's survives.

While this development was being undertaken by Vickers the War Office, WO, got its in-house firm – Royal Ordnance – working on tanks of a new specification, the A7, which was drawn up by the Tank Design Section at Woolwich under Major EML Clarke. The A7 was to be faster and lower than the 16 tonner. It is not obvious why the Royal Ordnance was instructed to undertake this work, but it may be suspected that the WO was looking for a cheap alternative to the Mediums.

While A7 could still, by some stretch of the imagination, be called a Medium. The next development slipped away from this. The A9 was initially planned to be the Medium Mk IV, to have the same firepower as the Medium Mk III, but be cheaper than the A7. The original specification was handed to Vickers in mid 1934, but by the end of the year the main armament requirement had altered to the 2-pdr. This indicated a distinct shift away from the concept of the Medium tank as a general purpose weapon, to what was to be called the 'Cruiser Tank' designed for a specialised role. The poor fighting capacity of the A9 was criticised by General Hobart, who was one of the leading lights of the Tank Corps, at the time commanding the Tank Brigade. However he seems to have soon reconciled himself to it.

The expression 'Cruiser' came from the naval analogy for armoured warfare popular at the time. It is possible that the expression pointed at the need for a heavier Battle Tank. The significant features of Cruiser tanks were high speed, thin armour and a too small main armament. The series continued until 1945 when the last to appear, the Centurion, was classified as a 'Heavy Cruiser'.

The Cruiser tank concept fitted well with the ideas expressed in Modern Formations and, as will be seen, the concept and the tanks seemed to work well in the early desert campaigns.

The A9 was classified as the Cruiser tank Mk I. The A10, Cruiser Mk II, was similar but with thicker armour for infantry support, which might indicate some confusion about the Cruiser/Infantry tank split. These tanks showed some similarity to the Medium Mk III, but being obviously cheaper were sometimes referred to as 'Woolworths Tanks'. The A9 had two MG turrets in the hull as did the Medium Mk III, but the A10 initially had no hull MG which is remarkable as these guns would seem to be more useful for infantry support, but this was soon changed. Both the A9 and the A10 could carry 3.7-inch howitzers for close support. It was quickly realised that the A10 was not well enough armoured for infantry support and it went into limited production, classified as a 'Heavy Cruiser'.

These tanks were soon replaced by the A13, Cruiser Mk III. The essential change was in the suspension which was of the Christie type. After the Mk III it became the fashion to give the tanks names, Cruiser tanks names started with 'C'. In view of this it was a pity that the Churchill, an infantry tank, was an exception to this convention.

Ignoring the Covenanter, the Cavalier and several other tanks that did not see action, the next significant tank was the Crusader, Cruiser Mk VI, or A15. This was the tank most associated with the desert campaigns. It was produced in, confusingly, three marks and the significant changes showed the experience of the desert fighting.

Mk I had the 2-pdr as main armament, one coaxial MG and one hull-mounted MG. The Mk II saw the hull MG removed and the extra space used for ammunition stowage, Mk III saw the 2-pdr replaced by a 6-pdr. This took up so much space in the turret that there was no room for a coax or a loader and that job had to be done by the commander.

The Crusader was a typical Cruiser with admirable speed and thin armour, but it was well known for lack of mechanical reliability. It was phased out in 1943, but some were converted into AA tanks and stayed in service until the end of the war. In the desert the Crusader was replaced by the American tanks, Grant and Sherman, but in Europe the new Cruiser was the Cromwell. This was the A27M, the 'M' refers to the Meteor engine.

The Cromwell was an excellent tank and, if it had been produced two or three years earlier, as it could have been, it would have been a war winner. Initially it was armed with the 6-pdr, but this was soon replaced by the 75-mm Medium Velocity gun. During the Normandy fighting the lack of a good dual purpose gun, firing both AP and HE ammunition, was making itself felt. A HE round was issued for the 6-pdr but it was not regarded as very effective, and it was the HE requirement that brought about the 75-mm gun. As the 75-mm was not very effective against tanks some Cromwells were modified to take the 17-pdr. These tanks were called Challengers and given the A30 designation.

An unfortunate aspect of the Cromwell's design was its narrow turret ring. This was important because it restricted the size of the gun that could be mounted in the turret. If the turret ring is too narrow the gun will not have room to recoil at certain angles of elevation, so a new turret must be built that will be high enough for the gun to recoil above the hull at all elevations. This resulted in the tall turret that gave the Challenger such an ungainly look.

The reason why turret rings in British tanks tended to be narrow was that in these tanks the hull sits between the tracks and does not extend over them. The advantages of this basic design were that the tanks were lower and more stable platforms for firing on the move, as was such the fashion between the wars. The disadvantage was the narrow turret rings.

The successor to the Cromwell, the Comet, A34, was a similar tank but capable of mounting the 77-mm gun, which was a cut-down version of the 17-pdr. The Centurion, A41, which followed initially carried the 17-pdr, but just missed the war.

After the Crusader the design of British Cruiser tanks became less important because of the issue of American tanks. The first was the Stuart or Honey, a light tank with the inadequate 37-mm gun. It should really have been a reconnaissance vehicle but was used as a Cruiser in the Crusader battle.

The Grant, a larger tank, saw extensive service in the desert, but not in Europe. It had a 37-mm in the turret and a 75-mm in the hull. The 75-mm was an American field artillery piece, not designed as an AT weapon and not very effective as one. Consequently the British opened the ammunition supplied by the Americans and replaced the propellant with chopped cordite. This increased the gun's muzzle velocity and made it reasonably effective even against the Panzer IV. The tank was certainly high, 10 ft, and this made it an easy target as, with the limited depression of the 75-mm, it could not take up effective hull-down firing positions. Its height was not so much of a disadvantage as it might seem. Because of the low position of the 75-mm gunner, and because of the desert dust blown up by the low-set gun, and the gun flash, the gunner could often not observe the fall of shot. This was done by the commander, high up in the 37-mm turret, who would give corrections via the intercom. Despite all this the Grant was well regarded and was christened 'Egypt's Last Hope'. It was certainly not a cruiser tank.

The Sherman was first issued in 1942 and became the most common tank in the British army. It was a reliable tank and popular. It had the 75-mm medium velocity gun which was sufficient for most targets, but hopeless against Panthers and Tigers. On some Shermans in the British service this gun was replaced by the 17-pdr and the tank called a Firefly, as sometimes was the Challenger. The 17-pdr was an excellent gun and could stand comparison with the feared 88. It was, though, a difficult gun to use because of its blinding flash. The round could travel hundreds of yards before the gunner could see its trace. The flash also had the disadvantage of making the tank more visible. German gunners, when they had the choice of targets, would always aim at the Firefly first. This was the reason why, when Fireflies were allocated one to a troop, the troop leader was ordered not travel in it. The propellants for German tank ammunition did not cause the flash that British ones did, this gave the Germans something of an advantage. The Fireflies were specialist AT weapons so only a small number of HE rounds was issued for their 17-pdrs, and they had to be deployed alongside 75-mm gun Shermans which had substantial HE ammunition. Also the hull MGs were taken out of Fireflies to allow more ammunition to be stowed, this further emphasised their specialist nature.

The Sherman's guns were provided with the Azimuth Indicator M19 and this allowed them to be used for semi-indirect fire, that is when the commander could see the target but the gunner could not, so the tank could be hidden behind a crest. This procedure would have been familiar to ex-Grant commanders, though for different reasons. The advantage of this in reducing the risk for the tank crew is obvious. This type of engagement was not all that easy. There was no trace on the 75-mm round so fall of shot was sometimes difficult to observe. In the desert this could be mostly due to heat haze; in France, due to the lie of the land or foliage. This, no doubt, improved with practice, but it did have the effect of making tanks little more than self-propelled howitzers. The tactical implications of this will be considered in Chapter 11. In Europe it was common to use Shermans to provide artillery barrages, each tank firing as many as 50 rounds as fast as the gun could be loaded.

The Sherman was thinly armoured and prone to bursting into flames when hit. The reason for this is usually thought to be the way that its ammunition was stowed in the turret, however it must be at least as much because of the petrol engine. Throughout the war British tanks were powered by petrol engines. This not only caused many fires but could make their resupply a nerve-wracking business. It was believed that diesel powered tanks had superior pulling power and speed, so naturally when some diesel Shermans became available they were very popular. However there were disadvantages, particularly for a tank crew in the desert. Replenishing with diesel fuel was a messy event compared to petrol, and with petrol no longer being so plentiful diesel was found to be a far inferior fuel for brewing up and cooking. It was also useless for washing clothes, diesel stains being irremovable. After the Normandy campaign the diesel tanks were reallocated to Canadian units to simplify supply. As events showed there is no doubt that the diesel powered Shermans were less likely to burn than the petrol powered ones.

To what extent the Sherman could be called a Cruiser would depend on the way it was used, but it can certainly be regarded as the tank the won the war.

After the war, in an attempt to beat the proverbial swords into ploughshares, the British government decided to convert 1,500 Shermans into agricultural tractors to be used for the Groundnut Scheme. The Shermans were to be converted by Vickers-Armstrong and the results called 'Shervicks'. It is not known how many were actually produced but they were not very successful, and the Groundnut Scheme was a disaster.

Some Vital Statistics

	Date	Weight Tons	Crew	Armament Main	MGs coax	MGs hull	Armour mm (max)	Speed mph
Medium D	1920	13.5					8	27
Medium Mk I	1922	12	5	3-pdr	1	5	6.5	15
Medium Mk III	1928	18	6	3-pdr	1	2	14	28
A7 prototype	1929	14	5	3-pdr	1	1	14	25
A9 Cruiser Mk I	1934	12	6	2-pdr	1	3	14	25
A10 Cruiser Mk II	1935	14	5	2-pdr	1	-	30	16
A13 Crusader Mk I	1938	19	5	2-pdr	1	1	40	27
Mk II	1941		4	2-pdr	1	-	49	"
Mk III	1942		3	6-pdr	-	-	51	"
A27M Cromwell Mk I	1943	28	5	6-pdr	1	1	76	38
Mk IV				75-mm				"
A34 Comet	1944	33	5	77-mm	1	1	101	29
Honey	1941	12.5	4	37-mm	1	1	65	35
Grant	1941	27	6	37-mm	1	(turret)	57	26
				75-mm	-	- (hull)		
Sherman	1942	31	5	75-mm	1	1	76	29
Firefly	1944	32	4	17-pdr	1	-	76	29

Chapter 4

Theory into Practice

The concepts expressed in Modern Formations were the result of large scale exercises. It is a pity that 1934 saw the last of these exercises before the start of the war. Even then the 1934 season was largely given over to experiments with voice radio [1]. However the last exercise of the year achieved a degree of notoriety and was held, particularly by Liddell Hart who revised his 'The British Way in Warfare' to give an account of it, to have damaged the general cause of British armoured warfare. The importance of the exercise, which became known as the 'Battle of Hungerford Bridge' is reflected by the large number of published accounts of it.[2] However they seem to be mostly based on the account Liddell Hart gave in 'The Tanks'. It is interesting to note that the one published before the Liddell Hart account was by no means so flattering to the RTC. Possibly the exercise made such a great impression because it was the last.

For this exercise the defenders, an infantry division with some mobile elements under command, were to hold a line roughly along the Kennet-Avon canal covering various installations close to Amesbury which the Mobile Force was to destroy. This had to be done in the manner of a raid in a very restricted timescale. The Mobile Force, which was based on an armoured brigade, had a motorised infantry brigade attached to make an ad-hoc armoured division, but unfortunately it had no divisional HQ.

The Mobile Force had to start from west of the Severn close to Gloucester. It was decided to break through the defender's front at Hungerford, which is around nine miles to the east of Marlborough. On the first night the infantry brigade drove there, a move of around fifty miles but across the defender's front. On the second night the tank brigade followed. Unfortunately the umpires judged that the Mobile Force had come under heavy air attack and would have to turn back. The defending mobile units, armoured cars and cavalry, sallied out to the north and planted road blocks and mines in the path of the retreating Mobile Force, which only escaped with difficulty.

The exercise had clearly worked out badly for the tanks, but it is not clear if the most important lessons were learnt from it. From the point of view of Cruiser Tank Warfare there were two. The first was the importance of proper HQs for armoured divisions. Secondly the exercise should have shown how vulnerable to counter-attack the communications of an armoured division could be.

In the event the commander of the Mobile Force, General Lindsay, being under something of a cloud, was sent out to India. A recent commentator, JP Harris, concluded that as General Lindsay was a supporter of the concept of the armoured division being a balanced grouping of all arms, his exile was a disaster for British armoured warfare and left the field open to the tank brigade commander, Brigadier Hobart, who was decidedly 'tank heavy'. However it is really impossible to judge the importance of this. Liddell Hart's judgement has already been noted.

Stopping holding large scale exercises with tanks was a pity because such exercises did force the tankmen into contact with the rest of the army, and without these exercises the RTC became a little introspective. It is true that individual battalions were lent out to infantry units to practise infantry support, but that was not the Modern Formations concept.

One of the reasons for the lack of exercises was that so much equipment was sent out to Egypt when the Mobile Force there, which ultimately evolved into the 7th Armoured Division, was set up. This was done over the 1935-36 period in response to the political crisis caused by the Italian invasion of Abyssinia. Unfortunately the North African desert was the terrain where infantry-tank co-operation was least required, but despite that many useful drills were worked out and valuable experience was gained in desert navigation.

The main problem with schemes in England for armoured units was either that they became parade ground-type manoeuvres on Salisbury plain, or that the vehicles were restricted to roads and did not have to worry about overcoming enemy demolitions or even natural AT obstacles. It was as if it was believed that the mobility of tanks would enable them to drive round such difficulties.

In real war artificial obstacles, like minefields, demolitions, such as blown bridges, or natural obstacles, such as rivers, would require the efforts of the Royal Engineers to get the tanks across. For the Engineers to work on the problem the area must be secured and this would require infantry to cross the obstacle and take up defensive positions on the far side. The conclusion should have been inescapable that the infantry should have been able to keep up with the tanks. The same was true for the engineers.

For the infantry to cross the obstacle they must be covered by artillery fire. The tank guns were not enough, so self-propelled artillery was called for. This supporting fire could never be enough so ground attack aircraft should be at hand, and a system developed to control them. Unfortunately these conclusions were not reached. Infantry had been deployed on schemes, but they were in buses, debussing miles away from where they were wanted and taking hours to come into action. The same was true for artillery. It was inevitable that the tankmen came to regard themselves as the only troops capable of mobile warfare.

Of course 'Modern Formations' had recognised that there were areas, towns and woods, which were unsuitable for tanks to operate in. At least, if they were to operate there they would be in support of infantry. The problem which was being ignored was how to get the infantry to operate in support of tanks in tank country; how to be, as Captain Liddell Hart put it in 1932, 'Land Marines'.

Further, it is an article of faith among tank historians that the army, or at least the higher ranks, were heavily prejudiced against tanks and resisted mechanisation. Of course there was a perpetual shortage of money but, within the realms of what was affordable, the tankmen got broadly what they wanted, even if they sometimes argued about what that was.

If the poor equipment of the other arms reduced the degree to which the tankmen were prepared to co-operate with them, the nature of the Vickers Mediums led the tankies into a grievous error. These tanks were thinly armoured but, for the time, fast. So it was assumed that their best protection lay in speed. This led to the conclusion that they should fire on the move. This meant accepting a low standard of main armament gunnery, and probably, sights. Certainly gunnery procedures were not given the attention they should have been, and this was to cost many crewmen their lives.

Practice soon showed that when firing on the move broadside fire was more accurate then head-on. This fact, and the presumed necessity to keep moving, resulted in tactical drills aimed at crossing the 'T' as in naval fleet manoeuvres. Such caracoling was irrelevant to real warfare, and would present to the enemy the entire side of the tank to shoot at. Worse it tended to suppress the requirement for thicker frontal armour.

Firing on the move can be useful in terms of its prophylactic effect, but this is for MGs, and possibly guns firing a reasonable HE round, in the hope that they might disturb the enemy gunner's aim. However it should have been obvious that a tank's main hope of survival lay in its main armament, and it is easier to hit a moving target from a stationary one than to hit a stationary target from a moving one, particularly before stabilisers. Ultimately hitting the target is what matters, and when firing solid shot, as was the standard British AP round throughout the war, a near miss does not count.

Brigadier, later General, Hobart was a great exponent of firing on the move, and he ensured the policy was rigidly taught. He trained the 7th Armoured Division for war though did not take it into action. He was subsequently to find fame as the commander of the 79th Armoured Division in North-Western Europe.

Unsurprisingly the perpetual problem was money, and most of what was available for armour was spent mechanising some of the cavalry regiments. There seems to have been a distinct trend at this time to prefer to issue infantry tanks to the RTC and light and Cruiser tanks, when they became available, to the Cavalry. If this was the plan it was only partly successful, perhaps it would have been more so given time. However there is no doubt that the infantry tanks were successful, and it might be that taking some of the more professional RTC officers away from the Cruiser service had a bad effect on it.

As has been seen Modern Formations concentrated on brigades and the structure of an armoured division was left to be decided locally. There were two types of armoured brigade, light and mixed. In 1938, in response to the threatening international situation, an armoured division was formed. It was called a Mobile Division (Armoured).

Essentially it contained:

Two Mechanised Cavalry Brigades (the new name for Light Brigades), each of three light tank regiments

One Tank Brigade (the new name for a Mixed Brigade) of one light and two Mixed Regiments

And insufficient divisional troops

This organisation was changed in 1939 to:

One Light Armoured Brigade (the new name for a Mechanised Cavalry Brigade)

One Heavy Armoured Brigade of three mixed regiments

And an even more inadequate Support Group.

This was changed in 1940 effectively replacing some of the light tanks with cruisers so that there were two armoured brigades each of three mixed regiments. The plan was for them to be all Cruisers as soon as possible. However this was changed again in 1940, after the withdrawal from France, by adding a motor battalion to each armoured brigade, and the division gained an armoured car regiment.

Experience in North Africa was to show that the armoured brigades needed extra firepower and there towards the end of 1941, as Operation Crusader was drawing to a close, the 'brigade group' concept was born. Each armoured brigade was now to include a motor battalion, a field artillery regiment and an AT battery. The armoured divisions, initially of course this only affected the 7th Armoured Division, lost their support groups, but retained a motor brigade.

In the UK in 1942 the establishment was changed to reflect experience in North Africa and divisions were reduced to one armoured brigade group, but gained an infantry brigade.

In 1943 an extra cruiser tank regiment was added to act as a reconnaissance unit, though there were some who thought this was just a subterfuge to get an extra armoured regiment in the division. This organisation lasted the rest of the war, but there are two points that must be borne in mind. Firstly all armoured divisions varied slightly from the ideal. Secondly, as all tanks now had radios it was easy to form ad-hoc tactical groupings, particularly of tank regiments and infantry battalions. Such battle groups would become the norm in the North-West Europe campaign.

The general trend of all these changes was to increase the number of vehicles in armoured divisions. This increased the logistics requirements of the divisions so making them less able to carry out the forays that were so much their original *raison d'etre.*

The finally resulting armoured division and its employment were described in July 1943 in the Military Training Pamphlet (MTP) Number 41 as:
'a mounted, hard-hitting formation primarily constituted for use against hastily prepared enemy defences, for exploitation of initial success gained by other formations, and for pursuit. It is designed for use in rapid thrusts against the enemy's vitals, rather than hammer blows against his organised defences. It is the rapier in the hands of the higher commander, rather than the bludgeon.'

But this description is anticipating events, and the history of 1940 was to show how fine phraseology could be meaningless in the face of practical difficulties.

Note 1,
At this time light tanks had the Wireless No 1 Set and the Mediums the MB Set. These gave a range for voice communications of, respectively, 2 and 5 miles, on the move using a eight foot rod aerial.

Note 2,
Accounts of this exercise can be found in:
'This, Our Army', Capt JR Kennedy, London, 1935

'The British Way in Warfare', Capt Liddell Hart, Penguin revised edition, 1935

'The Tanks', Capt Liddell Hart, London, 1959

'British Military Policy between the Two World Wars', B Bond, Clarendon Press, 1980

'The Tank Pioneers', K Macksey, Jane's, 1981

'The British Army and the Theory of Armoured Warfare', 1918-1940', RH Larson, Delaware, 1983

'To Change an Army', H Wilson, Brassey's, 1988

'Men, ideas and tanks', JP Harris, MUP, 1995, and possibly many more.

The 1st Armoured Division in France

At the start of the Second World War the BEF was sent to France. Compared to 1914 this was a leisurely deployment, particularly, although there is of course no direct comparison, in terms of armour. All three types of armour were involved. There were armoured reconnaissance regiments, some of armoured cars, some of light tanks and carriers. Infantry tanks were to make up the 1st Army Tank Brigade, because of the low rate of tank production this brigade was to consist of only two battalions, the second arriving in May 1940. Cruisers would be deployed in the armoured division.

The 1st Armoured Division, commanded by Major-General R Evans, with its Cruiser and Light tanks, was an essential part of the BEF, but its deployment was a huge exercise in muddling through. As Field Marshal Earl Kitchener commented about an earlier war, 'We had to make war as we must, not as we would like to do.' It started to arrive in France just after the second Infantry Tank battalion. The deployment was rushed and the division was short of many things, particularly artillery and radios, both for HQs and tanks. It was never to fight as a division.

The state of the tanks was worrying. The latest mark of Cruisers, A13, had only just been issued and the crews had not trained on them. Worse, the machine guns, new BESAs, and some of the 2-pdrs, only arrived just as the units were embarking. The guns that were still in their packing cases were covered in mineral jelly, and there was little cotton waste to clean it off with. After disembarkation the guns were mounted on the tanks, but there was no opportunity to zero them on a range. This was important for the 2-pdrs as, although the guns could be bore-sighted to line up with the sights, the location of the recoil buffers, above the barrels, caused the guns to fire a little low. So the first round was apt to fall short.

A further complication was that the .5-inch ammunition, required for some of the light tanks, was issued loose and had to be loaded into steel-link belts by hand. There was a shortage of 2-pdr ammunition and smoke grenades. All this, and more, was not helped by the internal lights on some of the tanks not working.

The division looked impressive on paper:

- 1st Armoured Division – Major-General R Evans
  - 2nd Armoured Brigade – Brigadier RL McCreery
    - The Queen's Bays
    - 9th Queen's Royal Lancers
    - 10th Royal Hussars
  - 3rd Armoured Brigade – Brigadier JG Crocker
    - 2nd RTR
    - 3rd RTR
    - 5th RTR
  - Support Group – Brigadier FE Morgan
    - Two infantry battalions
    - 101st Anti-Tank/Light Anti-Aircraft Regiment

The two AT batteries of the artillery regiment were each fully equipped with twelve 2-pdr AT guns, but the AA batteries had had to leave their 40-mm Bofors guns in the England. They were replaced by 96 Lewis guns. This was a significant loss to the division, the Bofors were not only excellent AA guns but, in 1940, were quite reasonable AT guns.

However even before the entire division had embarked for France the infantry of the Support Group and a Tank battalion, 3RTR, of 27 Cruisers and 21 light tanks, were detached and sent to Calais. They were permanently lost to the division, which finally deployed a total of 143 Cruisers and 114 light tanks, and no field artillery.

The leading troops had started landing at Le Havre on 15th May, but as that port was under attack from the German Air Force, the rest of the division was diverted to Cherbourg where it started to land on the 19th. It was to come, off and on, under French orders. It was presently joined by the 51st Highland Division and some ad-hoc units and fought a campaign entirely separate from that which ended at Dunkirk, and which, remarkably, has been largely ignored ever since.*(see Sketch 1)*

The division was initially instructed to take up a defensive position along a sector of the Somme, downstream from Amiens. Unfortunately the Germans had already established four bridgeheads across this river, and, in line with their standard procedure, had set to to make them tank-proof. Consequently it was decided to send the AA and AT regiment and the first available armoured regiment, the Bays, to the north of the Seine to take up a position to the east of Rouen to defend the line of the Andelle. This river runs north-east from the Seine and if it could be defended would prevent the Germans getting behind the troops on the Somme.

The Bays and artillery were transported by rail to the Seine and were on the Andelle on the 22nd. Next day the Bays were moved by General Evans to the line of the Bresle which runs parallel to the Somme, about 15 miles behind it. An order was received from the War Office to attack across the Somme, advance North-East to link up with other British units whose locations were a little vague. Not only was there this vagueness, but the French, with whom the armoured division would have to cooperate, had a basically different view of what it would do.

Fortunately the rest of the 2nd Armoured Brigade had landed and joined the Bays on the 24th. Like the Bays the two regiments were brought most of the way by rail, but still had to cover 65 miles on their tracks in 24 hours to be in time for the fighting. The brigade was given three companies of the 4th Battalion, the

Border Regiment, and took the division's artillery and some engineers under command.

The advance guard of the brigade, provided by the Bays, approached the Somme early in the morning. It lost two tanks on mines and found that all the crossings were mined and guarded. Attacks on three bridges were ordered, each undertaken by a company of the Border Regiment supported by tanks of the Bays. All the attacks failed, lives squandered pointlessly.

That night orders were received from HQ BEF to delay independent operations and be ready to cooperate with the French. Soon afterwards a message was received from the French to the effect that the 51st Highland Division was arriving from the Saar front. It was to be grouped with the armoured division and the resulting formation would hold the Somme from Longpre to the sea. Until this happened the 1st Armoured Division should eliminate the German bridgeheads. This was beyond the capacity of the division. Not only were the Germans steadily reinforcing their positions on the Somme, but they were patrolling forward, sometimes with armoured cars, as far as the Bresle. On 25th May the division came under the orders of the French 7th Army, and the next day it was to support the French attack on the Abbeville bridgehead.

By this time the depleted 3rd Armoured Brigade had come up. The two armoured brigades were parcelled out separately each to support a French light cavalry division (DCL), still partly horsed. The 2nd Armoured Brigade, with the 2nd DCL, was to capture the high ground south of the Somme immediately south-east of Abbeville. The 3rd Armoured Brigade, with 5th DCL, was to capture the high ground covering the Somme north-westwards to the sea. The French were to supply artillery and infantry, the British the armour, but with the language difficulties and the lack of time for rehearsals, the prospects of success were, at least, slim.

The action was ordered for the 27th May, but General Evans was not pleased with this plan, telling the French army commander that Cruiser and light tanks were not suitable for this kind of deliberate assault, but to no avail. It is possible that the French had heard about the Arras counter-attack and were expecting the armoured division's tanks to be Matildas.

The action was not a success. The 2nd Armoured Brigade, on the right, suffered heavily from AT fire in fortified villages with which the Germans had extended their Abbeville bridgehead. Some AT guns were sited to catch the British tanks as they came over ridges, a tactic which kept ranges short and time for tank commanders' and tank gunners' target acquisition short. The time of the attack was put back an hour but this message did not reach the 10th Hussars, the dispatch rider had been killed. This regiment advanced without infantry or artillery support and was quickly shot to pieces. A single 37-mm AT gun was credited with knocking out nine of the 20 tanks the regiment lost. The Bays attacked at the correct time with artillery support, but still lost 16 tanks. The 2nd Armoured Brigade made no real progress.

The 3rd Armoured Brigade met less resistance and was able to take up positions overlooking the Somme for the loss of 18 tanks. But the French infantry, which should have been supporting the tanks, dug in at least three miles to their rear. So the tanks withdrew.

By the end of the day the division had lost a total of 65 tanks knocked out by the Germans, and 55 tanks with mechanical breakdowns. Many of them were recovered, and the workshops, which had been set up close to Rouen, worked impressively, but there was a dire shortage of spare parts.

The French infantry, without the British tanks, renewed the attack the next day, but they were no more successful. The vehicle casualties in 2nd Armoured Brigade had been so heavy that the Bays and the 10th Hussars were amalgamated to form a composite squadron which was added to the 9th Lancers to form the 'Composite Regiment'. The 3rd Armoured Brigade was sent back to Rouen to refit. There can be little doubt that the tank losses along with the views expressed to the French Army commander by General Evans about the capabilities of Cruiser tanks resulted in little further use being made of the division by the French. This one action had gone a long way towards destroying the armoured division.

After the unsuccessful infantry attack the French 4th Armoured Division, commanded by General de Gaulle, arrived and on 29th May, and the next day, it attacked in the Abbeville direction, but failed on both days. It seems that both failures were due to poor infantry/tank cooperation.

While these French operations were continuing, the 51st Highland Division arrived. It and the 1st Armoured Division became the IX Corps of the French 7th Army. As neat as organisation looked, the British division commanders were as likely to receive orders from British sources as they were French.

There was now a short pause in operations. The Support Group lost the Borderers but gained the 2/6th East Surrey Regiment and ten 40-mm Bofors AA guns arrived at last. The 3rd Armoured Brigade took over seven Matildas which happened to be in the area, nominally a part of 1st Tank Brigade. To some extent this set up what was left of the division for the next phase of operations.

The Dunkirk evacuation was complete so there was no longer any requirement to drive north to link up with the troops there. The strategy now was to create a strong front to seal off the area captured by the Germans, and ultimately to advance north from it. The British contribution was to hold the line of the Somme from Abbeville to the sea, which involved having troops on the Bresle and the Andelle. Parts of this line were held by the

51st Division with the Composite Regiment and Support Group under command. It had two brigades along the Somme, and one on the Bresle with the Composite Regiment to its right rear. The 3rd Armoured Brigade deployed along the Andelle.

The French decided to renew the assault on the Somme bridgeheads on 4th June. The main thrust of the attack was to be mounted by the French to capture the high ground overlooking Abbeville. An infantry and an armoured division were to be used and the 51st Division would support them. The operation did not fare well. The Germans had had time to lay AT minefields and prepare their field artillery to engage tanks. When the French troops were recalled, only six out of 30 heavy tanks returned, and 60 out of 120 light tanks. It was plain that there would be no quick French recovery. The fighting caused heavy casualties among the British infantry, fortunately British tanks were not involved.

The Germans, now free of the Dunkirk operation, attacked followed the next day. The 51st Division was pushed beck to the Bresle, its situation would have been worse but for a counter-attack put in by the Composite Regiment. The Germans actually had little reason to attack the highlanders front, their main assault was to the British right in the direction of Rouen. Two panzer divisions and several infantry divisions were making excellent progress in that direction, and Rouen had the last bridge over the Seine before the sea.

There was an obvious necessity to withdraw the troops holding the Bresle and Andelle behind the Seine, but General Weygand, the Supreme Commander, vetoed this. As the situation became hourly more desperate there was another change in the chain of command. 1st Armoured Division came directly under General Altmayer, commander of a group of 7th Army divisions. General Evans spoke directly with him and agreed that his division would counter-attack to strike the flank of the German advance and prevent them outflanking the Bresle position.

At this time the division, still without the 2nd Armoured Brigade Composite regiment and Support Group, consisted of the 41 Cruisers, 7 Infantry tanks and 31 light tanks of the 3rd Armoured Brigade, and six light tanks of the Bays, probably a small number of light tanks of the 10th Hussars, and some lorry-borne personnel of the Hussars, which was all that was left of 2nd Armoured Brigade.

The counter-attack order was countermanded by General Weygand who insisted that the armoured division should defend a ten mile stretch of the Andelle to cover Rouen. General Evans had to recall his troops, the most advanced of which were in contact with German reconnaissance units. His force, missing infantry and artillery, particularly AT guns, was not well suited to such a defence. Fortunately there were British infantry of another division on hand. The light tanks of the Bays, supported by the Infantry tanks, covered river crossings. The rest of the armoured brigade pulled back from the river.

The desperate nature of the Allies' situation is illustrated by the increasingly bizarre command arrangements. There were three major British units involved: the Highland Division, the Armoured Division and the Beauman Division. This last was an *ad-hoc* unit which, in the circumstances, functioned quite well and some of its units were posted along the Andelle. Each of these units reported to different senior French officers. This was a mess that General Weygand does not seem to have been able to sort out.

The Andelle could not be defended against a serious attack. The front was too long and the AT weapons available too few. The river itself was not a serious obstacle to infantry. The Germans employed a *ruse de guerre* and broke through with captured French tanks. The Composite Regiment with the Support Group had just been returned to the Armoured Division. They were taking up their positions to the left rear of the Andelle when they ran into the advancing Germans. Both sides suffered losses, but the British had to pull back. There was now no possibility of restoring the situation by a counter-attack. Soon the Allies were in disarray. The 51st Division was cut off and the Armoured Division crossed the Seine mostly on the 8th of June. On the morning of the 9th the Germans entered Rouen and all the bridges over the Seine were down.

The effect of this was decisive. The 51st Highland Division with the rest of IX Corps was outflanked and surrounded, but its reduction did divert the Germans from attacking across the Seine so gave the Armoured Division a short while to sort itself out. On the 16th the remaining tanks of 2nd Armoured Brigade were loaded on a train which trundled off never to be seen again, at least by 1st Armoured Division soldiers. Next day a report was received that the French had requested an armistice. It was all over so the 26 tanks, 11 scout cars and 49 troop-carrying lorries of the 3rd Armoured Brigade drove the 200 miles by road to Cherbourg where they were evacuated. Only nine Cruisers made it back to England out of the 170 that left. This impressive move on its tracks was something of an answer to the critics of British tank manufacturers, but there is little doubt that this campaign had shown up the disadvantages of dividing medium armour into two types.

Due to circumstances now obscure one British tank turned up at St Nazaire, but it had to be left in France. It is to be hoped that the crew were not victims of the Lancastria disaster.

That ended the campaign. It is easy to imagine that, once the hectic pace slowed and the senior officers had a night's rest, they would have reflected on the importance of a simple chain of command, and on the general difficulty of Cruiser Tank Warfare.

It is interesting to consider the effect that a fully manned and equipped armoured division operating between the Somme and what was to be the Dunkirk perimeter might have had on the

Germans. However it should be borne in mind that it would have been difficult to supply a division there. Its main port, Le Havre, was within range of German bombers, and the bridges over the Seine and the Somme could have been attacked by dive bombers. Also its tanks, light and Cruiser, were vulnerable to the German 37-mm AT guns. The Arras counter-attack worried the Germans so much because the infantry tanks were not vulnerable to these guns.

Soon after his return to England General Evans recommended a substantial increase in the infantry and artillery component of an armoured division. This was totally unacceptable to the Armoured Corps which took the view that a balanced formation would be at the mercy of a tank-heavy one, and anyway the part played by the 1st Armoured Division was not really an example of Cruiser Tank Warfare, the division never having been deployed as a single unit. The success of Operation Compass, described in the next section, seemed to confirm the Armoured Corps point of view.

Keeping the tanks concentrated came to be a basic tenet of Cruiser Tank Warfare though the concept was only lightly mentioned in 'Modern Formations':
'The armoured fighting vehicle acts by fire and movement with the immediate object of creating an opportunity for decisive action and the ultimate one of securing a concentration of superior force at the decisive point.'

The operations in France showed how difficult maintaining this concentration could be. The Armoured Corps developed a dread of deploying in 'penny packets'[1], though if the requirement is to stiffen an infantry defence this kind of deployment can be highly effective.

Throughout the campaign it is difficult to see that General Evans had any alternatives to the actions he took. Nevertheless the failure of this campaign seems to have finished his career. It was different for his brigadiers. All three were to achieve high rank during the war.

Some of the 2nd Armoured Brigade's tanks came to light in 1945. They had been used as hard targets on a German tank range.

Note 1,
'Penny packets', an expression beloved of those writing about tank warfare, but not used by anyone else, seems to be an anglicization of *'en petits paquets'* first noticed, in this context, in *'Taschenbuch der Tanks, Erganzungsband 1927'* by F Heigl.

Operation Compass

While these disastrous events were occurring in Europe, the war was starting up in North Africa. Fortunately the danger posed by large Italian forces in Libya and Ethiopia had been noted and in 1938 steps had been taken to build up an armoured force in Egypt based on a mechanised cavalry brigade. This force was to become the 7th Armoured Division. Between September 1938 and November 1939 it was commanded and trained by General Hobart, and this training can be taken to have been in line with the most advanced RTC thinking.

This division was to take a major role in the 1940-41 North African campaign against the Italians and this campaign can reasonably be regarded as the most successful campaign the world has ever seen. However, when the campaign is viewed many decades later with the 20:20 vision of hindsight, the Italian forces can be seen to have had very little chance against the British forces. Their campaign was mounted more as a piece of political theatre than as a serious military undertaking.

The main problem was logistics. This was defined by the theatre, which was eastern Libya and the north-western sector of Egypt. Large tracts of these areas are desert, which is to say rocks with a thin covering of sand. The western area of operations, that of Jebel Akhdar, is more broken. There were settlements and some cultivation on the coast, but most importantly the only reasonable road ran close to the coast.*(see Sketch 2)*

The Italians received supplies mostly through Tripoli, but also through Benghazi and Tobruk. When the fighting started Tripoli was 1,200 miles away from the front line. As a round figure an armoured division required 10,000 tons of various supplies a month. Although it was feasible to land this quantity at the three ports, transporting it to the front line would be a considerable challenge. Considering this it is not surprising that few armoured units were expected to be deployed by the

Italians for their invasion of Egypt. This, though, resulted in the Italian forces having few troops able to manoeuvre and fight in the desert. Clearly the Italians could not have been expecting a serious fight.

Logistic difficulties and the lack of mobility of the Italian forces made it inevitable that their forces would be based on a series of field or permanent positions on, or close to, the coastal road, where they would wait to be attacked by the more mobile British, spearheaded by the 7th Armoured Division.

The fighting opened on 7th December 1940, at this date the major units of the division were:

7th Armoured Division – Major General M O'M Creagh
11th Hussars (armoured cars)
3rd RHA, less two batteries (25-pdrs)
106th RHA (anti-tank guns)
4th Armoured Brigade – Brigadier J Caunter
7th Hussars, one Cruiser squadron, two light tank sqns
2nd RTR, two Cruiser squadrons, one light tank sqn (from 3rd Hussars)
6th RTR, two Cruiser squadrons, one light tank sqns
7th Armoured Brigade – Brigadier HE Russell
3rd Hussars, one Cruiser sqn (from 2RTR), two light tank sqns
8th Hussars, one Cruiser squadron, two light tank sqns
1st RTR, two Cruiser squadrons, one light tank sqn
Support Group – Brigadier WHE Gott
1st KRRC
2nd RB
4th RHA (25-pdrs).

This list of units attempts to cover the mixing of units insisted on by General Hobart. Each light tank regiment swapped a squadron with a Cruiser regiment so that it would have the backing of its 2-pdr guns. This turned out to be a very important measure.

Apart from this division the only other armoured unit was the 7RTR, a regiment of infantry tanks, which came directly under the Corps Commander, Lt-Gen RN O'Connor.

The Italian forces in North Africa largely consisted of 14 infantry divisions none of which was motorised. They were not the best troops in the Italian army. Three divisions were 'blackshirts' and two were Libyans. These five divisions performed badly.

The most important of the Italian troops were the armoured units, of these there were two main ones. With the invading force, at Nibeiwa, was the Maletti Group. This contained 35 M11/39's and an equal number of M3's, the equivalent of the British Bren Gun Carrier. This group was totally destroyed when Nibeiwa was stormed, the opening act of the British operation. The M11's were not a match for the Matildas having only a machine gun in the turret and a 37-mm gun in the hull. Their crews were caught by surprise out of their vehicles, and even if they had been able to mount up they would have had to move their tanks to face the Matildas, then they would have found that their 37-mm rounds would have bounced off them as the Germans had done in the Arras counter-attack.

The other armoured unit was the Special Armoured Brigade, commander by General Babini, at Mechili. This unit was really in the process of forming. It was badly under strength, having 57 M13/40's when it should have had 120, but the group did contain three infantry battalions and some artillery. It was to cause the 7th Armoured Division more problems than the rest of the Italian troops in North Africa put together. In addition to these two groups there was a number of tanks around Tripoli and Benghazi which had been recently delivered or were being repaired.

Italian armour in general suffered from two main disadvantages. The main armament, either 37-mm on the M11, or 47-mm on the M13, was not quite as good as the British 2-pdr. Worse, few Italian tanks had radios. This made the control of units in action difficult and gave the British tanks a substantial advantage. Further, the fact that the Special Armoured Brigade, the Babini Group, had only recently been set up meant that it had had little opportunity for training.

This campaign will be briefly considered in an attempt to assess the degree to which it was an example of cruiser tanks warfare.

The Italians had invaded Egypt, but their invasion had been a slow and stately affair. They covered 60 miles in four days then stopped at Sidi Barrani and set up a series of fortified camps running southwards. During this period British light armour, mostly the 11th Hussars on Rolls-Royce armoured cars, harassed the Italians to a depth of many miles behind their lines. On one occasion, on 16th June, this regiment captured General Lastrucci, the chief engineer of the Italian 10th Army, and with him maps of the defences of Bardia. The 11th Hussars were to be so successful that an Italian air squadron was ordered to make the regiment's destruction its main duty. It carried out this task so well that an RAF armoured car company was attached to the regiment to make up for casualties.

The task of Operation Compass was to capture the fortified camps and drive the Italians out of Egypt. The limitation of the aim of the operation was necessary because the principal infantry unit, the 4th Indian Division, would soon be required elsewhere. The operation, originally thought of as a 'raid', was expected to last around five days,

Storming the camps was inevitably to be a task for infantry supported by artillery and 'I' tanks. It was to become standard that, once the tanks were inside the perimeter, resistance collapsed. Apart from a few large calibre AA guns, the Italians had little in the way of AT weapons that could cope with Matildas.

The role of the armoured division was to dominate the open ground between the Italian garrisons and prevent the Italians either withdrawing or reinforcing them. It would act against smaller Italian positions, prevent reconnaissance and guard against any counter-attack. But it could not attack the fortified camps or any of the Italian permanent fortifications. At the start of the operation General Creagh was ill and the division was commanded by Brigadier Caunter.

The attacking forces achieved total surprise due to meticulous camouflage and extensive deception measures, and these were successful because of the British ascendancy over the Italians gained by the 11th Hussars and other units in small scale actions in the desert.

The assault went in on 9th December 1940. The 7th Armoured Division's task was to swing to the south round to the rear of the Italian line to cover the left flank of the assaulting troops. It left its Support Group to watch Sofafi to prevent these troops interfering with the main assault. 4th Armoured Brigade captured the small post of Azziziya, containing 400 men, then took up a position on the coast road to the west of Sidi Barrani. The 7th Hussars were sent to patrol to the west of Sofafi to prevent the garrison withdrawing. The 7th Armoured Brigade was held back in reserve. An important aspect of this operation was the precise night marches of the Armoured Division.[1]

On the next day, 10th December, 4th Armoured Brigade detached 6RTR to assist the infantry attacking Sidi Barrani, a necessary move since 7RTR was down to seven serviceable Matilda tanks.

The remainder of the brigade swept the desert to the west of the Italian positions rounding up prisoners, though movement was hindered by sand storms. En route to Sidi Barrani 6RTR saw some scrappy fighting and Italian artillery caused several casualties, reducing the regiment to seven Cruisers and six light tanks.

During the following night the 7th Armoured Brigade less 8th Hussars was ordered to start along the coastal road to Buq Buq, and 4th Armoured Brigade was to assemble to the west of the Tummars prior to clearing first Sofafi and then the escarpment in the direction of Sidi Azeiz.

The 8th Hussars were sent to the west of Sofafi to prevent the escape of the Italians there, but the Hussars failed in this task, the Italians easily evading them at night. Troops of the Support Group found the position vacant next day. The retreating Italians were pursued by a squadron of armoured cars of the 11th Hussars, but the Hussars were halted by Italian aircraft firing armour piercing ammunition. The escape of this garrison was a significant disappointment.

During this night General O'Connor had driven to the armoured division's HQ to confer with Brigadier Caunter. He gave the order to proceed with the next stage of Operation Compass the capture of Bardia. This order was scarcely given when a signal arrived ordering 4th Indian Division's withdrawal. This eventuality had not been planned for but he decided to continue the pursuit with his remaining forces, the armoured division and Selbyforce, a brigade sized unit advancing along the coast.

On the morning of 11th December the 7th Armoured Brigade was preparing to attack the Italians at Buq Buq, when the 11th Hussars discovered that the Italians were evacuating that position. The brigade commander, whose tank had broken down, told Colonel Combe, the CO of 11th Hussars, to take command of the brigade and attack the Italians where found.

The result was a success, but nearly a disaster. Large numbers of were reported by 3rd Hussars who did not appreciate the strength of the Italian artillery. In best cavalry tradition the light tanks immediately charged, but unfortunately they did so over a salt marsh and bogged down. The Italian guns were destroying the stationary tanks, one after the other, when Cruisers from 8th Hussars, who had rejoined the brigade, came up and attacked the guns from the sea flank and a squadron of 11th Hussars armoured cars came up on the left flank. The fire from these destroyed the guns which were most courageously manned by the Italians.

The brigade was seriously embarrassed by the number of prisoners and had to call up some infantry from the Support Group to guard them. So far O'Connor's forces had captured 38,000 Italians and they were causing serious logistic difficulties.

There was a short halt while supply problems were sorted out and 4th Armoured Brigade was readied for its drive along the escarpment. This would be the first occasion in the war of British troops entering enemy territory, the original concept of Operation Compass had been swept away by events.

The brigade concentrated twelve miles south of Halfaya, it was commanded, in the absence of Brigadier Caunter, by Colonel Birks. He set up an advance guard to be commanded by Colonel Combe. This advance guard was to consist of the 11th Hussars, less two squadrons which would stay with the brigade, two batteries of the RHA and a squadron of light tanks from 2RTR. In fact it was becoming standard practice for the armoured cars of the hussars, which were armed with only machine guns, to be backed up by some RHA batteries.

The next phase started soon after midnight on 14th December. The brigade moved off and by 7:00 am was 20 miles to the south-west of Bardia. Combe's force went forward to find a route down the escarpment, but unfortunately it was attacked by planes and lost five armoured cars and two ancillary vehicles. It quickly recovered and was soon on the coast road to the west of Bardia. Soon the 4th Armoured Brigade had invested Bardia on its western side. Throughout this day the 11th Hussars were hit by aircraft many times and finally were temporally withdrawn from action, but they had cut the Italian telephone wires.

The 7th Armoured Brigade moved up to invest Bardia from the south. It was General O'Connor's plan that they should move quickly to prevent the Italian garrisons of Sollum and Capuzzo falling back to Bardia. They failed in doing this. This failure evoked an outburst from the General about the reluctance of armoured units to move at night, and how maintenance requirements should be decentralised to troop, or even individual AFV, level. Also he seems to have said that the officers messing together slowed the units down. If his strictures were justified they indicate a weakness of training in the brigade.

The defences of Bardia were essentially an anti-tank ditch, with a near vertical face of four feet. The ditch was of a zig-zag trace and was covered by many sunken pillboxes, a form of defence which would also be seen at Tobruk. Naturally the armoured division could not think of attacking it so they had to wait for Australian troops, who were replacing the Indians, and the Infantry tanks of 7RTR, to come up.

The 7th Armoured Brigade and the Support Group took over the complete investment of Bardia to allow 4th Armoured Brigade to be deployed elsewhere. The perimeter of Bardia was a little over 20 miles long and its garrison included three complete and elements of two infantry divisions, and a squadron of M13s. It can be seen how cowed the Italian command was to allow such a large force to be penned in by such a small one.

It could be speculated that 7th Armoured Brigade was given this static role because they were under a cloud following their 'stickiness' in allowing the Sollum and Capuzzo garrisons to escape.

On 16th December the 4th Armoured Brigade was sent off to Sidi Omar. This was not a serious fortification, being grouped around a Beau-Geste-type fort. The defenders' artillery consisted of 16 guns and was posted on the eastern side, and the garrison was approximately 1,000 men of a Black Shirt Fascisti battalion. Its capture should not have been a matter for light and Cruiser tanks, but there was no infantry available. So, after a few shells from the RHA, the tanks just charged from all directions except east, and resistance crumbled.

At this time the Division's strength was 120 light tanks, and 70 Cruisers.

Bardia was successfully assaulted on 3rd January. This was a fine feat of arms, but here it is enough to note that as soon as the tanks were inside the perimeter the end was in sight. It was at this point the Western Desert Force was renamed '13th Corps', and the scope of Operation Compass was expanded to include the capture of Benghazi after the fall of Tobruk, which was the next target.

On 5th January, even before the end of the Bardia battle, 7th Armoured Division was ordered to move off to isolate Tobruk. 7th Armoured Brigade drove, unopposed, along the Trigh Capuzzu to El Adem. The rest of the division followed as quickly as possible. The division took up positions around Tobruk unimpeded by the garrison: the Support Group to its west, 4th Armoured Brigade to the south-west, 7th Armoured Brigade to the south to cover against any possible counter-attack from the west. The Australians held the south-east from where they made their assault.

As with Bardia once the 'I' tanks were inside the perimeter the defence crumbled, but this fact should not hide the severe fighting that took place before that. The assault started on 21st January, the battle lasted two days. During this time the 7th Armoured Division was put in motion for the final stage of the campaign, the capture of Benghazi.

About 30 miles to the west of Tobruk the coastline bulges northwards and the ground becomes mountainous. This bulge is roughly semi-circular with a radius of 100 miles. It was known that there were Italian troop concentrations at Derna on the coast, and at Mechili, inland. Mechili was an obvious critical point, being at the junction of several tracks. 7th Armoured Division sent patrols to the west to reconnoitre between Mechili and Tmimi, on the road to Derna.

As soon as possible after the fall of Tobruk, Australian infantry took over the advance along the coast. The going had become too difficult for AFVs. One squadron of the 11th Hussars stayed with them. The pattern of operations was to be that the Australian infantry would pursue the Italians along the coast road. The Armoured Division would operate inland.

On 22nd January, at 2.0am, the 4th Armoured Brigade moved off in the direction of Mechili. Due to shortage of tanks the brigade had been down to two armoured regiments, as 6RTR and 8th Hussars from 7th Armoured Brigade had handed their tanks over to the other regiments, consequently the brigade took under command 3rd Hussars from 7th Armoured Brigade. The brigade had with it an infantry company. Unfortunately the night was moonless and the move resulted in several units becoming lost, but, by last light on the 23rd the brigade was closing in on Mechili.

The armoured cars of the 11th Hussars, approached Mechili from the north-east. They found that the Italians were present in strength both at Mechili and the high ground to its north. This came as something of a surprise, but fortunately the Italians could not respond fast enough to take advantage of it.

British reconnaissance concluded that the Italian force included a regiment each of infantry and artillery, and at least 50 tanks. When General O'Connor was informed of this he took measures designed at capturing the whole force and he ordered up 100 guns and an Australian brigade.

Next day, 24th January, there was a clash of armour. The light tanks of the 7th Hussars were sent to probe the Italian position, but a squadron of 22 M13's counter-attacked driving the light tanks back until they came under fire from some Cruisers of 2RTR and, being caught on the skyline, lost seven tanks in a few minutes. The final score was nine M13's, one captured, for six light tanks and two Cruisers.

Unfortunately during the night of 26/27 the Italians slipped away to the north, an essential move to save themselves from being cut off by the Australians on the coast. This was a great disappointment to the General who made his feelings known, and again criticised British armour's reluctance to move at night. The Italians, he observed, were not so reluctant. 4th Armoured Brigade pursued the Italians, but the broken country was handy for delaying tactics and the pursuit was called off. The result was that the Italian forces around Derna now had 60 to 70 tanks (M13s). Although Derna fell on 28th January it was plain that the fight along the coast road would be a long one. Consequently the headlong urgency was taken out of operations and the Armoured Division had a chance to refit.

Desert operations, involving as they do sand, are very wearing for machinery. The Cruiser tank strength of the division was down to around 50, and as some of these had exceeded their mileage allowance this figure could be expected to fall quite quickly. Total Italian tank strength was reckoned to be 100 medium and 200 light tanks, but only half of each category was believed to be runners.

However help was on its way. The 2nd Armoured Division was arriving in Egypt and two of its Cruiser regiments were due to arrive in Mechili on 7th and 9th February. To make the most efficient use of them all the 7th Brigade's Cruisers were handed over to 4th Brigade, as were a large number of light tanks, and the 3rd Hussars. One of the new regiments then joined 7th Armoured Brigade. The other was held in reserve. 7th Armoured Division now had two brigades, each the equivalent of one light tank and one cruiser tank regiment. The division was also reinforced by a squadron of armoured cars. While all this was proceeding the logistic situation was improving, Tobruk being opened sooner than expected.

After discussions with General Wavell, who was receiving questions from London as to the date British troops might be in Benghazi, General O'Connor decided on a bold stroke. Units of the 7th Armoured Division would strike out in the direction of Msus. This was well south of Benghazi. Troops there could either proceed westwards and cut the coast road, or advance north-west and attack Benghazi from, as it were, the rear. However it was not practical to advance on Msus before 10th February when the divisional reorganisation would be complete. It was planned to leave reconnaissance of the route to the last moment to preserve surprise.

This plan was certainly bold, but it must be observed that there was little scope for the deployment of armoured brigades in the broken country near the coast, so it was Msus or nothing. However the Italians upset General O'Connor's timescale by starting to withdraw their troops from the bulge to the north-east of Benghazi. If they were planning to concentrate at Benghazi this was not a problem, but if they were planning to go further they had to be attacked and destroyed otherwise the campaign would drag on and plans were afoot to send troops to Greece. This was soon reported to be the case.

The 4th Armoured Brigade was ordered to move off to Msus midday on 3rd February. Brigadier Caunter was back in command, General Creagh having returned from his sick bed. The brigade was to include a battalion of the Rifle Brigade, 4 RHA and an AT battery. The move did not take place on time due to fuel and ration problems. The brigade left at 7.00am next day.

When the brigade was finally in motion progress was slow and by 11.00am it was apparent that some changes had to be made, so an advance guard was organised to be commanded by Colonel Combe. 'Combe's Force' was to be as fast moving as possible. It consisted of:

Regimental HQ 11th Hussars, commander Lt Col JFB Combe
'C' Squadron 11th Hussars (armoured cars)
'B' Squadron KDG (armoured cars)
'C' Battery 4th RHA
Detachment of 106th AT Regiment (8 AT guns)
Detachment of 155th Light AA Regiment (3 AA guns)
2nd Battalion RB.

Considering the unreconnoitred state of the track, it is surprising that there were no RE units with this force. It should also be noted that there were no tanks.

Combe's Force arrived at Msus at 1.0am 5th February. 4th Armoured Brigade arrived around five hours later, with 50 Cruisers and 95 light tanks, followed by the Support Group. There was a halt because Italian aircraft had sown the area with 'thermos' mines which were a considerable danger at night. By this time it was plain that the Italians were withdrawing completely and a huge convoy was proceeding south from Benghazi. Seeing this, the divisional commander preferred to go south-west to Sidi Saleh. So away went Combe's Force to block the coast road there. The 4th Armoured Brigade followed at its best speed. The Support Group moved in the Benghazi direction but was halted by Italian resistance.

The result was a very near run thing. Combe's Force arrived only an hour and a half before the Italians, and the battle started at 2.30pm. The British had the advantage of surprise and the Italians were amazed to find them blocking their escape route. Presumably those first in contact with the British were administrative troops and not those best at mounting an attack at short notice. The first column easily surrendered after some escorting tanks were knocked out. This produced a prisoner problem for Combe's Force.

Shortly after 5.00 pm a much larger column came along and it quickly began to organise an assault. Colonel Combe contacted Brigadier Caunter asking him to send his brigade to Beda Fomm, around 10 miles north of the road block. Brigadier Caunter sent an advance guard of 7th Hussars' light tanks and six Cruisers from 2RTR, they went as fast as possible and came up at the rear of the column at around 6.00 pm. The tanks attacked the artillery firing at the roadblock, then drove along the east of the column firing into it. This put an end to any offensive action on the part of the Italians, and although large numbers of them surrendered most did not. Many of the tanks were running out of fuel, but this problem was solved, at least in the short term, by petrol found in some Italian vehicles.

There was something of an overnight standoff. The next day was to see heavy and continual rain that was cold and depressing. It hampered vision, probably resulting in the Italians missing some tactical opportunities. In the morning the Italians, who had been reinforced overnight mounted another attack on the roadblock, but this was easily held. The remainder of 4th Armoured Brigade was coming up and 19 Cruisers from 'A' squadron 2RTR took up a defensive position on a low hill just to the east of the Italian column about seven miles north of the roadblock. This feature was referred to as the 'pimple'. Other units of the brigade, 3rd and 7th Hussars, harassed the column to the north of the pimple.

The pimple became of critical importance as it prevented the Italians moving their tanks south to attack the roadblock. The Babini Group, which had eluded the British at Mechili, had been covering the rear of the Italian column. Now it was called on to save the column. Early in the morning a group of ten M13s tried to go south. The British tanks were waiting for them, just below the crest of the pimple. At a range of 600 yards the Cruisers edged forward till their main armament cleared the crest then opened fire. All ten Italian tanks were knocked out without firing a shot in return. The Cruisers then fell back east about a mile to another ridge, known as the 'Mosque Ridge', and repeated the tactic destroying seven more tanks that were trying a wider manoeuvre. A further Cruiser unit, 'C'sqn 2RTR, was arriving and this encountered and destroyed another ten Italian tanks and reoccupied the pimple.

While 'A'sqn had been away on the Mosque Ridge and not in a position to stop Italian movement, some Italian tanks had driven south so the squadron took off in pursuit, claiming a further ten. They arrived back at the pimple joining 'C' sqn at 11:15am. Both squadrons were very short of fuel and ammunition, some of both being supplied by HQ troop.

The Italians then brought up more tanks, three of which were quickly knocked out, but they preferred to stand off while artillery shelled the pimple. The RHA battery with the armoured brigade gave counter battery fire, reducing the effectiveness of the Italian artillery. The upshot of this was that the British tanks pulled back east a mile to the ridge abandoning three tanks: two hit by shells, one because of mechanical breakdown. They were met by fuel and ammunition trucks, and filled up with both. They then returned to the flank of the Italian column but at a point about a mile south of the pimple which had been occupied by the Italians who were moving artillery onto it.

No doubt things looked black to the Italian command, but the British situation was also looking desperate. Italian infantry were beginning to infiltrate round the roadblock, and 3rd and 7th Hussars, who had been very effectively harassing the column were almost out of ammunition and were being driven back by M13s. The Italian artillery on the pimple would soon dominate the battlefield, the British battery had lost its Forward Observation Post and could not engage the Italians.

At this point the commander of 7th Armoured Brigade, really now only 1RTR, arrived and contacted Brigadier Caunter. Unfortunately he came in a staff car with no radio and was out of contact with his brigade, but his brigade came on of its own accord and came into action against the Italians north on the pimple. The RHA's forward observer came back on the air and they blasted the Italians on the pimple then 2RTR again occupied it. This regiment was now down to four Cruisers. At 6:00 pm the Italians again occupied the pimple, the three surviving RTR Cruisers fell back a mile to the ridge, where fortunately more ammunition lorries had arrived.

Early next morning the Italians made their last and greatest assault on Combe's Force. They attacked with 30 M13s. It was a very near-run thing, the last surviving British AT gun knocking out the last Italian tank. This failure signalled the end for the Italians. The Australians were coming up behind them, 4th and 7th Armoured Brigades, fully 'bombed up' and refuelled, were to their flank, and Combe's Force immoveable to their front. They started to surrender.

This action really concluded the campaign. A campaign that had seen one corps of varying strength, but usually of two divisions, over a period of two months, advance 500 miles and destroy an army of ten divisions, capturing 130,000 prisoners, 180 medium and over 300 light tanks, and 845 guns of field calibre and larger. The cost was less than 2,000 casualties.

It was an amazing victory, at the time this must have seemed a resounding endorsement of 'Modern Formations'.

Note 1,

One of the most important armoured corps memoirs covering this period, 'Leakey's Luck' by Rea Leakey, Sutton 1999, mentions a two squadron tank action, Leakey having been one of the squadron leaders, by 1RTR on this or the next day, which resulted in the destruction of eight M13s. Leakey's account is quoted in P Delaforce's 'Battles with Panzers', Amberley 2010. The relevant squadron war diaries, which are held at the Bovington Tank Museum, show that this action did not take place. It is possible, of course, that Leakey made a mistake with the date of the action he describes, but it is by no means obvious what the real date could have been.

Chapter 5

Practice Considered

At the time of the surrender of the Italians at Beda Fomm the British army would have had total confidence in its armoured forces, and these functioned in line with the principles laid down in 'Modern Formations'.

As has been shown in the last two chapters, in the decade which had passed since the publication of 'Modern Formations' there had taken place a number of occurrences relevant to Cruiser Tank Warfare. There had been a cut-back in the exercises held by experimental mechanised forces. The Cruiser tank series had been designed in line with 'Modern Formations' requirements. The German successes in 1940 were not fully understood and seemed to confirm the validity of 'Modern Formations'. Even more so did the British successes in Operation Compass.

It will be necessary to briefly consider these four occurrences.

The cessation of large scale exercises was a pity. To date these exercises had shown that a mechanised force was greatly superior to a non-mechanised one. The lessons drawn from such exercises seem a little elementary now. They may not have seemed so at the time, but even so there is a distinct impression that there was not the 'Blimpish' resistance to mechanisation and tanks that is so often portrayed by the tank enthusiasts.

Probably inevitably, due to the high cost of these things, there were no exercised pitting two large armoured forces against each other. If there had been, or if the problem had been studied in Tactical Exercises Without Troops (TEWTs), it would have been realised that, because of demolitions and the need to deploy against small rearguards, the pursuing force must always move more slowly than the pursued. Also logistical considerations mitigated more against the pursuer than the pursued, who was falling back on his supply dumps. And this difference was greater for armour than for infantry. Consequently a retreating force could not easily be brought to battle by a pursuing one.

Further, 'Modern Formations' made a clear distinction between infantry and tank fighting. This would inevitably result in there being a definite time-lag between the enemy's front line being broken, by infantry and artillery, and the pursuit being taken up by the tanks. No matter how easy driving one large unit through another might seem in theory, in practice the result was chaos and delay.

The Cruiser tanks specification was an outcome of 'Modern Formations'. It may be the fact that a Universal Tank was too expensive and this resulted in the Cruiser/Infantry tank divide, but it is also the fact that the Infantry Tank Mk II, the Matilda II, was an excellent tank in 1940. After Dunkirk in the wake of German successes production emphasis was switched to Cruisers from Infantry Tanks, but this was the result of misreading experience.

The main feature of the Cruiser was speed, but in practice this is not the advantage it should be. In fact many soldiers who saw the Afrika Korps in motion were surprised at how slowly it moved. Providing a tank has enough power to jockey for position, it can put up with a top speed of less than 20 mph. Speed can never compensate for lack of armour. If 'Modern Formations' had not developed the concept of herds of tanks thundering around, then perhaps the specifications for the tanks would have been better thought out.

It is difficult to be sure of the extent to which the German successes in Poland and France were really understood. There was plenty of information disseminated, but it rarely went beyond obvious generalisations. It was appreciated that the Germans used armoured (Panzer) divisions in these campaigns and they were the keys to their successes. Therefore the British Army must deploy armoured divisions. Further, the panzer divisions contained mostly light tanks which, being fast and inadequately armed and armoured, could be regarded as the equivalent of Cruiser Tanks. However the bulk of the fighting undertaken by the panzer divisions, was done by the infantry and artillery units, ably assisted by airpower. When the German tanks were called on to fight, as in the Gembloux Gap battle, they were roughly handled. The panzer divisions had two great advantages over their opponents. One was that their commanders were well forward and, assisted by aerial reconnaissance, could make decisions quickly to take advantage of local opportunities. The other was their superiority in logistics, based on their experience in Poland and Austria.

The Germans analysed their experiences in the French and Polish campaigns and realised that their vehicles and organisation, which were good enough for Cruiser Tank Warfare, were not good enough for real armoured warfare, so they started on a program of up-armouring and up-gunning their tanks and improving co-operation between their tanks and AT guns. There can be little doubt that if the 7th Armoured Division in Operation Crusader in late 1941 had had to fight a panzer division of 1940, the Germans would have caused it little trouble, and there lay the problem. British equipment and training had not improved, but the Germans' had. They had found the Cruiser Tank Warfare concept wanting.

Finally there was the colossal success of Operation Compass, the Wavell Offensive. This success should never be forgotten or downplayed. However it was essentially a series of set-piece assaults on Italian permanent or field fortifications, by infantry supported by Infantry tanks. Significantly the RAF had played little part in the operation. There were few planes available, and Beda Fomm was beyond their range.

The 7th Armoured Division covered immense distances, and its logistic difficulties caused more trouble than the Italians who had few tanks, and they were of poor quality, and whose infantry was poorly trained, had few AT weapons, and was hopelessly out-classed. This is not to understate the Armoured Division's achievement in covering large distances and establishing blocking positions, and, at Beda Fomm, rounding up a defeated army. But Operation Compass, which was the finest example of Cruiser Tank Warfare, only succeeded because of the poor opposition.

However over ten years had passed and a good deal of experience had been gained since the publication of 'Modern Formations' so a new manual was produced in May 1941. This was the 'Army Training Instruction No 3, Handling of an Armoured Division'. This manual was less ambitious than 'Modern Formations', but rather came up with some practical procedures. It presumed an armoured division of two armoured brigades, each of three armoured regiments and a motor battalion, and a support group of one infantry battalion, a RHA regiment and an AT regiment.

At least this manual discussed the tank vs tank engagement:

'The decision whether our armoured forces are to seek action with those of the enemy will depend on the relative strength of armoured forces in the whole theatre of war. Once, however, an enemy armoured force is in a position to intervene effectively in the battle its destruction will be the main task of our own armoured formations. Its defeat is likely to have a marked moral effect, and to render considerably easier subsequent operations....

...Although air reconnaissance may give warning of the proximity of enemy armoured forces, there will often be little time for a deliberate plan or for detailed orders....

...The main requirements for success are superior fire power, combined with the good use of ground and immediate readiness for action. These will be obtained by effective reconnaissance and intercommunications, quick orders, and the ability to manoeuvre rapidly....

...Armoured action consists of manoeuvre which has as its object the utilisation of accidents of the ground to bring fire on the enemy. The action will consist of a series of such manoeuvres, each side trying to secure a commanding locality or to out-manoeuvre an opponent who may be in such a position already. The high ground and obstacles will play a great part in influencing such action and their skilful use may enable a smaller force to destroy a larger one piecemeal....

...Tanks, or infantry of the motor battalion or support group, and anti-tank guns, may sometimes be presented with an opportunity of checking the enemy frontally as the heads of his columns are crossing the defiles over an obstacle. While checked frontally, and with his force divided by the obstacle, the main attack by armoured units may be directed against his flank....

...Fire from stationary positions will always be more accurate than from a moving platform. At the same time, if firing is confined to 'hull down' positions, opportunities of engaging the enemy at a disadvantage will often be lost. It must be realized that no stationary position is of value for more than a few seconds since the enemy will always move to avoid fire by utilization of ground. When this situation occurs, armoured formations should be prepared to develop fire on the move in order to retain the advantage secured by the preliminary burst of fire....

...Success or failure in the series of fire fights which go to make up the battle as a whole will often depend on the initial deployment and disposition of the opposing forces....

...In action the leading part will be played by the armoured regiments. The artillery will seldom be in a position to help in the tank vs tank battle.'

This was a reasonably advanced statement in that it does envisage a role for the support grouping in the mobile battle, even if a very limited one. It will be seen to be far behind the 'Sword and Shield' tactics of the German Afrika Korps.

Remarkably the rather obvious statements that fire from a stationary vehicle was more effective than that from a moving one, and that tanks should continually move from one hull-down position to another, were direct contradictions to the RTC's policy. Unfortunately the statement that there was no place for artillery in the tank vs tank engagement was one of the reasons why the British tank units were so much less effective in the desert than were the Germans.

There was a much greater role for the division's infantry, particularly the motor battalions, but being in lorries their role was restricted. *'In the early stages of an armoured action the motor battalion, owing to its lack of armour, will be unable to accompany the rest of the brigade. It should remain in an area in which it can protect itself, but should be available to move forward at short notice. It should then concentrate on mopping up the lines of advance which wheeled vehicles will require to use to refill the armoured brigades. Purely defensive tasks should be taken over as early as possible by infantry of the support group or by bus-carried troops of the infantry division following behind....*

...When it is foreseen that opposition is likely to be met which cannot be overcome or avoided by armoured regiments – as, for example, in close country – the motor battalion should be working well forward in close co-operation with the armoured units. Such opposition is likely to be based on an

obstacle, and speed in launching the attack will be of primary importance in order to restore the mobility of the armoured units. Early decentralization of motor companies under the command of armoured regiments will assist rapid action; but a single company has little attacking power and, if resistance is considerable, the battalion should be employed as a whole to make an effective crossing on the front of one regiment – the attack being supported by intense fire from mortars and artillery, and possibly, by close support aircraft. It will generally be feasible for the operations to be limited both in extent and in depth....

....At night the motor battalions may be required to protect the armoured regiments in harbour; but they cannot be employed at night as well as by day except for limited periods.'

These roles should have been sufficient to keep the division moving as, at the time, infantry AT weapons were poor. The AT rifle had proven insufficient for the task and the Bazooka, and similar weapons often referred to as 'Shoulder Launchers', had not yet been invented. Even so it is surprising that the need for APCs was not identified.

The roles of the Support Group were in general defensive, and, as stated in the 'Army Training Instruction No 3', were to '*include:-*

(i) The occupation of a defensive position based on a natural obstacle to form a pivot of manoeuvre for the armoured brigades.

(ii) The protection of the armoured brigades in harbour

(iii) The protection of a flank

(iv) The holding of important ground secured by armoured brigades

(v) Mopping up after an attack by armoured brigades

(vi) Attacks beyond the scope of motor battalions to force obstacles or to overcome centres of resistance.'

In the advance the armoured brigades were to advance continuously, either, as the situation demanded, 'one up', with one brigade in front of the other, to allow the second brigade to be moved as a divisional reserve, or 'two up' to cover a large frontage and secure more ground for manoeuvre. Also each brigade could deploy its regiments one, two or three up as required.

The necessity for air support, bombing and reconnaissance, was recognised, but no method of achieving it was specified.

It was appreciated that an armoured division could not attack an enemy *'occupying a highly organised position'*, but would have to wait for other troops. But then *'The object will be to discover as early as possible the weak spots in the enemy dispositions, to break through at these spots, and subsequently to exploit success by breaking up the cohesion of the enemy formation – by attacking the nerve centre of its head quarters and by destroying its elements by attacking them from flanks and rear.'* Once again the concept of attacking HQs, so fine in theory, but of surprisingly little utility in practice. Later in this chapter, and in the next, it will be seen that brigade, division and even corps HQs could be scattered in the course of mobile operations, but due to the use of radios the confusion caused would only last a few hours and little permanent damage would be caused.

'Enemy defence will seldom have been located in great detail, and orders to leading formations must not tie their hands. It will generally be sufficient to give the intention and a general direction of advance, together with, in some instances, an objective. Commanders will then be at liberty to select lines of advance in detail and, by manoeuvre, to avoid striking the enemy from the direction expected and where preparations to meet the attack have been made....

...If resistance is encountered from tank proof localities (e.g. villages) which must be overcome to clear the line of advance for the rest of the division, artillery or close support bombing will be required. After the bombardment it will be necessary for the locality to be mopped up by the infantry of the motor battalion. If the resistance is strong, and the entries are mined or obstructed, a deliberate planned attack by the motor battalion, with all the fire support available, will be necessary....

...Surprise and enterprising action are of first importance in attacks on a river line or a railway. Such obstacles can often be crossed at the less obvious places. The sudden and unexpected appearance of tanks may cause the whole defence to crumble.'

It is remarkable that the last extract mentions railways as possible defended lines. This might reflect the British tendency to use them as such when constructing the Stop Lines in 1940. No other army seems to have used them like this.

In defence *'the action of armoured divisions......will always be offensive. They can therefore be used:-'*

For spoiling attacks. *'To attack and disorganize enemy forces in front of our own defensive position. Frequently the threat alone of armoured action will slow up and delay an enemy advance and gain time for the completion of our own preparations. The object of the divisional commander will be to cause the maximum loss and disorganisation to the enemy without becoming involved in a serious battle; he will successively withdraw and resume operations in other areas.'*

As can be seen the difference between this kind of attack and a raid, which was so deprecated in 'Modern Formations', can be difficult to define. This may point to sloppy thinking in at least one of the manuals. There is no instance of a British spoiling (pre-emptive) attack, unless the first phase of Operation Compass is considered as one. The Germans were too offensively, and manoeuvre, minded to be caught like that. 'As long as you attack them they cannot find the time to plan to attack you,' was a sentiment expressed by General Patton, and again, 'to keep the Germans from attacking, we had to attack.' The Germans carried out several spoiling attacks, an example of one is given in the chapter on the first phase of the Battle of Gazala. A significant disadvantage of spoiling attacks was that their tank casualties would be left behind when the attackers returned to their own lines.

And for counter-attacks. *'To counter-attack and destroy enemy forces that may penetrate into our position. Immediate counter-attack tasks will usually be allotted to army tank units'*

There were to be many armoured counter-attacks mounted in the desert campaigns, but none by armoured divisions, only armoured brigades. This will be considered in subsequent chapters.

There was a further role proposed for the armoured divisions in the early period after Dunkirk. This was to drive deep into occupied territory and their presence would spark off a huge anti-German uprising. Fortunately this concept was never put to the test.

After Beda Fomm the greater part of the armoured units was deployed to Greece, its place being partly taken by inexperienced units. It was known that there was a risk in this and it might have been justified had the German commander been anyone but Rommel, who attacked before it was believed he could and the British forces were either locked up in Tobruk, or bundled back to Egypt.

The situation in North Africa could be seen as desperate, the recent reverse had occurred at the same time as disasters in Greece and Crete. Consequently a convoy, 'Tiger', was sent carrying tanks and these were expected to restore the situation.

Before the arrival of 'Tiger', Wavell decided to launch Operation Brevity. The logic being that the Germans were experiencing logistic difficulties and an immediate counter-attack might be a success. The 7th Armoured Division was to operate on the southern flank, but it was weak, only possessing 29 Cruisers. The Germans were found to be stronger than expected and the operation was called off.

After the arrival of 'Tiger' and the re-equipping of the 7th Armoured Division, came Operation Battleaxe. The convoy brought 21 light tanks, 135 Matildas and 82 Cruisers. Of the Cruisers 50 were of the latest model, Mark VI, the Crusader. Unfortunately the Crusaders arrived without tool kits and manuals, and many without radios. On top of these problems the regiments were rushed into action before they could fully familiarise themselves with the new tanks. Not surprisingly Battleaxe was to be a disaster for the division and a triumph for the defenders. There were not enough Cruisers for both armoured brigades of the division, instead 4th Brigade had two regiments of 'I' tanks, 7th Brigade had two regiments of Cruisers.

4th Armoured Brigade provided a column to attack Capuzzo and other locations, and some tanks to support an infantry assault on the Halfaya Pass. 7th Armoured Brigade was to operate on the desert front.

The Matildas, hitherto the Queen of the Battlefield, had only patchy success. The Cruisers could make no progress against the German defences which were a series of strongpoints set up for all-round defence and each containing several AT guns, and some 88-mm AA guns in the AT role. They were fortunate that the German counter-attacks were not so well coordinated as usual.

Operation Battleaxe should have shown the importance of AT guns and the necessity of greater cooperation between the arms, particularly tanks and artillery, to destroy them. Unfortunately because it was easy to see tanks and difficult to see AT guns, partly because they were small, and partly because of heat haze, it was believed that the only important targets were German tanks and cooperation between the arms was unnecessary.

These three relatively small actions did little to prepare the 7th Armoured Division for its next major action, Operation Crusader.

Operation Crusader
The first seven days

In November 1941 occurred one of the great British battles of the war. In it the 8th Army, now fully equipped with modern tanks, was to destroy the major axis forces in the desert and relieve Tobruk, which had been besieged since 10th April 1941. This operation was codenamed 'Crusader'.

This operation turned out to be the most complex battle of this size fought to date. It lasted much longer than was originally planned, and in the end, despite both sides being exhausted, it was a British victory. Tobruk had been relieved and the surviving Axis forces driven out of Cyrenaica. However, during the first phase of the battle, a period of seven days, the British Cruiser tank units were all but annihilated. How this happened will be considered in this chapter.

The Terrain

In contrast to Operation Compass this operation took place almost entirely in classic desert conditions. The ground was flat and hard so that vehicles, both tracked and wheeled, could be driven anywhere as required. The pattern was different to the north. On a line running roughly east-west, and about five miles south of the Tobruk perimeter was a series of ridges or escarpments. These are not high but their northern faces are steep enough to be impassable to vehicles except at a small number of places. There are three escarpments, one on each side of the Trigh Capuzzo, an old arab track, and the third roughly three miles to the south so that the southern two escarpments were each side of the Sidi Rezegh airfield. A modern road, the Via Balbia, runs to the north of the ridges, close to the sea. North of the ridges the country is much more broken, and difficult for tanks. Although many map features are actual geographical features, there are many others, like Gabr Saleh, which are only expanses of sand. This made navigation sometimes very difficult. *(see Sketch 3)*

Tactical Implications

The open nature of the terrain resulted in surprise being difficult to obtain, and the opening of Crusader, as with most battles, would depend on surprise. The answer was deception and a great deal of trouble was taken to mislead the enemy. In particular the British tanks were fitted with framed canopies, referred to a 'sunshades', that gave them the appearance of lorries.

The range of engagement, mirages and dust, frequently made AFV identification difficult. The poor quality of radios made reconnaissance less effective than it should have been. The radios of the time had only enough range for voice communications within the squadrons or back to RHQ. For transmission back to brigade it was necessary to use morse code. This slowed everything down and gave commanders the opportunity to ignore orders they did not agree with, saying they were not received [1]. The difficulties of navigation made the resupply of fuel, ammunition and rations to the fighting units unreliable and a perpetual worry for the commanders.

Remarkably British tank units were usually better than the Germans at desert navigation. This was because of the use of sun compasses fixed on the turrets. The Germans did not use them but made more use of light reconnaissance aircraft. So if they made a mistake, it was a bigger one.

The two airforces provided little direct ground support during the period in question. The lack of landmarks caused difficulties, but the main problem with the RAF, was that a workable system for controlling ground attack aircraft had not been set up - a case of culpable negligence. The RAF did, though, by shooting down a number of Stukas prevent Axis ground attack.

German aerial reconnaissance was remarkably ineffective. Initially this was caused by the heavy rain making their airfields unusable, though later on it was only partially explained by the RAF's numerical superiority. Ground attack suffered from the same problems and, as will be seen, on the critical day Rommel's HQ was scattered, upsetting the command system. German aircraft sometimes machine gunned British tanks, but that was to indicate their position to German tanks. German AA artillery could provide little assistance in the fight against the RAF. Most of its guns were in use in the AT role.

The supply of fuel was made critical by the vast distances travelled by the tanks. The centre line of the 4th Armoured Brigade extended over a total of 1,700 miles during Crusader. Some of its individual tanks clocked up 3,000 miles. The British army supplied petrol in four gallon cans. These were made of welded thin sheet steel. They were referred to as 'flimsies' because of their tendency to split and leak. They were usually packed in wooden crates, two to a crate. This did not always improve things as nails in the crates could sometimes puncture the cans. It has been estimated that 30% of the petrol sent to the troops in the desert was lost because of leaking flimsies, and the vehicles delivering it were sometimes wet with petrol, increasing their already worrying vulnerability. The flimsies were made locally in Egypt, presumably as an economy measure. On the other hand the Germans (Jerries) preferred not to waste fuel like this and used the more solid 'Jerrycan' (*Wehrmachtskanister*). This was a robust 20 litre pressed steel container, with a neck so that it was easier to use without a funnel. It is still in service in most armies today.

The Germans had constructed a defensive system based on a series of strongpoints running south from around Sollum. It played a large part in defeating Operation Battleaxe. Since then it had been extended to a total length of 25 miles, and this ensured that if the British outflanked it to the south they would be well away from the German supply route close to the coast, and their own supply situation, particularly for fuel, would be more difficult.

The days were short, 7.00 am to 5.00 pm being the period it was light enough for operations. Also there tended to be a two hour break at noon due to the distortion of vision caused by the shimmering heat. These factors resulted in the indecisiveness of many actions. It was dark before a decision could be reached.

A further implication of the wide-open spaces was the large frontages covered by the armoured brigades. Tanks were supposed to deploy 100 yards apart. Consequently a regiment advancing with two squadrons 'up' and deployed in extended lines would have a frontage of approximately 3,000 yards. A brigade with two regiments up would cover 6,000 yards. Such, of course, was an imposing sight which commanders in the subsequent Tunisian, Italian and North-Western European campaigns would never see. The photogenic nature of the desert campaigns no doubt played a major part in making them popular with the public and historians. Unfortunately this wide dispersion and the dust inevitably thrown up by moving tanks made the units difficult to control, and difficult for them to generate heavy firepower. This, together with the short winter days, contributed to the indecisiveness of desert fighting, and British tanks had to learn to drive more slowly to avoid creating dust clouds.

Artillery was, as usual, the God of War. As the surface of the desert was, under a thin layer of sand, hard rock the explosion of shells was more lethal that it would be in Europe. There was not the soft soil to dampen the explosion, instead, the rock provided extra fragmentation. The same facts of geology naturally made it difficult for infantry being shelled to protect themselves by digging in. Conversely the open nature of the desert, and the lack of reference points, made the application of fire more difficult. Also as soon as the guns opened fire they raised clouds of dust, giving their positions away and inviting counter-battery fire.

The Germans had a great advantage in artillery terms. Their Panzer IV could deliver significant HE fire. The British were particularly vulnerable to HE fire because their AT guns, the 2-pdrs, were rather tall and difficult to conceal and shield. Also their Cruiser tanks were vulnerable because of their thin armour. German tanks would usually not attack until their target had been given a good pounding with HE.

German artillery was usually kept concentrated under a single commander, particularly the medium guns, whereas the British artillery was scattered among the divisions. In general the German artillery can be regarded as the more effective, the more so as the British 25-pdrs were often pressed into doing duty as AT guns, being taken away from their normal role. When considering armoured warfare it is easy to forget what a battle winner a concentrated artillery barrage could be.

Finally there were the climate and the weather. The days were hot, as expected, but the nights were cold. This came as a shock to the most recently joined troops. Worse, it rained heavily on many of the days in question. This reduced visibility, grounded aircraft, made going difficult, particularly for wheeled vehicles, and made life miserable for the soldiers. Tank crews stowed their bed rolls and blankets on the outside of their tanks. So they became sodden and cold and the little sleep the crewmen got was rendered less comfortable. Lack of sleep ultimately results in a decline in daytime performance.

As the nights were long their utilisation was more important, and the Germans used them much more efficiently than did the British. The British procedure was at nightfall to go into leaguer, or 'laager up'[2]. They concentrated their tanks, filled the tanks with fuel and ammunition, had a meal and a night's rest. Shortly before dawn they deployed into tactical formations. The Germans, however, stayed in tactical formation all night, moving as necessary. Their recovery teams scoured the desert for knocked out vehicles and often worked on them *in situ*, providing light by sending up flairs. The consequence of this was that the British often knew where the Germans were, but they seldom took advantage of this.

Tactics

These have been covered in an earlier chapter. It is enough here to note that, because of their belief in the cooperation of arms, the Germans manoeuvred as complete panzer divisions, masses of vehicles moving slowly, at the pace of the slowest artillery tractor. This could present a very intimidating sight. Conversely the British armour, manoeuvring by brigade or individual regiment, moved much faster, but lacked the punch. Both sides were to find that, in desert conditions, once a division was broken up it was very difficult to reunite, but on the other hand inhibiting independent brigade actions could result in tactical opportunities being lost.

The British Troops

The British offensive was to be carried out by the 8th Army. This army had two corps. One, the 13th Corps, was infantry. The other, the 30th Corps, was based on armoured brigades.

The principal units were:

Eighth Army, commander Lieutenant General Sir A Cunningham
- 13th Corps - Lt Gen AR Godwin-Austen
  - 4th Indian Division – Maj Gen FW Messervy
  - New Zealand Division – Maj Gen BC Freyberg
  - 1st Army Tank Brigade – Brig HRB Watkins, which included two tank regiments with a total of 147 infantry tanks.
- 30th Corps – Lt Gen CWM Norrie
  - Three armoured car regiments, two allocated to 7th Armoured Division
  - 7th Armoured Division – Maj Gen WHE Gott
    - 4th Armoured Brigade – Brig AH Gatehouse
      - Brigade HQ, 10 Honeys
      - 8th Hussars, 51 Honeys

3rd RTR, 51 Honeys
5th RTR, 51 Honeys
One regiment of 25-pdrs, one anti-tank regiment
2nd Scots Guards
7th Armoured Brigade – Brig GMO Davy
Brigade HQ, 9 Cruisers
7th Hussars, 37 Cruiser and 20 Crusaders
2nd RTR, 52 Cruisers
6th RTR, 49 Crusaders
Two batteries of 25-pdrs, one anti-tank battery
One infantry company
22nd Armoured Brigade – Brig J Scott-Cockburn
Brigade HQ, 8 Crusaders
3rd City of London Yeomanry,
47 Crusaders and 4 CS tanks
4th City of London Yeomanry,
43 Crusaders and 5 CS tanks
2nd Royal Gloucestershire Hussars,
47 Crusaders, 4 CS tanks
One battery of 25-pdrs, one anti-tank battery
One infantry company
7th Support Group – Brig JC Campbell
Two infantry battalions
Three batteries of 25-pdrs
One AT regiment
22nd Guards Brigade – Brig JCO Marriott
Two infantry battalions
one regiment of 25-pdrs, one anti-tank regiment
1st South African Division – Maj Gen GE Brink

These figures give 30th Corps a total of 489 tanks in the field. In addition to these there was a substantial reserve of 92 cruiser types, mostly Crusaders, and 90 Honeys in workshops which could be fed into the battle.

The 4th Armoured Brigade was originally a part of 13th Corps, but came under 7th Armoured Division for Crusader. It was an experienced unit with reliable tanks.

In the other brigades the condition of the British tanks was variable. In 7th Armoured Brigade three quarters of the Cruisers were old A13s, and the remainder even older A10s. These tanks could be expected to be very unreliable. In 22nd Armoured Brigade the Crusaders were newly arrived from the UK and had been hastily modified for desert conditions. It is not obvious why this could not have been done in England. The delay caused meant that their crews had had little or no training in Africa, neither had Brigade HQ, and the lack of training at this level would make itself felt at Bir el Gubi.

The South African Division had been included in the corps because it had a large establishment of vehicles, so could be expected to be highly mobile. It was, though, not well trained for armoured corps operations. The Guards Brigade was to defend the Lines of Communication.

The Axis Troops

The situation for the Axis was complicated by there being two nationalities involved, the desert being fought over was theoretically owned by Italy. The overall commander was Italian, Marshal Bastico. Under him were:

- The 20th Italian Mobile Corps – Gen Gambara
  - Ariete Armoured Division, 146 M13/60s and 50 light tanks
  - Trieste Motorized Division
- Armoured Group Africa, commander General E Rommel
  - 21st Italian Corps – General Navarrini
    - four infantry divisions
  - German Africa Corps (DAK) – Gen L Cruwell
    - 15th Panzer Division - Maj Gen Neumann-Silkow
      - Panzer Regt 8, 38 pz II, 75 pz III, 20 pz IV
      - four infantry battalions

21st Panzer Division – Maj Gen von Ravenstein
Panzer Regt 5, 32 pz II, 64 pz III, 15 pz IV
three infantry battalions
Africa Division – Maj Gen Suemmermann
Two infantry regiments. This division, which became the 90th Light Division, was in the process of forming. It appears to have contained a large number of ex-French Foreign Legion troops. It was not very important to the period being studied here.
Savona Italian Infantry Division.

Disregarding the Italian light tanks it can be seen that the Axis had 390 tanks in the field, though the panzer II's and the M13/60's were no match for the British tanks. The great problem was that they did not have the reserve of tanks that the British had, and this meant that they were worse placed for a sustained battle. It can be presumed that the Germans had some idea, if not a perfect knowledge, of this mismatch.

As can be seen initially the Italian Mobile Corps did not come under Rommel, but as soon as serious fighting started this was changed.

The Axis forces were not well placed to receive an attack. The four divisions of the 21 Italian Corps were deployed round Tobruk maintaining the siege. The Italian Mobile Corps was to the south of Tobruk, with Ariete at Bir el Gubi, and Trieste to its west. The 15th Panzer Division was close to the coast where it was preparing for the assault of Tobruk. The 21st Panzer Division was on the Trigh Capuzzo, to the west of Sidi Azeiz. Rommel's Head Quarters was at Gambut. The Savona, and elements of the 21st Panzer Division were manning the defences on the frontier at Sollum and to its south.

The reason why the Axis forces were not well placed to receive an attack lies with the impression formed of British intentions by Rommel during Operation *Sommernachtstraum,* a raid which turned into a reconnaissance in force, which he led in mid-September. Although he was lucky to return alive from this jaunt he concluded that the British were not planning an offensive in the near future. This was a preconception he was to be reluctant to abandon.

The General British Concept of Operations

The offensive was to involve both corps. 13th Corps was to advance over the broken country north of the Trigh Capuzzo, 30th Corps over the open country to its south. Initially the role of 13th Corps was limited, possibly 'I' tanks were under something of a cloud following Operation Battleaxe in which they suffered heavy casualties caused by German heavy AT guns. Consequently Crusader was expected to be essentially a 30th Corps affair.

The essence of 30th Corps' plan was to drive to the area around Sidi Rezegh, which was judged to be of great importance to the Germans who would then be enticed into a huge tank battle. Such a battle as this, with its swirling squadrons of modern chivalry clashing at close range was what the armoured brigades had been created for, and it was confidently predicted that, with their numerical superiority, they would wipe out the Axis tanks. Once this had been done, Tobruk could be relieved.

The simplicity of this plan was chipped away by the 4th Armoured Brigade being given a separate mission. The 13th Corps, despite its large infantry tank component, was concerned about the vulnerability of its left flank to armoured forces striking northwards from the desert and wanted 4th Armoured Brigade under its command as a defence against them. 30th Corps wanted 4th Armoured Brigade in 7th Armoured Division. A compromise was reached whereby the armoured brigade was in 7th Armoured Division, but was to be deployed to cover 13th Corps' left flank.

The Course of the Battle

18th November 1941

Operations on this day went according to plan. Gaps were blown through the frontier wire to the south of Fort Maddalena outflanking the German defences and, despite the heavy overnight rain, the 7th Armoured Division started to pass through them at 6 am led by the armoured cars of the King's Dragoon Guards and the 12th Lancers. By 12.00 the recce units were in contact with their German opposite numbers who pulled back in front of them, skirmishing fitfully. By the end of the day the division as a whole was around Gabr Saleh. The 7th Armoured Brigade, after an advance of over 40 miles, was approaching Sidi Rezegh. 22nd Armoured Brigade was to the south of Bir el Gubi, where the Ariete was, and 4th Armoured Brigade was closing on Gabr Saleh. During this advance the 7th and 22nd Armoured Brigades, lost respectively, 49 (29%) and 22 (14%) of their tanks due to mechanical breakdown. The figures for 4th Armoured Brigade are not known, but can be assumed to be much lower due to the shorter distance travelled and the greater reliability of its Honey tanks. As 7th Armoured Brigade had the oldest tanks some were brought to Gabr Saleh on transporters. Naturally most of these broken down vehicles would be repaired and rejoin their units during the battle. The armoured brigades went into defensive laagers

The figure of 22 tanks lost by the 22nd Armoured Brigade includes one Crusader that spontaneously combusted while it was being filled with petrol. The procedure was to draw the required number of cans from the dump, then drive away to a safe distance before refuelling. Fortunately this procedure was followed in this case.

The remarkable aspect of this day's events is that Rommel did not react to them. The German reconnaissance troops must have reported the British movements, but the weather was too overcast for aerial reconnaissance, and the airfields too muddy. A British soldier captured in the frontier defensive zone revealed the whole plan. Despite all this, in what may be a case of wishful thinking rather than cold calculation Rommel decided that the British advance could be ignored while he concentrated on plans for the assault of Tobruk. General Cruwell, acting against Rommel's wishes, did not ignore it and sent an armoured regiment from the 21st Panzer Division to Gabr Saleh to reinforce the reconnaissance troops.

There is a certain irony in that the British had taken extensive deception measures to mislead Rommel, and now the very success of these measures was prejudicing the operation.

19th November
The lack of any reaction on Rommel's part seems to have caught the 7th Armoured Division off balance. The armoured brigades were given separate tasks, keeping the division dispersed and surrendering the initiative.

4th Armoured Brigade, like the division, showed a tendency to disperse. At first light a squadron from 3RTR was sent off to support the Kings Dragoon Guards, one of the divisional armoured car regiments, which was driving the German armoured cars back to Sidi Azeiz. Then the other two squadrons were sent east after a suspected enemy convoy. That convoy did not exist, but they swung to the north-east, came across an axis supply convoy that was driving along the Trigh Capuzzo, and gave pursuit. They destroyed the column, but inevitably a feature of the Honeys, their short road range of 70 miles maximum, made itself felt, and soon the bulk of the regiment was immobilised waiting for fuel.

Throughout the morning Rommel had still not been convinced that the British movements constituted a real offensive, but he did allow 15th Panzer Division to move to the south of Trigh Capuzzo, and a battle group of 21st Panzer Division to go to the aid of the armoured cars close to Sidi Azeiz.

This battle group, commanded by Col Stephan, was built around the panzer regiment Gen. Cruwell had ordered south the previous evening. It consisted of from 80 to 90 tanks with some artillery support. It ran into the 4th Armoured Brigade to the north of Gabr Saleh. Perhaps if the brigade has stayed united things would have been better, but unfortunately with one regiment, 3RTR, wildly galloping after the supply column and another, 5RTR, moving so as to be able to support 3RTR if necessary, there was only one regiment, 8th Hussars, available to fight the Germans. The Honeys were hopelessly out-gunned and could only hope to bring effective fire to bear by charging to close range, something the Honeys were well able to do. Predictably they fared badly. The Hussars lost 20 tanks knocked out. 5RTR, which came quickly to their support, lost three, two being mechanical failures. Twelve of these tanks were repaired within 48 hours. The battle faded away as night came on and 3RTR returned, in dribs and drabs. They laagered up separate from the rest of the brigade.

The British crews claimed to have knocked out 26 German tanks, but the actual figure was eight, and only two of these were destroyed. The German recovery crews were, at this time, more efficient than the British. Their low-loaders followed the tanks into action and were quickly on hand to pick up vehicle casualties and take them back to where the fitters could work on them. The German tanks had practically run out of fuel and ammunition.

7th Armoured Brigade seems to have done little in the morning, its movements were slow as the overnight rain had left the ground in front of it very soft. Around 1.0 pm it was ordered to capture the airfield, which had minimal AT defences, to the east of Sidi Rezegh, which it did capturing 19 Italian aircraft. It then established itself on the ridge above Sidi Rezegh

22nd Armoured Brigade's original orders reference Bir el Gubi involved little more than masking it and concentrating on getting to Sidi Rezegh. This was changed early in the morning when General Gott visited the brigade and instructed it to assault it ASP. The Italian position at Bir el Gubi was not to be despised. It stood on a low ridge, around 15 feet high, two miles long running north to south, and consisted of three battalion sized strongpoints, two well dug in, the third under construction. Italian armour in the form of the Ariete Division was know to be in the area, its tanks were of poorer quality and of roughly similar numbers to the British tanks, but their artillery was superior. The infantry was equipped with 47-mm AT guns and was supported by 75-mm and 105-mm field guns. Remarkably the Italians deployed seven truck mounted 102-mm naval guns. These guns were designed to defeat ships' armoured plating and would have no difficulty with lightly armoured cruiser tanks. Also the Italians made some tank traps by soaking patches of sand with oil to cause tanks to bog down.

The strength of the Italian position was known to the brigade command, as it had been scouted and reported on by an armoured car regiment, the 11th Hussars. Consequently the decision to try to rush the position with Cruisers was rash. Perhaps General Gott, who had played a major part in Operation Compass, was not taking the Italians seriously enough.

The armoured brigade spent the night roughly 10 miles to the south-east of Bir el Gubi. At dawn it set off in widely separated formations with 2RGH taking point, 4CLY on its left and 3CLY to the right rear, and at 11.00am drove back a screening company of Italian tanks. Three of these tanks were left burning, seven more were hit but could return to the Italian lines. At around midday the leading regiment, 2RGH, met some 11th Hussars in their armoured cars at a point in the desert where the Italians had set a red flag. No-one thought to take this down. The Colonel of the 2RGH, an ex-17th/21st Lancer, spoke directly to the CO of the 11th Hussars, then immediately ordered his regiment to attack, shouting over the air, 'Royal Gloucestershire Hussars, the enemy are in front of you. You will attack and destroy them...Charge!'[3] The regiment went in with 4CLY echeloned back to the left and 3CLY nowhere to be seen. The brigade HQ seems to have had no part in this decision. The red flag must have been an artillery range marker because as soon as the regiments passed it they were shelled. This assault was said to have taken the form of a high spirited charge with minimal artillery support. There was actually little point in waiting for the artillery, it was only one battery of eight field guns. Each squadron was in an arrowhead formation, each regiment formed an arrowhead of its three squadrons. The brigade, according to one of the squadron leaders, Viscount Cranley, was a magnificent sight. The advance was somehow redolent of the whole Cruiser Tank concept.

The RGH struck the left battalion position, and in the face of heavy fire veered to its left to hit the right battalion which was not well dug in. Here they started to be successful and many Italian soldiers tried to surrender, but there were no attacking infantry available to accept their surrender so they returned to their weapons and were on hand to capture dismounted tank crews. There is a point in an advance that, when it suddenly comes under defensive fire, it is more sensible to charge than to pull back. This situation was covered in 'Troop Training for Cruiser Tank Troops, Military Training Pamphlet No 51, 1941':

'Action on encountering hostile anti-tank defence
In open country

Immediate action
The principle governing this action is that of fire and movement. The leading tank should immediately open fire on the enemy gun, at the same time moving forward to a covered position or, if no cover is available, closing immediately with the enemy. Isolated cover from view is a trap if the tank can be seen entering it.

The troop leader should, without checking, make the best use of the available ground and cover to outflank the enemy gun and attack it with his own and his reserve tank. Smoke bombs may be valuable if natural cover is non-existent. Speed is the essence of the action. Wide flanking movements cause delay, and are liable to create a mixture of sub-units. Remember that armour, and the sheer speed of attack, will confer a considerable degree of immunity on the attackers.

Tanks will never halt in the open.'

Anything other than a charge would have been inimical to the spirit of Cruiser Tank Warfare. Perhaps it was then, when the Italian fire was becoming effective that, to urge his squadron forward, Viscount Cranley shouted over the air, 'Let them have it they're only Eyeties'[4]. But, alas for *élan*, the frontal attack ground to a halt. One squadron of 4CLY tried to work its way round the southern flank but was stopped by mines and artillery, and, worse, by running out of fuel. The self-propelled 102-mm guns were camouflaged as ordinary lorries and their fire came as a considerable surprise. As the brigade was halted the tanks of the Ariete Division were sighted to the north, around 3,000 yards away. These tanks launched a counter-attack and started driving the British tanks back. Brigade HQ came up and ordered 3CLY to from up on the right of 2RGH but, for reasons unexplained did not. They had already lost one squadron leader to fire from Bir el Gubi, and perhaps were engaging the Ariete in their own private battle. At 4.30 the brigade pulled back, defeated.

The 22nd Armoured Brigade had 25 tanks knocked out and a further 45 immobilised either by battle damage or mechanical failure. A number of tanks were recovered, which implies a fairly supine attitude on the part of the Italians who lost 34 tanks destroyed, 15 damaged, and 12 guns. This was not excessive in view of the difference in quality of the British and Italian tanks. The impression this action gives is one of gross overconfidence and a brigade HQ that was not yet up to the job. The result was that the brigade was badly weakened and spent the night close to where it spent the previous one, at least ten miles away from where it should have been.

The British believed that as a result of this action the Ariete gave a performance throughout the remainder of Crusader of at best average. How reasonable this was is impossible to judge, but any lack of effectiveness of this division can realistically be put down to its small number of radios. It was at its best in a small tightly controlled action like Bir el Gubi, in wider manoeuvres it could easily get out of hand.

The real lesson was that properly set up field defences could not be easily rushed, but would need a set-piece attack. This was a truth that would be demonstrated three days later be 13th Corps at Sidi Omar, and by the Ariete itself at Bir Hackeim the following May.

By evening the 1st South African Division was taking up position at Bir el Gubi, and the 22nd Armoured Brigade moved to its north. The Divisional Support Group was ordered to Sidi Rezegh.

Rommel was finally getting an idea of the scale of the advance of 30th Corps. His perception no doubt being helped by a BBC news broadcast at 9.00pm which announced that a major offensive planned to destroy the axis forces in Africa had started. He ordered the two panzer divisions of the DAK to destroy 30th Corps. General Cruwell decided first to deploy them against the troops close to Sidi Azeiz.

20th November, Cambrai Day

It is always easy, with the benefit of hindsight, to be critical, but in mobile operations when the situation is unclear it is best to concentrate one's mobile troops and wait till the fog of war clears. Rommel would not wait. His kind of generalship, leading from the front and making quick decisions, can be very effective, but it has its limitations.

General Cruwell's appreciation of the situation, which must have been shared by Rommel, was wrong. He identified four British armoured groups. These were the three armoured brigades and a spurious one to the north of Sidi Azeiz. No doubt exaggerated reports from the reconnaissance units and the destroyed supply column had magnified 3RTR into an armoured brigade. General Cruwell decided to destroy the imaginary armoured brigade first. Had this brigade existed this would have been a reasonable decision, he could have deployed two panzer divisions against it so the outcome would have been in little doubt. Then having destroyed the unit closest to the frontier and cut the British troops off from their supplies, he could have destroyed the remaining armoured brigades, one after the other.

Cruwell's plan was a good one. The 15th Panzer Division was to move east to face the supposed Armoured Brigade from the north. The 21st Panzer Division was to go south-east in the Sidi Omar direction, to get to its south, and the troops on the frontier should prevent its escape to the east.

As good a plan as it was it failed because no British troops were within this planned encirclement. The day started with a battle with 4th Armoured Brigade. At daybreak 5RTR had been informed of an enemy unit close and to the west of their position. They were ordered to engage it. 'C' squadron identified the German tanks at a range of around 3,000 yards, and despite the German artillery it closed to 1,200 yards to commence the firefight. 'A' squadron was ordered round on the right flank and the brigade artillery was brought up to give fire support. 'C' squadron advance to within 700 yards of the Germans but was running out of ammunition so was replaced by 'B' squadron. The Germans started to move round the southern flank of this squadron but were held back by artillery fire. 'A' squadron also started to run short of ammunition and had to withdraw. This left 'B' squadron in an exposed position so it withdrew a short way, but at 9.00 the 8th Hussars came up on the left and some 3RTR tanks on the right. This forced the Germans back and they proceeded to the east according with Cruwell's plan.

The Germans advanced slowly against a screen of armoured cars, until the 21st Panzer Division stopped, out of fuel. Rommel wanted both divisions to halt, but Cruwell advanced cautiously with the 15th Panzer Division only. The British had intercepted enough radio messages to know that the 4th Armoured Brigade was about to be attacked, and at 11am General Norrie ordered 22nd Armoured Brigade to reinforce it. This would seem a remarkable decision. As far as the British command knew they were about to engage the entire armoured strength of the DAK and sent only two armoured brigades to do it. The 7th Armoured Brigade was not withdrawn from Sidi Rezegh, even though there was no axis armour in the vicinity, and the Support Group could have held the position. The 7th Armoured Brigade had actually been roughly handled during the morning by German infantry who had advanced to the north of the airfield overnight and dug in some guns. The brigade pulled back to the south but the Support Group arrived at 10.00 and restored the situation. The Ariete was to be covered by a brigade of the South African Division, the other brigade of which was, next day, to move to Sidi Rezegh.

The decision to send the 22nd Armoured Brigade to reinforce the 4th flew in the face of the basic concept of Crusader, which was to destroy Rommel's armoured forces before relieving Tobruk. And the destruction of Rommel's armoured forces would require the concentration of all the British armoured brigades. Perhaps this decision was the result of a military *folie de deux*. Both Generals Cunningham and Norrie were in a rush to proceed to the next stage of the operation, that stage after the tank battle. Norrie, believing the reports of heavy casualties inflicted on the Axis tanks and their fuel shortage, wanted to start the Tobruk action as soon as possible before they could recover. Cunningham, believing false aerial reconnaissance reports that the Axis units around the frontier with Egypt were retreating westwards, assumed that if 30th Corps could link up with the Tobruk garrison then the bulk of the Axis forces would be surrounded and forced to surrender.

Whatever the case may be, German capabilities were greatly underestimated and a tactical opportunity lost. It is interesting to note that the New Zealand Division of 13th Corps offered to assist 4th Armoured Brigade with 'I' tanks and AT guns. This offer was turned down by General Gatehouse, who probably thought that infantry divisions had no place in tank battles. The next day, as the situation deteriorated, 30th Corps was glad to receive a squadron of Valentines from 13th Corps.

In all this can be detected the influence of 'Modern Formations', the belief that great things could be achieved by driving Cruisers around without the necessity of battles. Events would show that between evenly-matched opponents this is just not the case.

Just before midday the 4th Armoured Brigade started to advance roughly north towards Bir el Barrani, and arrived there at 4.0pm to be attacked by the Germans. This attack came as a complete surprise. The Germans had made a wide loop round the north of the brigade and came in from the west, from the setting sun. The German use of the blinding effect of the sun like this was at that time a novelty for the British, but it soon became standard. The Germans hit 3RTR first on their left flank. 5RTR came up to cover this flank, and 8th Hussars on their left. The Hussars actually charged the Germans to force a close range melee on them. This was not cavalry élan but a necessity brought on by the short range of the Honeys' guns. The tactic does not seem to have unduly worried the Germans. The three regiments, being out-gunned, fell back. Some units retreated fighting stubbornly, fire and movement by alternating squadrons, some didn't.

The British came to believe that the Germans liked to attack out of the setting sun partly because of the blinding light and partly because it would soon be dark and their recovery crews could get quickly to work. But in situations changing as quickly as they did in the desert campaigns it is hard to believe that even the Germans could organise this.

Although the brigade soon lost 26 tanks, destroyed and damaged, the speed of the Honeys and the lateness of the hour made it impossible for the Germans to win a major victory and the battle petered out in darkness just as 22nd Armoured Brigade arrived. Shortly before dusk a German supply column arrived in the distance. The German tanks pulled back to it, covered by their AT guns. Because of the short range of their guns the British tanks could do nothing about this, it is not known why the artillery did not try. The emphasis the Germans placed on defending vulnerable vehicles with AT guns was commented on in 'Notes from Theatres of War':

> *'following his usual practice, he replenished his tanks behind a screen of anti-tank guns. He placed his anti-tank guns in such a manner that it was not possible to take the opportunity of attacking him whilst he was replenishing'*.[5]

On one of the knocked out British tanks the Germans found written orders and a map giving information about lines of advance and supply dumps. This helped to clear the fog of war for the DAK, but it does not seem to have been passed up to Rommel, judging by decisions he took during his 'Dash to the Wire'.

The British believed they had knocked out 30 German tanks, but this was wildly optimistic, the Germans probably had none destroyed, another case of inflated estimates of German tank casualties. However while this battle was in progress General Gott issued orders for the Tobruk Garrison to break out the next morning.

7th Armoured Brigade had stayed around Sidi Rezegh all day. The previous night enterprising German infantry had wheeled up some AT guns in the broken ground to the north, and at dawn they knocked out three 2RTR tanks. As the Support Group did not come up till late afternoon, and this was a job for infantry, there was not a lot that the brigade could do but pull back and wait. When the Support Group did arrive the Germans were too well dug in to be moved.

The full scope of the British offensive was now plain to Rommel, and he now made the first of several major mistakes when he assumed that the 4th Armoured Brigade had been destroyed. He ordered General Cruwell to move the DAK to Sidi Rezegh next morning.

21st November

The 7th Armoured Division, that is the 7th Armoured Brigade and the Support Group, was to attack northwards at 8.30am in support of the break-out from Tobruk. Its initial aim was to secure the ridge overlooking the Trigh Capuzzo from the south, then 6RTR would drive on to meet the break-out. Two units were involved, an infantry battalion on the right and 6RTR on the left. The defenders were part of the 155th Regiment of the Africa Division.

Around 8am German tanks were seen approaching from the South East. This was the DAK, now at last fully united, having been ordered by Rommel away from the 4th Armoured Brigade at Gabr Saleh. Its arrival at Sidi Rezegh this early was a considerable achievement for General Cruwell. It started its move overnight, abandoning two panzer IIs. 4th Armoured Brigade seems to have had the impression that the Germans were in retreat and followed up at a leisurely pace, 5RTR on the right and 3RTR on the left. At 9.00 a column of German tanks, either towed or on transporters, was sighted. One panzer III was abandoned. The German column found refuge behind a screen of AT guns which 'B' squadron 5RTR identified at a range of 2,000 yards. The brigade artillery was called up, and under its cover 5RTR advanced 1,000 yards when the Germans abandoned the position. This gave 'A' and 'B' squadrons the chance to charge in and collect some prisoners and a gun. The prisoners belonged to 15th Panzer Division.

Further pursuit by 4th Armoured Brigade was slowed down around midday because of fuel shortage and because 3RTR had suffered some casualties. Although the pace picked up early in the afternoon it was halted at 4.00 due to a downpour of rain which reduced visibility to 400 yards. At 4.30 the brigade laagered up, much to the relief of the echelon whose vehicles were starting to bog down.

As can be seen the 4th Armoured Brigade did not hinder the DAK to any significant extent in its march to Sidi Rezegh. Unfortunately for 7th Armoured Division the sortie from Tobruk had already started so the attack by 6RTR could not be called off, so Brigadier Davy ordered the other two armoured regiments, 7th Hussars and 2RTR, to face the approaching German tanks. This battle lasted all day. The Germans first fell on the 7Th Hussars which suffered heavy casualties, the colonel being killed. 2RTR tried to swing round to the south and hit the German left flank, but ran into a *pakfront* and suffered heavy casualties, mostly from the 50-mm AT guns. While 15th Panzer Division was fighting 7th Armoured Brigade, 21st Panzer Division moved to the southern escarpment and attacked units of the Support Group. They inflicted heavy casualties but lost six tanks to porteed 2-pdrs. This was the action in which Lt Ward Gunn won his posthumous VC.

The advance on Tobruk had started well even though the sortie from Tobruk, which had gained some ground, was less successful than hoped. 6RTR had achieved its initial objective, but came under heavy AT gunfire from the opposing ridge. The guns were 88s, ordered there by Rommel. 6RTR quickly lost three quarters of its tanks, and was halted. The survivors, reorganised as a composite squadron, joined the rest of the brigade facing the Germans, as did the artillery of the support group. By evening the brigade was down to 28 tanks, but still held the airfield.

For a while the situation, though perilous for 7th Armoured Brigade, seemed to present a major opportunity for the British. The other two armoured brigades, which had remained in the Gabr Saleh area, were ordered to close on the Germans. This should have resulted in the DAK being surrounded and destroyed. They failed to achieve this, partly due to shortage of fuel, and they only came into action at dusk.

The 22nd Armoured Brigade was ordered to Bir er Reghem at dawn but there does not seem to have been any urgency attached to this. At 3.00 this was changed to getting to Sidi Rezegh ASP, but the brigade was slowed by passing through 5th SA Brigade, and by the rain.

The situation also appeared to be a magnificent chance for the Germans to destroy 7th Armoured Brigade and the Support Group, but in the end they suffered from lack of fuel and ammunition as did the British. The presence of 4th and 22nd Armoured Brigades had made resupply difficult. Dusk fell on one of the most perplexing situations in modern warfare.

This situation may be summarised as, working left (north-east) to right (south-west), British forces trying to break out from Tobruk, axis troops fighting against them, 7th Armoured Brigade trying to break in, DAK units attacking 7th Armoured Division troops for the possession of the Sidi Rezegh airfield and 4th and 22nd Armoured Brigades coming to its defence. This, of course, is a simplified way of seeing the situation. For the troops involved it meant that when a column of vehicles was sighted, no-one knew which side it was on until it came quite close.

Despite everything the situation seemed promising for the British and 13th Corps had started its advance. The sortie from Tobruk had been halted but even so it had gained 4,000 yards, and the usual over-optimistic reports had the DAK in a very bad way. The 7th Armoured Division still had 209 tanks fit to fight. On the next day, once the DAK had been finished, the advance on Tobruk would continue.

General Cruwell was correspondingly pessimistic, he wanted to pull the DAK back to Gambut, but Rommel, who was mostly concerned with the break-out from Tobruk, insisted that it stayed where it was to prevent 7th Armoured Division assisting it. In the event the DAK pulled back north-east a few miles though some tanks were immobilised due to lack of fuel. 15 Panzer Division pulled back in the direction of Gambut, and 21st Panzer Division towards Belhammed.

22nd November

Rommel was still mostly concerned to prevent the relief of Tobruk and wanted to continue hammering at Sidi Rezegh, but Cruwell was reluctant to see his tanks being drawn into a positional battle. To try to build up a reserve he ordered 15th Panzer Division back to Gambut, leaving its panzer regiment, the 8th, to the south-east of Sidi Rezegh to cover the withdrawal. The 21st Panzer Division stayed close to Belhamed to the north of Sidi Rezegh.

The morning saw some inconclusive sparring as 8th Panzer Regiment pulled back and 22nd Armoured Brigade arrived. 5th SA Brigade also arrived to the south of Sidi Rezegh. The situation for 30th Corps seemed to be steadily improving. The German tank forces were apparently beaten and the British infantry were coming up to continue the march on Tobruk. This illusion would soon be shattered. Rommel arrived at 21st Panzer Division around midday. He ordered its infantry, battle group Knabe, to attack southwards and drive the British troops off the escarpment to the north of Sidi Rezegh. The armour,

5th Panzer Regiment with 57 tanks supported by a battery of 88s, was to make a wide detour and attack the airfield from the west.

The attack went in at 2.20 pm. The effect at the airfield was stunning. The attack first fell on 7th Armoured Brigade. This brigade had only about 30 tanks and the weight of the defence seems to have been born by 25-pdr batteries. Soon 22nd Armoured Brigade, with over 70 tanks, came up from the south, counter-attacked gallantly and quickly took heavy casualties. Perhaps they were charging in the gallant way they had done at Bir el Gubi.

As the situation at Sidi Rezegh deteriorated General Gott called in 4th Armoured Brigade which had spent a good deal of the night driving around the desert after non-existent German columns. At 11.00 the brigade was ordered to the south-east of Sidi Rezegh, and seems to have proceeded slowly. At 3.00 this was changed to proceed to Sidi Rezegh ASP. Its progress was slightly slowed by reports of an unidentified column moving parallel with it to its north. This column was to remain a mystery.

At 4.00 the brigade was two miles to the south of the airfield and its commander, Brigadier Gatehouse, met the commander of 7th Armoured Brigade. The orders agreed were that 5RTR was to swing round to the north of the airfield and 3RTR, on its left, was to clear the airfield. The brigade arrived to look down on the airfield from an escarpment. The view was amazing, a near total chaos of burning and exploding vehicles, guns firing and destroyed, men fighting and casualties, the atmosphere thick with smoke and dust. The first tanks to arrive, a two-tank troop commanded by Captain Crisp, were met by the Support Group commander, Brigadier 'Jock' Campbell. He instructed the troop to follow him as he stood upright in an open car hurtling through the debris of battle to the western edge of the British battle area. There they could plainly see 60 to 70

German tanks apparently advancing steadily towards them. The troop sergeant's tank was almost immediately knocked out by a round penetrating the glacis and killing the driver, it drove away erratically with the dead man's foot on the controls. The situation was desperate, but the British did not realise that the Germans were out of fuel. They were not, however, out of ammunition.

Brigadier Gatehouse's orders were easy to give but the chaos of the moment made them difficult to carry out. The regiments set off gamely, but 5RTR veered southwards receiving AT gunfire from the north. The tanks of 3RTR and 5RTR became intermingled. Smoke and dust limited visibility, radio communications became difficult, the two regiments were on different frequencies, and there was an unfortunate 'blue-on-blue' incident when the cruisers of 22nd Armoured Brigade fired on the Honeys. As the Germans were making no progress and with the agreement of the brigade commander 3RTR and 5RTR disengaged and rallied to the south-west of the airfield.

Just as the day's fighting seemed to be dying down the two regiments were informed of a German infantry assault on the airfield that was threatening the brigade's guns. The regiments swept back across the airfield but found no infantry only some AT guns, one or two of which might have been destroyed. 'B' squadron, 5RTR, contacted some German tanks but night was falling and visibility was down to fifty yards so the regiments were called back to their rallying point. The brigadier returned to his HQ which was with 5RTR's echelon.

The day had been a disaster for 3RTR which was down to four tanks, 5RTR was down to 26. Meanwhile the 22nd Armoured Brigade was ordered south to support the South Africans. They spent a cold night in their tanks expecting an attack at any time, but it did not happen. Next morning the brigade was reorganised as a composite regiment.

Only 3RTR and 5RTR had gone to Sidi Rezegh, it would have been better if 4th Armoured Brigade had moved en-bloc to Sidi Rezegh as, later in the afternoon the 15th Panzer Division came swinging to the south to attack Sidi Rezegh from the east. It was not seen by the armoured cars, and just as 4th Armoured Brigade was laagering up for the night the German tanks crashed, literally, into brigade HQ and the 8th Hussars of which regiment only four tanks survived. They had obviously not been responsible for their own safety, as enjoined by 'Modern Formations'. The brigade was scattered. The Brigadier drove back to the rallying point to try to organise a counter-attack. He decided that 3RTR was not capable of further action, and he started back with 5RTR.The night was moonless and as they approached the site of brigade HQ, easily identifiable by burning vehicles, they ran into a German tank unit. The result was a confused action which lasted for 10 to 12 minutes, then a withdrawal southwards. 16 tanks rallied to the south that night, a further six returned to 3RTR and stayed with them a few days. The day had been a disaster for 4th Armoured Brigade. The Germans claimed to have captured about 50 tanks.

For the next day the brigade ceased to exist. The other two brigades, 7th and 22nd, had only, respectively, 10 and 34 tanks still fit to fight. The Germans had 173, and also had the vital ground around the airfield.

The situation was looking better from the German point of view, but due to 13th Corps operations Rommel was increasingly worried about the garrisons on the frontier. He was eager to be done with 30th Corps and to go to their aid. He ordered General Cruwell to attack with the whole of the DAK in the direction of Bir el Gubi to catch the British tanks between it and the Ariete. Unfortunately there was a break down in communications during which Cruwell was hatching his own plan. He preferred to take the 15th Panzer Division and the tank regiment from the 21st, join with the Ariete, then sweep north to catch the British tanks against the infantry and artillery of the 21st Panzer

Division which he placed on the southern escarpment. When he received Rommel's orders it was too late to make any changes. This change of emphasis marked the end of what is commonly known as the first Battle of Sidi Rezegh.

23rd November, *Totensonntag*, the German day of remembrance for the dead of previous wars.

In the event General Cruwell started without the 21st Panzer Division's tanks (5th Panzer Regiment), but left for Bir el Gubi with only 15th Panzer Division. *En route* he encountered the now very understrength support group and scattered it. Next he hit the transport of the 5th South African Brigade and scattered that. The German tanks swung to the west pursuing the soft skinned vehicles contrary to orders. General Cruwell had a chance here to alter his plan and strike the South Africans from the north. It may be that some minor counter-attacks by 3RTR persuaded him otherwise. Perhaps it would have been different if Rommel had been present, but his whereabouts at this time were obscure. The corps HQ had been overrun by the New Zealanders at 5.45am and he was presumably trying to sort out the resulting confusion. This event might have been the reason why the Axis airforces took no part in the coming action.

The result of all this was that 5th South African Brigade, which was to the north of Bir el Gubi, roughly half way to Sidi Rezegh, was very much on the alert, and was soon under infantry attack from the north.

General Cruwell gathered his tanks and continued south. He met the Ariete close to Bir el Gubi around 12.35, and the 5th Panzer Regiment arrived soon after. He had planned to start the sweep north at 2pm, but it was 3pm before the move started.

The advance was one of the most impressive of the war. The Ariete on the left with 90 M13s, 8th Panzer Regiment in the centre and 5th Panzer Regiment on the right. There was a total of 162 German tanks. This represented a loss of 88 tanks since the start of Crusader.

The German target was the 5th South African Brigade, supported by the 22nd Armoured Brigade, and the very weak 7th Armoured Division Support Group. Assistance was requested from 4th Armoured Brigade, but this unit was so scattered that the brigadier refused until the situation clarified. The South Africans had had time to prepare but unfortunately they were hardly able to dig in, there were only a few inches of sand then it was solid rock. The brigade had a total of forty-six 25-pdrs and twenty-four 2-pdrs. Of these twelve 25-pdrs and twenty-one 2-pdrs, and also two 18-pdrs as AT guns, were on the south front to face the German armour. As they could not be dug in the 2-pdrs were all kept mounted on their *portees*. Unfortunately the guns were less effective at short range than they should have been because, initially, they were masked by the transport vehicles, then later the smoke and dust were so thick that visibility was down to just a few yards.

The Germans advanced and the firefight began around 3.15. The weight of fire caused the Germans to falter but finally panzer regiment 8, on the German left, got in among the South African guns. The real breakthrough for the Germans was when panzer regiment 5 veered to the right and penetrated the South African perimeter's eastern front. This panicked the transport which had, presumably, been a little highly strung since the morning's disaster. The result of this was that ammunition could not be brought up to the guns. And without guns, infantry could not fight against tanks. The Ariete had veered to its left and taken little part in the assault on the infantry position. Naturally it was criticised by the Germans for this, but it might have been a result of so few of the Italian tanks having radios. Certainly the Ariete prevented 22nd Armoured Brigade intervening against the Germans which could have been disastrous. By nightfall the 5th South African Brigade had ceased to exist. The 22nd Armoured Brigade lost at least 10 of its 34 tanks, 2nd RGH was down to four tanks. The Germans lost over 70 tanks destroyed or damaged and sustained very heavy officer casualties. The two panzer regiments, 5 and 8, were down to, respectively, 32 and 15 operational tanks.

The heroic defence by the 5th SA Brigade and associated units, though unsuccessful, was the crucial turning point of the battle. Because of it both commanders misjudged the situation. As will be seen Rommel decided that the 30th Corps could be ignored for the next few days. Following similar reasoning the British commander decided that he no longer had the superiority in tank numbers that was the basis of the Crusader plan, so it seemed that Crusader in its original conception could no longer proceed. Consequently General Cunningham flew to Cairo to discuss future operations with General Auchinleck. Auchinleck declined to end the operation, but instructed 30th Corps to maintain operations against German armour until it ran out of tanks. But he altered the emphasis of the operation onto 13th Corps which now took over some infantry units from 30th Corps, and had the responsibility for the relief of Tobruk.

24th November

Fighting continued in the Sidi Rezegh area, but less intensely than on the previous day. Both sides were very disorganised, in fact some of 22nd Armoured Brigade's wheeled vehicles did not stop till they had reached the wire well to the south of Sidi Omar. The 4th Armoured Brigade was coalescing and at 9.00 am was ordered to send 5RTR to the assistance of 22nd Armoured Brigade which was being threatened from the north. 5RTR formed up on the right of 22nd Armoured Brigade, but within minutes it was recalled to 4th Armoured Brigade which was itself under threat. Luckily this threat was found to be a column of 5th South African brigade survivors. A further scare sent the brigade driving pointlessly around the desert, but later in the afternoon, at 3.00, a German column was pursued and defeated, around 40 vehicles of all types being destroyed.

At 6pm General Cruwell at last made contact with Rommel and proposed that he keep up the pressure on 7th Armoured Division, which was now practically destroyed, and totally finish it off.

Rommel disagreed and made one of the boldest, and worst, decisions of his military career. He decided to make his counterstroke, his 'dash to the wire'. He ordered the DAK, and the Ariete and Trieste divisions, to mount a sudden thrust east, roughly along the Trig Capuzzo to relieve the frontier garrisons. This decision seems bizarre, but only a few months earlier, during Operation Battleaxe, a similar manoeuvre, but on a smaller scale, had worked. A sudden thrust deep behind the British fighting troops relieved the Halfaya garrison and unhinged the British plans to the extent of forcing them to retreat. However manoeuvres that work on a small scale are not always successful on a larger one.

The result of the dash to the wire was that the pressure was taken off the 7th Armoured Division, and the armoured brigades, which hardly existed, were given the chance to recover knocked out and broken down tanks, and absorb reinforcements from base workshops.

Subsequent Actions

Although the fighting on the 24th and the German withdrawal of their tanks from the Sidi Rezegh area concludes the main narrative of this chapter it did not end the battle. Among the many actions that followed there is one further event that is of particular interest to any study of British armour.

Rommel's counterstroke had ended in failure, he was forced back to the Sidi Rezegh area and continued the battle for a few more days. However the balance had swung against him and finally he had to abandon the siege of Tobruk and withdraw to the west. He took up a fairly strong position with his left on the coast at Gazala.

By this time the 30th Corps HQ had been withdrawn and the surviving armoured forces came under 13th Corps. The commander of this corps, General Godwin-Austen, was anxious to pursue the Axis troops and drive them as far to the west as possible. Consequently he mounted an example of the standard desert war manoeuvre. He attacked the Axis position frontally with infantry units, and sent his armour, in this case the 4th Armoured Brigade in a wide out-flanking sweep round the south of the Axis position. Its task was to destroy the Axis armour, which was believed, fairly accurately, to be around 50 tanks. The brigade had 90 Honeys, so Godwin-Austen could be optimistic.

The result was a failure. On the first day, 15th December, the brigade had to cover nearly 70 miles. The country was very rough, this resulted in a shortage of fuel and that evening General Gott ordered the brigade to pull back next day to meet the petrol vehicles which were having difficulty crossing the rough ground. This put the start of meaningful operations back to the afternoon of the 16th. When they did start it was too late, the German tank units had already retreated. As a secondary option General Godwin-Austen told the brigade to break the coast road at Tmimi. This was done by an armoured car unit and some Honeys, but they only stayed there a short time and the raid hardly seems to have been noticed by Rommel. Their prolonged presence at Tmimi was pointless as they could see the British troops advancing and there were no axis troops to cut off.

This inconclusive skirmishing seems to have achieved nothing and was a great disappointment to General Godwin-Austen who, though little known, was one of the best of the British commanders in the desert.

The crews involved were told that the foray had been a success and had forced the Germans to abandon the Gazala line.

Note 1,
The standard British tank radio set of the time was the Wireless Set No 19. This was, in its day, a very advanced system. It comprised three facilities in the one box: the 'A' set for communicating back to regiment, the 'B' set for inter-tank communications, and an intercom within the tank. The 'A' and 'B' sets gave voice communications ranges of 10 miles and 1,000 yards, respectively, using an eight foot rod aerial. The 'A' set could reach 15 miles with morse.

Note 2,
'Laager' is the term currently favoured by the Royal Armoured Corps, and it was used in Modern Formations. During the war 'leaguer' was used in the desert and 'harbour' in Europe, 'laager' seems a reasonable amalgam of these terms, and will be used in this study.

Note 3,
See 'Rogue Male', G Gordon-Creed DSO, MC and R Field, page 48

Note 4,
This is credibly reported in 'Before I forget', Roy Cawston, 1993, but is not reported in the relevant officer's own book, 'Men and Sand', The Earl of Onslow, 1961

Note 5,
'Notes from Theatres of War No 4: Cyrenaica, November, 1941/ January, 1942', The War Office, May 1942

Chapter 6

More Practice Considered

It has been shown that the first seven days of Operation Crusader were a disaster for 7th Armoured Division. The case might, just, be made that the division's organisation and procedures were reasonable, just the command was at fault, and German generalship that much better. But it must not be forgotten that the battlefield was the most favourable in the world for Cruiser Tank Warfare, and this was the type of warfare 7th Armoured Division was designed for.

In considering the action, General Gott, who commanded the division, drew three lessons.

Firstly, because of the open nature of the battlefield and the high mobility of tanks, it is easy for one side to avoid an armoured battle. Consequently, if the aim is to bring about such a battle, the method must be to seize some ground that is vital to the enemy so that he is forced to try to recapture it.

Secondly, when the ground involved is not vital to the Germans they were reluctant to be drawn into fighting for it, and particularly would not make the death-or-glory charges characteristic of British armour.

Thirdly, Lines of Communication must be carefully situated.

As with all aspects of warfare these three points are simple in principle, but do stand consideration in greater detail.

In the first case, seizing the vital ground and inviting the enemy to attack to recover it, the strategic offensive and the tactical defensive, has been a basic part of German thinking since the Seven Week War of 1866, but its application to tank warfare is problematic. It is a matter of scale. Tanks are best used offensively. So if the defending force is a corps of two infantry divisions and an armoured division then the infantry can be dug in and the armour used for counter-attacks. If the defenders are only the armoured division then its armoured brigades will be forced to manoeuvre, and do so probably at a disadvantage, to prevent the support group being crushed. General Gott's point was sound in that it could force the enemy into a battle of attrition, but in Crusader this worked out to the British disadvantage.

In the second case it seems that the General has missed the point. The standard German tactic was to lure the British tanks into the attack then move their own tanks away to a flank, so that the British would come up against the German AT gun screen. This would halt the British and the German tanks would then attack them from the flank. When the Germans could not employ this tactic they would rather not get involved.

Finally, supply is naturally of supreme importance. Ideally the division's centre line for supply should be at right angles to its front, and right at its centre. To attack it an enemy must make a long and wide flanking march. This was certainly not the case in Crusader.

A moment's consideration shows how much more vulnerable to disruption of supply are tank units than are infantry. An armoured division requires around 900 tons of supplies a day, a fully mechanised infantry division required only half of that. Also the distances the supplies have to be moved tend to be greater in the case of the armoured division. Worse, infantry may be able to improvise, but tanks have to have fuel and ammunition and are useless without them.

The supply tonnage required by an armoured division stayed fairly constant regardless of the type of operation it was involved in. If it was a pursuit, fuel requirements would be high, but not ammunition. If it was involved in static fighting then these would be reversed, but the total tonnage would remain much the same.

A point related to the one about supply is recovery and repair of AFVs. The side holding the battlefield at the end of the fighting had the chance to put many of his vehicle casualties back on the road, the opposing side cannot do this. One of the results of Rommel's 'Dash to the Wire' was the phoenix-like recovery of 7th Armoured Division. Later Montgomery's insistence that captured German AFVs should be destroyed beyond repair might seem unnecessary, but did ensure that they were permanently lost to the Germans.

Operation Crusader should have been a great triumph for Cruiser Tank Warfare and, although the operation as a whole was a British success, in fact it was a disappointment. A senior officer involved in the battle, Colonel, at the time, Belchem, concluded that the Germans were beaten 'not by the competence of the British Army', but by supply difficulties, specifically caused by RAF raids on Benghazi and Tripoli[1]. But then Belchem was a dedicated Montgomery man. That there was a problem with British armour was appreciated by General Auchinleck who believed that the armoured divisions should employ the tactical co-operation of arms as did the panzer divisions. To this end he increased their infantry and artillery components, there being field and AT artillery permanently attached to both the armoured and infantry brigades. The brigades were now termed 'brigade groups'. As a natural result of this thinking he insisted that armoured divisions fought as divisions. Shortly before the Gazala battle he wrote to Lieutenant General Ritchie, the 8th Army commander, 'I consider it be of the highest importance that you should not break up the organisation of either of the armoured divisions. They have been trained to fight as divisions, I hope, and fight as divisions they should. Norrie must handle them as a Corps Commander, and thus be able to take advantage of the flexibility which the fact of having two formations gives him.'

Unfortunately the very act of setting up the brigade group structure resulted in the armoured brigades having a greater tendency to act independently.

A well regarded modern military commentator, Dr Paddy Griffiths, has blamed the incorrect use of British armour during Crusader on three main errors:

> The belief in the tank's invulnerability,
> Poor tactics,
> Slow and extended tactical 'command path'.

It can be seen that these three points added up to a mismatch on the battlefield. The first resulted in a futuristic, Cruiser Tank Warfare, concept of operations. The second meant that it would not work, and the third, with the endless series of face-to-face briefings down the chain of command, meant that it could not be controlled.

Command and Control was largely ignored in 'Modern Formations'. Certainly the manual pointed out that *'Skilful manoeuvres, intelligently conceived and rapidly executed, may well confuse the hostile commander for producing uncertainty in his mind.'* But procedures for issuing orders by radio were not investigated. This will be considered, in terms of the 'Boyd Loop', in Chapter 7.

'Modern Formations' can be held to have delayed the development of effective co-operation between tanks and the other arms by the way it showed a near contempt for AT guns. In 1931 when 'Modern Formations' was published there were few such guns but that changed and manuals did not keep up with the changes. The 1931 view was that:

'Tank brigades depend on speed and fire power to overcome the defence. Open and undulating ground is therefore most favourable to them, since it presents few obstacles to tank movement and offers little cover to anti-tank weapons. On ground of this nature, anti-tank weapons should be rapidly neutralized, and then destroyed by a well co-ordinated and energetic attack by a tank brigade.' In view of this it is not surprising that tank brigades felt they only needed minimal assistance from the other arms.

In the early desert fighting some British armoured regiments did not help themselves. They had only recently converted from horses on a peacetime footing and, being social units as much as military, refused to accept replacement officers from other regiments, particularly the RTR. As officer casualties tended to be unnecessarily heavy in these units due to their exuberant cavalry spirit, this meant that their performance quickly fell off. Although under force of circumstances changes were made and officers were transferred around the Armoured Corps, this attitude partly explains why so many regiments were rotated out of the desert, sometimes after only a short time, with the resultant loss of experienced units.

The number of British tanks increased, there were now two armoured divisions, and two Army Tank Brigades equipped with Infantry tanks. Also the quality of the tanks improved as American Grant tanks started to arrive. These tanks had a 37-mm gun in their turret and a 75-mm in the hull. Great faith was placed in these tanks, the 8th Army believing that at last it had a tank that could defeat the panzers. Crews called them 'Egypt's Last Hope'.

The Grants were so well regarded that each regiment had to have some, but there were not enough to fully re-equip the armoured divisions so the regiments were mixed, Grants with Cruisers or Grants with Honeys. The resulting resupply and spare parts problems made life difficult for the quartermasters even on the most basic nuts-and-bolts level, and on this level American Coarse and American Fine just do not go with Whitworth and BA.

There was a further problem with Grants. Because they carried American radio sets they used a different frequency from that used by the Cruisers. This problem was handled by attaching a Cruiser to each Grant squadron to at as rear link, but the potential was there for communications breakdown. This was made worse by the low cross-country speed of the Grants. On roads they could keep up with Crusaders, but not in the desert. This could cause squadrons to become widely separated, to the detriment of communications.

As the Grants presented bigger targets – with the hull-mounted 75-mm capable of limited depression they could not take up good hull down positions – and as they were the most dangerous tanks, German gunners concentrated their fire on them.

German tanks were also being improved, though on a much more modest numerical scale. This improvement was the issue of a small number of panzer IV 'specials', initially there were only four of them, and they were short of ammunition. They were standard tanks but with long-barrelled high velocity 75mm main armaments. These tanks could defeat even the Grants at long range, up to 1,500 yards. Naturally, as the British were to find in Normandy with the issue of Fireflies, tanks with long gun barrels attracted enemy fire, so panzer IV specials, while they were rare, usually moved with their guns depressed as far as possible in an attempt to hide them. In action specials were screened with panzer III's in the '*panzerglocke*' formation and commonly only used against Grants.

In an attempt to improve control on the battlefield British regiments started to set up their own reconnaissance troops. This happened in an irregular way, some regiments only getting theirs towards the end of the North African campaign. In the initial fighting in the desert when regiments had light tanks and Honeys then any troop with these vehicles could be nominated as a regiment's recce troop. Later, regiments received, or provided, between 10 and 20 scout cars or carriers, or turretless Honeys, to form their recce troops. These troops were very useful in the desert even though there was a shortage of radios for them, but they were to be found less useful in Europe.

Shortly after the close of Crusader, Rommel bounced back and re-conquered Benghazi and western Cyrenaica. This was serious, because of the loss of airfields it made the provision of aerial support for Malta that much more difficult. Consequently General Auchinleck was ordered, and nagged, by Winston Churchill to drive the Germans back out. This was to be Operation Buckshot. At the same time Rommel was straining every nerve to prepare his forces to attack the British and capture Tobruk, which would be essential to the supply of his campaign against Egypt.

Although the British were thinking basically in offensive terms they had set up a defensive position consisting of thick minefields and infantry 'boxes' in what was termed a 'cow-pat' layout, running inland, south, from the Mediterranean roughly forty miles. The minefields contained about 1,000,000 mines. The boxes were around two miles wide and defended by a brigade with a significant amount of artillery. They were well supplied and were expected to hold out for several days if surrounded. Unfortunately they were too far apart to be mutually supporting. The extent to which they could be compared to the Italian fortified camps of the Sidi Barrani line would depend upon how well supported they were by the Infantry tanks of 13th Corps.

The British placed a series of large numbered oil barrels in the desert behind the field defences as aids to navigation, so that a unit at a particular barrel would know its exact map reference. Remarkably this common sense system does not seem to have improved anything and is seldom mentioned. Perhaps the Germans knew about it and destroyed or moved any such barrels they came across.

The Gazala Line, as these defences became known, had two defects. One defect, the standard one in the desert, was that it could be outflanked to the south. The other was that the defenders placed too much faith in minefields, particularly when they were not covered by fire, as was the case with large sections of the Line. Only a few anti-personnel mines were laid and no anti-disturbance devices were set so paths through the minefields could be easily cleared, even by the tank crews themselves.

The change of season since Crusader had resulted in a change of weather. Naturally the days were longer and the heavy rains stopped, but now there were frequent sandstorms. These storms were based on the seasonal wind, the *Khamsin*, the name of which was derived from *chamsoun*, the Arabic for fifty, and this, probably coincidentally, was the approximate time in hours they lasted. They were extremely unpleasant and made movement impossible.

Rommel attacked first. On 26th May 1942 his tank and motorised forces swung round south of the Gazala Line and quickly overran three isolated British brigades. This action started the Battle of Gazala which was destined to become even more complex than Crusader, and a staggering success for Rommel.

For simplicity the battle breaks down into a number of phases. The first three of these phases will be summarised below in terms of their relevance to Cruiser Tank Warfare.

Note 1,
'All in the Day's March', Major-General D Belchem, Collins, 1978.

The Battle of Gazala
Phase 1, Operation Venezia

When the Gazala battle started, on 26th May 1942, the British forces involved can be summarised as:

Eighth Army, commander Lieutenant General NM Ritchie
- 5th Indian Division – Maj Gen HR Briggs
- 13th Corps – Lt Gen WHE Gott
  - 1st and 32nd Army Tank Brigades
  - Three infantry divisions
- 30th Corps – Lt Gen CWM Norrie
  - 1st Armoured Division – Maj Gen H Lumsden
    - 2nd and 22nd Armoured Brigade Groups
    - 201st (renumbered from 22nd) Guards (Motor) Brigade
  - 7th Armoured Division – Maj Gen FW Messervy
    - 4th Armoured Brigade Group
    - 7th Motor Brigade Group
    - 3rd Indian Motor Brigade Group
    - 29th Indian Infantry Brigade Group
    - 1st Free French Brigade Group

Although Brigade Groups are properly so called, the word 'Group' will be left off from now on.

The two armoured divisions together with their immediate reserves had a total of 573 tanks, comprising: 167 Grants, 149 Honeys and 257 Crusaders. The two Army Tank Brigades had a total of 276 Infantry tanks.

The Axis mobile troops, not including the infantry divisions facing the Gazala Line, can be summarised as:

Armoured Group Africa, commander Field Marshal E Rommel
- German Africa Corps (DAK) – Lt Gen Nehring
  - 15th Panzer Division – Lt Gen G v Vaerst
  - 21st Panzer Division – Maj Gen G v Bismarck
- 90th Light Division – Maj Gen U Kleeman

The 20th Italian Mobile Corps – Gen E Baldassare
Ariete Armoured Division – Gen G de Stefanis
Trieste Motorised Division – Gen Azzi

The German armoured divisions had 332 tanks: 50 Panzer IIs, 242 Panzer IIIs and 40 Panzer IVs.

The Ariete was to come as something of a surprise for the British who may have been relying too much on institutional memories of Beda Fomm. It contained 138 M14 tanks that were inferior to the British Cruisers, but its artillery component had been substantially increased. There were more field guns, but more significantly there were some 88s on loan from the Germans, a new battery of eight 90-mm AA guns that, like the German 88s, could be used as AT guns, and six new 47-mm AT guns. There were twenty-six more 20-mm AA guns and a company of 24 Semovente de 75/18 self-propelled guns. These were a new class of vehicle that would be called that 'Assault Gun'. The Semovente was a 75-mm field gun mounted on a M13 medium tank hull. These vehicles would give the Ariete tanks a chance against Grants. Overall these changes significantly improved the Ariete's firepower.

The essence of Rommel's plan was to swing round the south of the Gazala Line, which was the French strongpoint of Bir Hackeim, then turn north and cut the coast road to the west of Tobruk. Then engage and destroy the infantry forces to the west, on the Gazala Line, then assault Tobruk.*(see Sketch 4)*

When Rommel was formulating his plans his intelligence was woefully inadequate. He greatly underestimated British strength. He believed there was only one Army Tank Brigade rather than two. Worse, he knew about 4th and 2nd Armoured Brigades, but not 22nd or 1st which was in reserve. Nor he did not know about several infantry units, most importantly 150th Brigade which was manning a box on the Line between Trigh Capuzzo and Trigh el Abd. Had his reconnaissance been better he might have made less ambitious plans.

The British armoured forces were not well place to meet the assault. This is believed to have been the result of lack of understanding down the chain of command. Essentially General Auchinleck believed the German assault would come in the north. He wanted the armoured brigades concentrated to the north of the Trig Capuzzo. General Ritchie was not totally convinced. He wanted to cover the possibility of the Germans coming round the south of the Line. To that end he moved 7th Armoured Division a little to the south, expecting the Corps Commander, Norrie, to concentrate the two armoured divisions once the main thrust of the German attack was identified.

There were several factors that would prevent the British armour working in harmony. The human factor is commonly dwelt on and was probably the most significant. The corps and divisional commanders did not have much regard for the army commander, but they did for General Auchinleck. If Auchinleck said that the threat was in the north that is where it was, and they were reluctant to cover any supposed threat in the south. Secondly the corps commander, General Norrie, seems to have had little control over his divisional commanders, in fact it is tempting to wonder of this extra level of command was just a nuisance. Finally the two armoured division commanders disliked each other. In particular General Lumsden thought Messervy to be incompetent and was very reluctant to see any of his troops coming under his command.

Two factors militated against Auchinleck's insistence that armoured divisions should fight as divisions. One was his own actions in adding artillery, both field and AT, to the armoured brigades. Naturally this made the brigade groups more independent, so less likely to function as a part of a division. Another was the unfortunate location of some infantry brigades of the 7th Armoured Division. These were scattered to the south and would be easily overrun by Rommel's troops unless armoured troops were rushed to their rescue, and this would inevitably happen before the armoured divisions had time to concentrate. As will be seen the support groups were not employed in a mobile role in conjunction with the armoured brigades, as were their opposite numbers in the DAK.

Just before the battle started two General Routine Orders were issued. One was to the effect that nobody was to call Rommel a good general. The other was that no battle-worthy tank was to pick up the crew of a knocked out tank. The first of these orders was merely fatuous, the second, if enforced, would have been very detrimental to the morale of the tank crews. Fortunately few Colonels passed these orders on to the troops.

27th May 1942
The battle really began at 8.30 pm on the previous evening. This was when Rommel instructed the Armoured Group Africa to start its move. This move went remarkably smoothly and by daybreak the 10,000 or so vehicles had rounded Bir Hackeim and were poised to surge north. Only one division was missing, the motorised infantry Trieste, which was still following earlier orders and working its way through the minefield to the north of Bir Hackeim.

Rommel probably flattered himself with the belief that he had achieved surprise. He hadn't. His movements had been reported to 7th Armoured Division and the 30th Corps, but so strong was the effect of Auchinleck's prediction that the Germans would attack in the north that the Axis movements were taken to be solely attempts at deception. Perhaps the German feat of moving through the night baffled the British command.

The huge force formed up with Ariete on the left, DAK in the centre and 90th Light Division on the right, then it started north. The first action was the Ariete overrunning the 3rd Indian Brigade. It then swung west in the direction of Bir Hackeim. On the right the 90th Light Division overran the 7th Motorised Brigade. By 9.0 am this division had progressed a further 10 miles north and captured the Advanced HQ, 7th Armoured Division, along with the divisional commander. Fortunately General Messervy, posing as a private soldier, managed to escape after only a few hours, but even so during this critical period the division's GOC was missing.

The DAK, in the centre, struck 4th Armoured Brigade. The brigade had received a warning order at 2.30am and within an hour the regiments had been ordered to be ready to move at first light. The regiments stood to at 5:45 but no further orders were received until roughly 7:30 when they were ordered to their battle positions. The implication is that this hiatus was the result of arguments between the generals. As the regiments started to move the left hand regiment, the 8th Hussars, was struck by the bulk of the German force. This regiment had only deployed its Honey squadron, it fought gallantly but was badly hit. When the two Grant squadrons came up they were soon reduced to two tanks. The regiment had ceased to exist as a fighting force.

The destruction of the 8th Hussars had taken time and this gave 3RTR the chance to form a line and the bulk of the remaining fighting fell on them. This regiment, with its Grants, forced a stand-up fight with the Germans. The Grants had come as a considerable surprise to the Germans which had not been dispelled by the action with the 8th Hussars and which accounts for the overconfident way in which the Germans attacked 3RTR. In common with the 8th Hussars, 3RTR had a Honey squadron (16 tanks) and two Grant squadrons (12 tanks each). RHQ had two of each type of tank. When the regiment finally pulled back, being entirely out of ammunition, there remained six Grants and 10 Honeys in the squadrons and one of each type in RHQ. The 5th RTR, which had been stationed five miles to the north of 3RTR, joined the battle later, relieving 3RTR, and fighting what was really a delaying action, suffered no casualties.

It is sometimes hinted that the disaster to 4th Armoured Brigade was the fault of the 8th Hussars. It is not beyond the bounds of possibility that this was because this regiment was cavalry and the other two armoured regiments were RTR. However the 8th Hussars were the most experienced armoured regiment in the desert, and had done everything right. They were just unlucky.

The brigade pulled back eastwards to a designated RV, but was too scattered for further united action that day. Some subunits did have skirmishes with passing German columns.

This action forced a delay on Rommel and he was critical of his commanders for accepting such a slogging match rather than covering the British with AT guns and out flanking them with tanks. This was what they finally did, bringing up three batteries of 88s.

The DAK progressed north for 10 miles then hit 22nd Armoured Brigade, catching it totally by surprise. The brigade was positioned to face north. The southern-most regiment, the 2nd Royal Gloucestershire Hussars, was in reserve but was actually the first hit. Oddly the British tanks were ordered not to open fire because it was thought that the German tanks were the survivors of 4th Armoured Brigade, a mistake that was soon rectified. In an action that only lasted 20 minutes the regiment sustained heavy casualties, the Grant squadron being reduced to one tank. The survivors withdrew to the Knightsbridge box. The other two regiments of the brigade did not join in but pulled back to the north-east to join 2nd Armoured Brigade. They were pursued by the Germans and, because of the slow cross-country speed of the Grants decided to stand and fight. The battle lasted 30 minutes, around 13 of the brigade's tanks were knocked out and the survivors continued their retreat towards the 2nd Armoured Brigade which was yet to move, but the Germans lost some tanks and their progress was checked if only for a short time.

It was now early afternoon. The Ariete had tried to steam over Bir Hackeim, as 22nd Armoured Brigade had tried to do six months earlier at Bir el Gubi, but had lost 40 tanks, and was now stationary. 90th Light was pursuing broken British units to the east and north. The DAK had taken substantial casualties from 4th Armoured Brigade, but was now heading north. Two infantry brigades had been destroyed, and two armoured brigades scattered. It had been a pretty impressive performance, but the Germans would find, as was shown in Operation Crusader, that it is difficult in the desert to totally destroy an armoured formation, it can always pull back further than the victor wants to follow it.

The inevitable result was that the DAK was running out of fuel and ammunition, but their supply columns were finding themselves under attack by fragments of units scattered in the morning's fighting. Worse, a large percentage of what fuel was getting through was being appropriated by the Ariete, even though this unit was now stationary in front of the French defences at Bir Hackeim.

As the DAK was worrying about resupply it was attacked from the east by 2nd Armoured Brigade and survivors of the 22nd. The 2nd had finally moved and come to the south of Knightsbridge. The DAK was also engaged from the north and west by Matildas of the 1st Army Tank Brigade stationed in support of the Gazala Line. The DAK seems to have coped easily with these attacks. The Tank Brigade lost 18 tanks, but the armoured brigades seem to have been more circumspect and, as night came on the fighting ground to a halt.

Rommel was a worried man. In the evening he was at Bir Harmat, south of the DAK. He was joined there by the Ariete, greatly weakened by its disaster at Bir Hackeim, but the 90th Light was out of touch, somewhere east. DAK was down to 110 tanks, though by morning this number should be increased by the recovery crews. His greatest worry was supply.

28th May
The day was to be something of an anticlimax following the high drama of the 27th. The 22nd Armoured Brigade attacked again from the east, this time going to the south of the DAK. They struck the Ariete, but were driven off by heavy AT guns. The Ariete was also attacked by 1st Army Tank Brigade, but held its own, and the 90th Light fell back to Bir el Harmat, escorted but not driven by 4th Armoured Brigade.

The actions of 22nd Armoured Brigade had the fortunate effect of scattering Rommel's Advanced HQ, but it is difficult to judge the result of this.

While all this was happening Rommel was roving the battlefield determined not to let the initiative slip away. To achieve this and regain momentum he ordered the DAK to continue its drive north to the coast road, but after visiting and ascertaining its condition he sent 21st Panzer Division by itself. This was a decision hard to understand. He must have known that he had a sizeable British armoured force in a position to place itself directly across his communications. He knew, because of the Knightsbridge box he could not outflank this force, and he knew that his supply situation was bad and this order would make it worse. It is difficult to see what he thought one understrength division would achieve. It is a military truism that the outflanker is also outflanked. Had his original estimate of British forces been accurate, it may have been that placing his armoured troops across the supply route for the Gazala Line troops might have been decisive, but just sending one division could not be, and it was not.

The 21st Panzer Division arrived at the escarpment, but found it could not get down it. So shelled some traffic, overran a small infantry box, and returned to its starting point. Much more useful, if less photogenic, the Trieste Motorised Division had driven a gap through the minefield north of Bir Hackeim. This would provide a welcome supply route.

Events were much slowed down in the afternoon due to a sandstorm.

Through the 28th British actions had been disappointing. They could be reasonably pleased with their performance of the previous day, but their success seemed to be the result of actions taken by armoured brigade commanders, and even commanders at a lower level. In the case of 7th Armoured Division this was fairly inevitable in view of General Messervy's brief captivity of the previous day, and the scattering of his Advanced HQ. It was less creditable in the case of 1st Armoured Division where General Lumsden's chief concern seems to have been to keep his armoured brigades out of action in case they came under 7th Armoured Division's control. Neither division used its infantry in co-operation with its tanks.

It is difficult to believe that the great opportunity available to 22nd Armoured Brigade of cutting the DAK off from its supplies was not apparent to the corps commander, yet it was let slip.

29th May

This day saw the Axis supply situation eased. Rommel actually led one fuel convoy himself up to the DAK. Feats of *Rommelei* like this played a great part in maintaining the German troops' morale. He had decided to concentrate his armour in the area of Bir el Harmat. It was a great misfortune that this was the area that 2nd Armoured Brigade was launched into. The battle started around 11.00 am, soon the brigade had 15th Panzer Division to its west, 21st Panzer to its north and the Ariete to its south. After an hour 22nd Armoured Brigade arrived to reinforce it, unfortunately 4th Armoured Brigade had been withdrawn and put in reserve, and arrived too late. A sand storm, then night, put an end to the fighting, the two armoured brigades fell back to Knightsbridge. This action had been an undeniable defeat for the British. It was not obvious at the time, but with hindsight it can be seen as the decisive point of the Gazala battle.

While the armoured battle was afoot the Italian infantry to the west of the Gazala Line mounted some attacks on it. Most were ineffective, but one division breached the minefield where the Trigh Capuzzo crossed it. Rommel realised that this was a promising supply route, he also realised that his initial plan for Operation Venezia had failed. He decided to abandon the offensive and pull back into the area around the breach in the minefield.

The Battle of Gazala
Phase 2, Operation Aberdeen

29th May

Rommel acknowledged that his plan to reach the coastal road had failed and his forces needed a break. He decided to pull back to the 'Cauldron' which was an easily defensible area backing on to the Gazala Line, bounded to the north by Sidra Ridge and to the east by Aslagh Ridge. Its greatest width, east-west, was about 10 miles. The Germans called the Cauldron the '*Wurstkessel*', perhaps they likened the Gazala line more to links of sausage than a series of cowpats! During the day Rommel concentrated his armoured forces, delivering a sharp defeat to 2nd and 22nd Armoured Brigades *en route*, and pulled back that night. The basic idea was that by defending the two ridges a strong position on the east of the Gazala Line could be maintained, and a route cut through the Line to allow resupply and reinforcement. After a few days the battle would be continued.

The plan was very nearly a total failure because at the point where the Cauldron backed onto the Line it was defended by a strong infantry box, the 150th Brigade. This came as a surprise to Rommel who had no choice but to assault it. The battle was desperate, lasting two days. His forces became short of everything, specially water, and he was within a few hours of surrendering his forces when the defence started to crack. The British, who also had suffered badly in phase one of the battle, did not realise what a desperate situation Rommel had been in.

The northern face of the Cauldron, Sidra Ridge, was occupied by the 21st Panzer Division, and Aslag Ridge by the Ariete. 90th Light faced the 150th Brigade and 15th Panzer Division was in reserve, generally facing south.

30th May
The day after the German retreat the two armoured brigades of the 1st Armoured Division, 2nd and 22nd, following the Germans up, put in an attack against Aslagh Ridge, nine regiments 'up', formed up in full view of the defenders. It was held off by the Ariete's artillery, the division's tanks were not involved, they had taken heavy casualties at Bir Hackeim and may well not have been fully reorganised. The British made little progress, not surprisingly considering their casualties of the previous day, and they retreated after running out of ammunition, covering their retreat with smoke. The Italians dragged some derelict tanks up onto the ridge to give British patrols something to shoot at over the next few days.

4th Armoured Brigade, because of the heavy casualties it had suffered, took no part in this fight, but sent part of the brigade south where it recovered some abandoned tanks.

As far as British armour was concerned the day was one of wasted opportunities. The 150th Brigade battle was just getting started and Rommel's troops were vulnerable to a determined assault, but the chance was let slip as it was on the next day as well. General Lumsden, reluctant to see his armour shot to pieces, wanted a night attack to be made by infantry to neutralise the Axis AT guns and open a way for his tanks. This plan was too ambitious to put into practice at such short notice. Perhaps the reactions of the British armour would have been faster if the HQs of the 8th Army and 30th Corps were not forty miles away to the east.

1st June
The survivors of 150th Brigade surrendered. While this was happening a squadron of the 4th Armoured Brigade – 'A'sqn, 5th RTR – with six Honeys, drove round Bir Hackeim and capture an Axis supply convoy of sixty vehicles, and brought them all back, a poor recompense.

After the destruction of 150th Brigade Rommel's next task was Bir Hackeim. Its capture was necessary to free up routes for supplies and reinforcements. The 90th Light Division and other troops were sent to reduce it, but it proved a more difficult task than expected and the fighting dragged on.

2nd June
While the Bir Hackeim battle was in progress, 21st Panzer Division was sent north, presumably this was a spoiling attack to disrupt the British preparations for the inevitable assault on the Cauldron. Returning to the Cauldron it struck a squadron of the 8RTR, in Valentines, then hit 4th Armoured Brigade, which was sent to its assistance, and destroyed a Honey of 3RTR, 19 Grants of 5RTR and most of the guns of 'B' battery, 1st RHA, without loss, though the brigade reported that it had knocked out a similar number of German tanks. In this action the Colonel of 5RTR was killed and the regiment reduced to one Grant and two Honeys, fortunately some new Grants were delivered next day. The other two regiments of the brigade, 3RTR and 8th Hussars, had already been amalgamated because of heavy losses, so now they were joined by the depleted 5RTR and the 3rd/5th RTR became the only regiment in the brigade.

Because of heavy casualties the 1st Armoured Brigade, which had been ordered forward to join 8th Army, was used as a pool for reinforcements for the other brigades, an expedient which inevitably disrupted the chain of command. This unit is not to be confused with the 1st Army Tank Brigade, which was largely destroyed with 150th Brigade.

3rd /4th June
By this date Rommel had 130 serviceable tanks, less than half the number he started the battle with. The British had about 400. Despite this superiority there was a lack of decisiveness in the command structure. The British had the initiative but knew, with the loss of 150th Brigade, it was slipping away. There was a number of alternative courses of action, in particular General

Auchinleck wanted an infantry assault through the Gazala Line close to the coast. Because of the confused situation General Ritchie felt that alternatives had to be discussed with corps and divisional commanders. In the end he decided that, because he could not be sure of preventing the German armour counter-attacking, the best course to follow was to eliminate the Axis forces in the Cauldron as soon as possible. This was to be Operation Aberdeen.

Inevitably the operation would involve troops from both corps, from 13th Corps in the north and 30th Corps in the east. It would have been most sensible to have had one commander for the whole operation and General Gott was asked to do this but would not accept. So General Ritchie decided to retain overall command himself with the fighting being controlled by either the armoured division commander, General Messervy, or the infantry commander, General Briggs, depending on whether the fighting was in the initial, infantry, stage, or the later, armoured, stage. The 30th Corps commander, General Norrie, seems to have been left out of the chain of command.

While the British were sorting themselves out, so were the Germans. They not only repaired tanks but cleared lanes through the minefield to the south and east of the Cauldron for the use of counter-attacking troops.

The bulk of the fighting on the 30th Corps front was to be done by the 22nd Armoured Brigade which had 156 tanks, a mixture of the three types. It had been transferred from 1st Armoured Division to the 7th to replace the 4th Armoured Brigade which had been withdrawn due to heavy casualties.

The essence of the British plan was an infantry brigade assault on the Aslagh Ridge, it would carried out at night and would be supported by the Valentines of 4RTR. Following this, at dawn, the 22nd Armoured Brigade would burst through into the centre of the Cauldron, destroying any Axis armour it met, and finish up at point B104 just to the south of Sidra Ridge. It would be followed by an infantry brigade which would dig in to consolidate the ground taken by the armour.

A secondary assault was to be mounted by 13th Corps on Sidra Ridge. It was to be carried out by 32nd Army Tank Brigade supported by an infantry battalion, its left flank being covered by the depleted 4th Armoured Brigade. This action was not coordinated with that of 30th Corps.

5th June
The 13th Corps operation started in the early morning. The artillery barrage started at 2:50 and by dawn the leading infantry were on the ridge. Unfortunately the weight of the artillery preparation had fallen on empty desert, the Italian defenders had decoyed the British into thinking their defences were half a mile in front of their real locations. The real fighting started at dawn and the infantry suffered greatly but it was judged that they had carried out their task and the 22nd Armoured Brigade was sent through.

The tanks covered around two miles then ran into the German and Italian artillery. The only reason they were not annihilated was that the shells raised so much dust that the gunners could not see their targets. It also made it harder for the tanks to fire back. All this caused them to swing north but here they ran into the AT guns of the 21st Panzer Division and pulled back behind some infantry who were digging in. The brigade had lost 60 tanks out of its initial strength of 156.

The withdrawal of the armour left the infantry vulnerable and the German and Italian armour counter-attacked causing devastation. Because of the convoluted command structure, all armoured forces were temporally under 1st Armoured Division's control. The armoured brigade, which had been told to give absolute priority to engaging Axis tanks, refused to help the infantry, which was finally forced to retreat, its 2-pdr AT guns, not dug in, being easily knocked out. The armour then pulled back with it. The assault here had failed.

Afterwards one of the two infantry brigade commanders commented that in the desert a brigade needed 48 hours to set up a tank proof position, that is one able to survive without armoured support. The armoured brigade did not seem to understand this.

The attack of the 32nd Army Tank Brigade on Sidra Ridge was a disaster. 70 infantry tanks advanced in broad daylight, with minimal artillery support, against the 21st Panzer Division, and ran into a minefield. They lost 50 tanks and achieved nothing.

By mid afternoon the British attack had ground to a halt. There had been a chance to throw in the 2nd Armoured Brigade which had been 20 miles away to the north. It was brought up and placed under 7th Armoured Division, but it received from it a number of contradictory orders and was not used. As it only had one regiment of tanks it would probably not have achieved much.

At 5.00pm Rommel ordered a general counter-attack. The 21st Panzer Division attacked to the north, passing the wreckage of 32nd Tank Brigade. It then swung to the east, then to the south to hit the flank of 22nd Armoured Brigade and the two infantry brigades on the Aslagh Ridge.

The Ariete in the middle attacked eastwards towards Aslagh Ridge, pinning down the infantry brigades there. Elements of the 15th Panzer Division, under the direct command of Rommel, passed through the minefield to the south of the ridge and at this point the Germans were joined by a battlegroup withdrawn from the Bir Hackeim fighting. They overran unit after unit and also overran the HQ of the 7th Armoured Division. This was one of the few double envelopments that modern warfare has seen.

The defence against such an envelopment should be troops and artillery positioned to fight, as it were, sideways to prevent the line being rolled up, and a reserve. As it was all the artillery was close to the ridge and facing the Cauldron, and the 2nd Armoured Brigade was left without orders. The nearest significant unit, the 201st Guards Brigade, was hit by the Luftwaffe and immobilised. The Germans mopped up the remaining infantry units of the Aslagh Ridge next day.

Around half of the 22nd Armoured Brigade escaped, again giving no assistance to the infantry. It is just possible that, with some Rommel-type leadership, it could have joined the 2nd Armoured Brigade and perhaps some of the 201st Guards Brigade troops and counter-attacked to allow the escape of some of the surrounded units, but the reality is that routs take a long time to halt. And there is no doubt that it was a rout. It could be that desert fighting results in a frame of mind that prefers movement to fighting for every foot of ground, and certainly some units fell back too quickly. Some fought very well. When the Ariete tanks assaulted Aslagh Ridge, one group of four 25-pdrs stayed in action to the end, the last gunner running from one gun to another until he, in his turn, was killed.

The Battle of Gazala
Phase 3, Knightsbridge

The end of the Cauldron fighting was followed by the fall of Bir Hackeim on 9th June. After that it was plain that the initiative was in Rommel's hands. Unfortunately the British command was still optimistic.

In the few days available before Rommel resumed the offensive it would have been impossible to realign the British forces to cope with the new situation. Ideally the Gazala Line would have been evacuated, the troops and such mines and wire as were available sent to defend Tobruk. Tobruk was Rommel's obvious target. The armour should have been concentrated into one division, and some infantry boxes, such as Knightsbridge, retained and strengthened to act as pivots for the coming tank battles when Rommel tried to surround Tobruk.

There were some minor changes made to infantry positions, but little more. The three armoured brigades were grouped round Knightsbridge, they contained a total of 185 tanks, comprising: 77 Grants, 52 Crusaders and 56 Honeys. In addition were 63 Infantry tanks of the 32nd Army Tank Brigade. They were to confront Rommel's 200 tanks, but this total included 85 second class tanks, either Italian or Panzer II's. The result of the coming action should not have been a foregone conclusion.

11th June
Phase three of the Gazala battle started mid afternoon. Rommel's first move seems to have been something of a gambit to see which way the British would jump. He did not keep the DAK together, but left 21st Panzer Division in Sidra Ridge, and sent 15th Panzer Division to the north-east, from Bir Hackeim, towards El Adem. This division was supported on its left by the Trieste Motorised Division. On its right went the 90th Light Division. Presumably this division, now down to 1,000 men,

was to establish itself to the east of Tobruk. The British were very sensitive about this area because of the supply dump at Belhammed.

The route of the 15th Panzer Division and the associated units was right between the 4th Armoured Brigade and the 7th Motorised Brigade and other 7th Armoured Division units. The armoured brigade started south from Knightsbridge but halted at Naduret el Ghesceuasc which, if not high ground, is slightly higher than the surrounding desert. The 15th Panzer Division had also halted and the two forces spent the night within extreme range of each other.

12th June
In the morning General Norrie ordered 2nd Armoured Brigade to join the 4th . These two brigades, containing 56 Grants and 84 light tanks, should have been able to strike a major blow against 15th Panzer Division, while 22nd Armoured Brigade, with 27 Grants and 39 light tanks, held 21st Panzer Division and the Ariete in check. The 32nd Army Tank Brigade could be called on to help.

This plan was sensible and realistic but failed utterly because the two brigade commanders would not accept General Messervy's plan. This was for 2nd Armoured Brigade, in the east, to pin down then 15th Panzer Division while 4th Armoured Brigade swung round to the west, linked up with 7th Motor Brigade, then attacked the Germans from the flank and rear.

This plan, in its turn, was a good one, but it seems that 4th Armoured Brigade was reluctant to leave the high ground of Naduret el Ghesceuasc, and 2nd Armoured Brigade did not want to get involved in serious action away from 1st Armoured Division. The two brigades remained stationary. General Messervy, having failed to get his orders accepted, drove off to see General Norrie, ran into a German reconnaissance unit and spent the rest of the day hiding in a well.

The situation with the British armoured brigades was bad enough but their radio procedure made it worse and, via his radio intercept service, Rommel was soon aware of the hold-up in the British chain of command and he set out to exploit it.

Up to midday the armoured brigades and 15th Panzer were stationary, in long range contact, the superior armament of the Grants deterring the Germans. Then two things happened. General Norrie, realising that General Messservy was missing, put General Lumsden in command of all three armoured brigades. General Lumsden ordered 22nd Armoured Brigade south to join the other two. Rommel ordered the 21st Panzer Division to drive to the east with all speed, which it could do now that 22nd Armoured Brigade was no longer watching it, and engage the tanks facing the 15th Panzer Division.

The Germans were faster, probably because both Rommel and Nehring were driving them as hard as they could. The result was that the armoured brigades were hit on the south and the east, and some of the 21st Panzer Division started to lap round to the north. Not surprisingly casualties were heavy among British tanks. The Grant, with its main armament in the hull, could not take up a hull down firing position and, being on slightly higher ground, would have risen above any heat haze, and been an easy target. The DAK had recently received some Panzer III's with the longer barrelled 50-mm guns which, having a higher muzzle velocity, could penetrate the frontal armour of the Grants.

The situation of the 2nd and 4th Armoured Brigades was desperate, but they received a little respite when 22nd Armoured Brigade joined the fray. This gave 4th Armoured Brigade a chance to pull back, which it did with such vigour that it reached the Tobruk by-pass road, but with only 15 tanks.

The 2nd and 22nd Armoured Brigades, fighting all the way, fell back to the east and north-east of Knightsbridge. This box was judged to be untenable without the support of strong British armour, and it was evacuated on the night of 13th/14th. The Gazala Line was then in danger of being cut off, so that too was evacuated, and since Tobruk was no longer defensible, it was lost.

Some comments on the Gazala Battle.

The basic concept of the British forces for the battle seemed to be a common sense one. It involved a strong front line with two armoured divisions behind it ready to destroy any German forces that penetrated or outflanked that line. It was, though, not the best deployment for Cruiser Tank Warfare.

The alternative would have required the acceptance of the principle that there was no point in holding desert, but rather the purpose was to destroy Rommel's mobile troops. To achieve this, the armoured divisions should have been given a secure base by fortifying Tobruk and the coastal area back to the east along the escarpment as far as Bardia and Sollum. This should have been no more difficult than to create the Gazala Line.

Once this secure base had been set up Rommel could not advance past it without exposing his supply troops to destruction by the armoured forces lurking within the fortified area, and he could not attack this base without risking the British armour attacking his flanks. His supply situation would have been precarious compared to that of the British whose tanks were close to three harbours. Finally, when the time was judged right the British armour could have sallied forth for the tank battle it always thought in terms of.

Rommel's fixation with the capture of Tobruk shows that he agreed with this analysis. It is sometimes written that Rommel needed Tobruk as a supply port but this cannot be his main motive. Tobruk, when fully functioning, could handle 600 tons daily, but when on the offensive Rommel's troops consumed ten times that. As a port Tobruk was not worth the bother.

The general plan outlined here was not adopted and the more conventional approach was. The result was a defeat. As will be seen the Gazala battle was the last opportunity for what can reasonably be called Cruiser Tank Warfare, though this was not obvious at the time.

It is possible that British armour could have been more effective if the Grants had been concentrated in all-Grant units. The Grants were by far the most effective British tanks and they came as a shock to the Germans. Rommel, it seems, knew about them but did not fully appreciate how good they were. An all-Grant brigade should have been more than a match for a panzer division, but scattering the Grants among all the armoured regiments resulted in squadron after squadron of Grants being destroyed individually, and does not seem to have increased the effectiveness of these regiments to a commensurate degree.

Chapter 7

Cruiser Tank Battles

In the period after Knightsbridge and before El Alamein British armoured operations were characterised by failures in Command and Control. Worse, they were up against Rommel and the Afrika Korps at the very peak of their form.

After Alamein British operations settled down to a pattern. The infantry divisions would close up to a German position, bring up artillery and ammunition dumps, stage a set-piece break through. Then the armoured divisions would pursue the beaten enemy as far as their next defensive position. Then the procedure would be repeated.

The extent to which the new pattern of operations was due to the limitations of technology or to the preferences of General Montgomery, does not alter the fact that Cruiser Tank Warfare had been superseded because it had failed. Worse, it had failed in the theatre most suitable for its application.

The causes for this failure may be considered under two headings: Command and Effectiveness.

Command

In modern times it is usual to lump Command with Control, Communications and Intelligence. This is a reasonable way of looking at the whole process: finding out the facts, making a decision, passing the orders on to the troops, and ensuring the orders are carried out. The process is on-going. The situation is perpetually changing and decisions will constantly need updating. This process has, in the past, been referred to as the 'Boyd Loop'. It is now usually called the Observation, Orientation, Decision, Action loop (OODA). The requirement is to pass through the loop as quickly as possible, more quickly than the enemy so that he is always being presented with a new situation and does not have time to react to it. This was what the British armoured divisions failed to do. Most notably, as had been shown, in mounting the assault of the 'Cauldron'.

There were several reasons for this failing. One was the predilection for dispersion. The armoured brigades were spread far from each other and the regiments within them were also well separated. This might have been sensible in terms of camouflage, but it made control much more difficult. In the early stage of the Gazala battle 5RTR was five miles away from 3RTR and had to drive that distance to respond to orders.

Another of the reasons was the lack of Standard Operating Procedures (SOPs). If these had been well thought out, practiced and adhered to then the whole machine would have responded to orders faster and more reliably, and disasters like the failure of infantry/tank cooperation in the Cauldron action may have been avoided. Further, rigid adherence to SOPs would have simplified the passing of orders by radio, very necessary in view of the poor quality radios of the time.

Probably the most significant of the reasons was the conference ethos. Before a battle conferences are essential so that all senior officers know the aim and can make informed independent decisions if required. However during an action, as before the Cauldron assault, they only interrupt the Boyd Loop, as generals briefed brigadiers, then brigadiers briefed colonels, and so on.

Worse, conferences can result in a general loss of grip, this happened before the Gazala Battle when the armoured division commanders, having been told that General Auchinleck was anticipating an attack in the north, were less than whole-hearted in accepting General Ritchie's plan to counter an attack from the south. This resulted in compromise in planning and dispersion for the tanks.

Once the conferences were over and the battle had started it was usual for a commanding officer to leave subordinate officers alone as much as possible, almost as if intervention would have been regarded as ill mannered.

German methods in general, and Rommel's in particular, may be contrasted with the British. Rommel commanded from the front. To an extent this was forced on him by the lamentable state of the Italian maps, the only ones available, which meant that it was all but impossible to command highly mobile operations from anywhere else. He kept his two most powerful units, the two panzer divisions, united in the DAK, and he went with it. Being right at the front, and taking decisions instantly, he was always able to outpace the British Boyd Loop, even though his methods made life difficult for his staff. It also meant that he sometimes made decisions without having all the available facts in front of him, and got it wrong, as with his 'Dash to the Wire'. It is significant that the DAK was recalled from this venture by Colonel Westphal, the operations officer, when the staff could not contact Rommel. When Rommel heard of the order he was extremely annoyed, but approved it when he found out details of the tactical situation.

Rommel was not the only German commander who liked to be well forward. General von Thoma, who was to command the DAK, believed that the armoured force commander should be 'in the midst of his tanks', and, like a cavalry-man, give 'saddle orders'[1]. General von Thoma was captured at Alamein.

Again in contrast with British methods, it was common for German senior officers, particularly Rommel, to be well forward, badgering and driving subordinates, ensuring that everyone was doing his best. Rommel, in particular, could use this method of command in North Africa because he could travel in a Storch army co-operation aircraft which could easily find landing rounds where he could alight and talk to local commanders having done his own reconnaissance.

At this point it might be mentioned that the widely accepted view that the Germans were very much in favour of directive control *(auftragstaktik)*, was not demonstrated by Rommel whose command style was that of direct orders. To what extent it is true that the German army as a whole accepted the principle of directive control is still a little vague.

There is a final point about the difference in command between the British and German armies, one that affected all modes of warfare but most conspicuously mobile operations. This was the way that the Germans would identify the critical point (*schwerpunkt*) and ruthlessly drive their units to succeed there almost regardless of casualties, cold-bloodedly taking troops from less important areas knowing that losses there were of secondary importance. The British never achieved this intensity and ruthlessness, and so let several opportunities for tactical success slip. This was illustrated during the Tunisian campaign on 10th April 1943.

The North African campaign was entering its last phase. The 1st Army had almost fought its way eastwards through hills and mountains to the coastal plain, and 8th Army was attacking from the south. On 9th April the German armour, having comfortably held off the 8th Army, was streaming north. The commander of the 6th Armoured Division was ordered to burst through the last of the German defences in the hills and engage and hopefully destroy the panzers. The division was led by 26th Armoured Brigade which attacked gallantly. The leading regiment, 17th/21st Lancers, had very heavy vehicle casualties, mostly due to mines, and was effectively *hors de combat.* The other two armoured regiments lost only seven tanks between them and finally fought their way through. Some German armour made a small counter-attack, they were easily beaten off. Then the brigade, and the rest of the division, laagered up.

Next morning, at 8.45, the brigade resumed its advance, sweeping majestically across the plain. It exchanged a few long range shots with the German rearguard. A huge opportunity to end the campaign had been missed, an assessment agreed with by General Kramer, the relevant German commander. It is hard to imaging a commander like Rommel allowing this. He would have had the fuel tanks of all non-essential vehicles drained to keep the tanks running, and he would have driven the tanks until they were all knocked out rather than let the enemy just slip away.

Remarkably the commander of the 26th Armoured Brigade, Brigadier Roberts, went on to command the 11th Armoured Division, and was generally regarded as the best of all British armoured division commanders.

Effectiveness

The main difficulty with the British armoured force in the desert, which is to say usually the 7th Armoured Division, was getting it to fight as a division, the armoured brigades were too used to operating independently. This lack of control was largely caused by the division(s) being so large and widely deployed that effective communications between the brigades could not be maintained with the radio sets of the day. During the Crusader period when the artillery was concentrated in the support group this resulted in the armoured brigades having no artillery support. Once the artillery was scattered among the armoured brigade groups these brigade groups were better equipped for independent action, and were less likely to fight as a part of a division. The result of this was that, time after time, armoured brigades were defeated by larger German units.

Even when a British armoured formation met a German panzer unit of similar size the Germans tended to win. The reason for this is not hard to see. The Germans practiced cooperation of arms through well understood battle drills. The most striking aspect of German tank tactics was what is often called 'sword and shield' tactics, cooperation between tanks and AT guns. The scenario would be that the German tanks would make contact with a British tank unit. The AT guns would deploy behind the tanks, which would then fall back through them. The British might oblige by charging the AT guns, but even if they did not, the German tanks could manoeuvre behind the shield of AT guns and strike the British force from a flank.

The British could not match this kind of tactics as their AT gun, the 2-pdr, was of a less mobile design. It fired from a pedestal mount, which gave it a 360 degree traverse, rather like a stationary tank turret, but meant that it took some time to set up. When it was set up it had a high, hence vulnerable, profile.

When the German tanks attacked AT guns or dug-in troops they had a great advantage over British tanks in that the Panzer IV could fire 75-mm HE shells. Before the arrival of Grant and Sherman, British tanks were restricted to firing AP shot. The Panzer IVs would engage a battery from the front, driving the gunners from their guns, while lighter tanks assaulted it from a flank.

Also the German issue of AP rounds for their tanks' MGs made them more effective against the shields of British AT guns than the normal issue British 303 ball ammunition was against the German AT guns. Armoured corps Besa 7.92-mm AP ammunition, which became more common over time, was as good as the German AP ammunition.

On top of this there was the higher standard of German tank gunnery. Perhaps this was an indirect result of the British faith in firing on the move, or perhaps it was a result of the way the accuracy of the 2-pdr shot fell off at longer ranges. As has been mentioned in Chapter 4 the bore sighting procedure for the 2-pdr did not help. The bore would be lined up with the sight, but as the recoil buffers were on top of the barrel, the barrel dipped a fraction on firing and the first shot fell a little short. The sights, of course, could have been corrected by test firing on a range, but there is no reason why the bore sighting procedure could not have been improved.

The 2-pdr was reputed to be more effective against German tanks than it actually was. German tanks in the field usually had extra armoured plated bolted on their fronts. When 2-pdrs were tested against captured or knocked out German tanks these plates were removed. This produced spuriously good results for the 2-pdrs. This would not have improved the reputation of the gun among tank crews.

Even when German tanks had been knocked out they were more likely to be recovered, repaired and returned to the fray than were British. This was partly because they had well designed firewalls between the fighting compartment and the power pack, and partly because of the excellent recovery crews that followed in their low loaders closely behind the fighting units.

The critical factor was to retain control of the battlefield where the wrecks were. This was illustrated when Rommel staged his 'Dash to the Wire'. That left the shattered 7th Armoured Division on the battlefield among their wrecks, and gave them a few days to work on them and stage a phoenix-like recovery.

This points back to the salient point about Cruiser Tank Warfare in the desert. It was almost impossible to destroy an opposing armoured force. This accounts for the to-and-fro nature of the campaign which was only ended after the Axis forces were pinned down and destroyed at Alamein in a battle which showed a greater resemblance to the fighting of 1918 than to anything described in 'Modern Formations'.

Note 1,
As quoted by BH Liddell Hart in 'The Other Side of the Hill', Cassell, 1948

Chapter 8

Cruisers in the Breakthrough

From the earliest days it was never intended that armoured divisions should be used for breaking through prepared positions. This was implied in Mechanized and Armoured Formations by the theoretical separation of the army into 'mobile troops' and 'combat troops'. More significantly it was stated in Modern Formations: '*guns will always outclass armour, and the accuracy of stationary guns will always be greater than that of those in movement, direct frontal assault on prepared positions will be costly unless supported by adequate covering fire.*'

The concept that armoured divisions should not be called upon for breakthroughs was reinforced by the types of vehicles they were issued with, light tanks and Cruisers. These tanks, as Modern Formations put it '*can best deal with obstacles to their movement by circumventing them.*' The more heavily armoured 'I' tanks were not issued to armoured divisions.

Remarkably the concept of using armoured divisions for breakthroughs does not seem to have been seriously considered during the 1930s and, perhaps, too much was expected from Medium and Cruiser Tanks. General Martel, who had a significant influence on tank design, and hence on their capabilities, observed some Red Army manoeuvres in 1936 involving a large number of the Soviet equivalents of Cruisers. He commented that trying to stop such a formation with AT guns would be like a sportsman trying to stop a covey of partridges by shooting into it. Presumably he considered that a mass of Cruisers would be able to barge through any opposition and, in particularly favourable circumstances, as with the Tebaga Gap battle of March 1943, this may be possible. However if the defence has any depth and the defenders have had time to organise their AT weapons, the Cruisers are much less likely to be successful.

Efforts were made to develop heavy tanks to lead breakthroughs, but, apart from work on the 'I' tanks, these developments were soon halted. Consequently the armoured divisions of the late 1930s, including as they did large numbers of Cruiser tanks but little in the way of infantry, artillery and engineers were poorly equipped to fight their was through field defences.

The reluctance of armoured divisions to attack field defences is repeated in the Army Training Instruction No 3 of 1941. *'Armoured Divisions may be set the task of attacking infantry divisions, or they may have to undertake it during the performance of other roles. If the enemy is occupying a highly organised defensive position the task is unsuitable for an armoured division. Suitable tasks would be to exploit success when the crust of the enemy resistance has been broken by other troops, to break through the rearguard in a pursuit, or to drive in a protective screen of outposts.'*

Clearly it was basic to armoured corps thinking that infantry divisions, supported by 'I' tanks, should break into and through the enemy positions, leaving the breakouts to armoured divisions. However there were two operations during the war in which armoured divisions were thrown at German defences to achieve breakthroughs, Operations Supercharge and Goodwood. The first of these will be considered in this chapter.

There are two criteria for a successful breakthrough. One is that the assaulting troops should be through the enemy's line and out in the open while most of the defenders are still in the line. The alternative is just to push the enemy back. The other is to break through in such a way that the defenders cannot deploy their reserves to either seal off the rupture in their front or counter-attack to restore the situation.

The question of reserves hardly occurred with either of the two operations listed above, but it is fundamental to any consideration of a breakthrough. So long as the defenders have a significant and mobile reserve then the operation will fail as a breakthrough, even though it may be a success in other ways. The defeat of the Gothic Line was a case in point. The assault on the line by V Corps should have conformed to the standard model of the defence being opened up by infantry and an armoured division, in this cast the 1st, bursting through. However things turned out differently.

The real problem was that the strength and depth of the German defences were underestimated by the British command. The assault broke down into two phases, in each phase the infantry almost achieved its objectives, but when the armour was unleashed the Germans had managed to rush up reinforcements, including AT guns, and the tanks took heavy casualties and failed. In the second phase the leading regiment, the Bays, had an entire squadron wiped out in their final assault on the Ceriano ridge. The day after this anti-tank success the Germans started evacuating the Gothic Line.

Operation Supercharge

The battle of El Alamein started on 23rd October 1942. Unlike previous desert battles there was no open flank to the south and the British forces had no alternative to battering their way through the Axis positions. There were three major problems to contend with: Axis minefields, AT guns, and armoured counter-attacks. The plan for the initial assault involved driving lanes through the minefields and establishing bridgeheads beyond them for two armoured divisions' worth of tanks to pound through and take up positions behind the defending infantry to prevent the Axis armoured forces from launching counter-attacks to support their infantry, who would be being battered to pieces by the attacking infantry and artillery.

The plan did not work. It was far too ambitious to accomplish in one night, and the Axis forces fought back too well. For the next few days there was fighting on a much smaller scale. Most importantly that carried out by the Australian troops at the north of the line. This was due to its closeness to the coast road, a naturally sensitive point for the defenders.

By 1st November it was starting to appear that the Axis forces were weakening and General Montgomery decided to launch an armoured assault in the hope of achieving a breakthrough. This assault was Operation Supercharge.

The original concept was for the assault to be made in the north along the coastal road, but it became plain that Rommel was massing his best troops there, so it was moved south. In planning the operation the lessons of the first assaults were considered. It was believed that the failures on 24th October were caused by a lack of reserves to keep the advance moving at its critical stage. Consequently Supercharge was to comprise of three phases, each phase being a new wave hitting the defences.

> Phase I, an infantry assault to break through the minefields and forward defences.
>
> Phase II, an armoured brigade assault to destroy the AT defences deployed in depth.
>
> Phase III, a major armoured unit to pass through the static defences and engage, and destroy, the Axis armour, then cut the coastal road.

The last phase was naturally the most important, without it all that would be achieved would be pushing the enemy back a bit. Montgomery was very alive to the necessity of destroying Rommel's armour, but wanted to do it in a tightly controlled way, on the battlefield and not in wide-ranging Cruiser manoeuvres that he did not trust his generals to carry out.

Phase III was to be undertaken by 10th Corps. The Corps commander, General Lumsden, decided not to use both armoured divisions of the corps for the breakthrough, but only one, the 1st, commanded by General Briggs. For this operation it was reinforced with an extra armoured brigade, the 8th from 10th Armoured Division. The armoured division was expected to pass through the German defences and take up a position on the slightly elevated ground to the west of the Rahman track. It should have one armoured brigade on the Tel el Aqqaqir, another two miles to the north-west. It could be assumed that, as the Rahman track was important to the defenders, they must attack the armoured division there even though they would be at a disadvantage and within range of the British artillery. After this successful engagement the armoured division would swing to the north to cut off the Axis retreat in the area of Ghazal station. The armoured division was to be accompanied by several armoured car units which would forge ahead carrying out reconnaissance tasks and causing general chaos. Because the break-in was an infantry affair the first part of Supercharge was to be under 13th Corps, more specifically under General Freyberg, the commander of the New Zealand Division. At 9.10am this was to change and all tanks would come under 10th Corps.

Clearly the success of Supercharge depended on the Axis front crumbling in front of it, and this was what Montgomery anticipated. All previous experience of positional warfare had shown how vulnerable a salient could be. Consequently it was emphasised that Supercharge could only work if the 1st Armoured Division, commencing Phase III, could pass through the 9th Armoured Brigade, which would just have completed Phase II, at 6.45am, before dawn.

The infantry assault of Phase I was made by two brigades, 152 Brigade to the south, and 151 Brigade to the north, supported by the Valentines of the 50th RTR and 8th RTR respectively. They were to attack due west, the centre line being roughly six miles south of the coast road. Their final objective was between 300 yards and a mile to the east of the Rahman track. The artillery support was impressive, provided by 296 field guns and 48 mediums, but because Axis positions had not been perfectly located, it took the form of a creeping barrage with some counter-battery fire. Before the barrage started the infantry withdrew 1,500 yards and formed up in line to simplify the fire plan, reduce the possibility of map reading errors and ensure that no enemy locations were missed.

The barrage started at 1.05am on 2nd November 1942. The infantry had 4,000 yards to advance, an epic by any standards. They were on their objectives on time, at 3.45, having captured several dug-in tanks and a German tank recovery unit *en route* but due to rocky ground they found great difficulty in digging in. Taking advantage of German disorganisation a regiment of armoured cars managed to get two squadrons through the German front on the southern flank of the salient. They spent the day spreading alarm and despondency behind the front. After the infantry had gone firm there was a planned wait of two hours, to just before dawn, when the tanks of 9th Armoured Brigade, an independent armoured brigade attached to the New Zealand Division, should pass through the infantry front line, commencing Phase II.

9th Armoured Brigade - Brigadier J Currie
- 3rd The King's Own Hussars
- Royal Wiltshire Yeomanry
- Warwickshire Yeomanry
- Motor battalion

The task of 9th Armoured Brigade was to destroy the AT screen which was taken as located around the Rahman track, with a final objective of a position around 2,700 yards in front of the infantry. It was important for the tanks to be among, or even past, the AT guns before dawn as that was when they were most vulnerable. Their bulk stood out against the lightening sky whereas the dug-in AT guns remained invisible. The armoured brigade had the advantage that the majority of its tanks, Grants and Shermans, could fire 75-mm HE and hope to destroy the AT guns. Also their armour, though not thick, was reasonably proof against 37-mm and 50-mm AT projectiles. Even so it was appreciated that carrying out its task would cause the armoured brigade heavy casualties. Montgomery was said to have been prepared for 100% tank casualties.

The armoured brigade had left its laager late, 10pm, the previous evening. Its strength was 123 tanks: 46 with the Warwickshire Yeomanry, 44 with the Royal Wiltshire Yeomanry and 33 with the 3rd Hussars. Unfortunately a 46 of these consisted of Crusaders just returned from workshops and their guns had not been zeroed and other checks not done. Many fell out on the march up. This march was an exceedingly difficult one. Not only was it made at night, through or past minefields, but the fine dust produced a blinding fog. The Warwickshire Yeomanry got lost and had to retreat out of a minefield, losing four tanks in the process, this resulted in them veering a little to the south. The 3rd Hussars were shelled, the resulting chaos temporarily cost them their motor company.

The mishap to the Warwickshires caused the brigade commander, no doubt thinking how thin on the ground his brigade was on a front of 4,000 yards, to request a delay of 30 minutes even though the other two regiments were on the start line and eager to move off before the sun rose. The 3rd Hussars were on the right, the Royal Wiltshire Yeomanry in the centre and the Warwickshire Yeomanry a little far out on the left. The Brigadier, Currie, posted himself with the Wiltshires. The barrage started at 6.15, just before dawn, and advanced at 100 yards each three minutes. The regiments advanced with their Crusader squadrons leading. The barrage was too slow for the nine tanks of the Royal Wiltshire's Crusader squadron and they drove through it on to the Rahman track, but there its troubles began. It was by then light enough for the dug-in AT guns to see their targets and the Crusaders, mostly being armed with 2-pdrs that did not fire HE ammunition and were separated from their Grants and Shermans that did, could do little but charge the muzzle flashes of the AT guns. A few Crusaders had 6-pdrs and these were issued with a small proportion of HE rounds, which were not regarded as very effective and certainly made little impression on the battle. The squadron, fighting gallantly, was wiped out, the other tanks fired smoke to cover the escaping dismounted crews. As the heavy squadrons came up they were hit by even heavier fire. The Crusaders may have destroyed some AT guns but these were of smaller calibre. There were twenty-four 88-mm guns deployed further west and as the day grew lighter their fire became more deadly. In the end the regiment was reduced to four tanks, but its motor company with its AT guns, dug in around the Rahman track and stayed there all day.

The 3rd Hussars on the right were luckier. Their Crusader squadron was only three tanks strong. They surged ahead with the Royal Wiltshire's, but the Germans let them pass, they were waiting for the Grants and Shermans. The Crusaders seem to have made little contribution to the battle, not surprisingly as they could see the heavy squadrons being massacred particularly by fire from their right flank. The regiment was reduced to the three Crusaders and nine Shermans and Grants.

The Warwickshire Yeomanry had drifted to the south and had arrived actually behind some German guns. At dawn they came under fire from three sides but remarkably managed to destroy all the guns shooting at them. Perhaps the low rise of Tel el Aqqaqir shielded them from the 88s. Even so by the time they closed up to the Royal Wiltshire Yeomanry they had only seven tanks of all types left.

It cannot be said that the brigade was unlucky as everything that it endured had been anticipated in the planning of the operation. However in one instance it had been very lucky. As a part of the German reaction to Operation Supercharge the 21st Panzer Division had moved north and taken up a position behind Tel el Aqqaqir. Had it launched an immediate counter-attack the results for the 9th Armoured Brigade would have been catastrophic. Fortunately Afrika Korps HQ, mistaking its location, told it to wait, and when the Warwickshire Yeomanry joined the Royal Wiltshires the opportunity was lost.

The brigade had really ceased to exist and only held its position because of this German error. Of the 94 tanks that had crossed the start line, 75 had been knocked out. Its total casualties were 31 officers and 198 other ranks. This might seem a high proportion of officers but actually roughly reflects the proportion of officers and other ranks involved. The officers would not have stayed with the tanks that fell out on the march up, but transferred to other tanks. The brigade's success can be judged by the fact that 35 knocked out AT guns were found within 100 yards of the wrecks of its tanks

Phase III

- The 1st Armoured Division - Major-General R Briggs
  - 2nd Armoured Brigade - Brigadier AF Fisher
    - The Queen's Bays
    - 9th Queen's Royal Lancers
    - 10th Royal Hussars
    - Motor battalion
  - 8th Armoured Brigade - Brigadier ECN Custance
    - 3rd RTR
    - Sherwood Rangers Yeomanry
    - Staffordshire Yeomanry
    - Motor battalion
  - 7th Motor Brigade - Brigadier TJB Bosvile
    - Three battalions

As can be seen the armoured regiments of the 2nd Armoured Brigade had not changed since the French campaign.

Unfortunately the sacrifice of 9th Armoured Brigade was not taken full advantage of. Phase III started late. At 7.0am the 2nd Armoured Brigade was taking up a position 600 yards behind it to the right. From the south the regiments were the 10th Hussars, the 9th Lancers and the Queen's Bays. By this time the sun was fully risen and the 88s deployed to the west of the Rahman track and not engaged by the 9th Armoured Brigade, could dominate the battlefield even with the sun in their eyes. So 2nd Armoured Brigade settled down to a long range HE duel with them, each regiment being supported by a battery of self-propelled artillery. This was really the only realistic way of countering this threat. Later in the war these large AT guns would have been quite easily and quickly destroyed by the RAF. It was a pity that the RAF could not manage to do it in 1942. It did, though, mount a series of bombing raids during the afternoon that played a major part in hindering the German counter-attack.

It may be that this duel would have worn the defenders down, but it did not have the chance. At 9.35 radio intercepts picked up that the Germans were massing for a counter-attack which started at 11.00. By this time the second brigade of 1st Armoured Division, the 8th, was coming up, to form up on the left of 2nd Armoured Brigade. However some German tanks were approaching from the north, on the right flank of the salient and the leading regiment of the 8th Armoured Brigade, the Staffordshire Yeomanry, facing north behind the other two armoured brigades, forestalled them. This was a very lucky deployment and was only possible because the brigade was late. The other two regiments, 3RTR and the Sherwood Rangers Yeomanry took up position by the Staffordshires as they came up. As this threat abated they were sent to their planned posts by a direct order from General Montgomery. The Staffordshires joined them later.

The surviving tanks if the 9th Armoured Brigade were formed into a single regiment and posted on the right. The few surviving Valentines of the 8th RTR and 50th RTR were also in the firing line, respectively in the north and south, and some AT guns were brought up. The British tanks were still being backed up by their artillery concentration, and the Germans by their 88s. The German counter-attack was the greatest clash of armour of the Battle of Alamein and in the end both sides were fought to a standstill. The 1st Armoured Division did not pass the Rahman track, but had fairly light casualties: 14 tanks destroyed and 40 damaged. The Afrika Korps was down to 35 tanks and its two panzer divisions were really fought out. The Italians were in a worse state and down to 20 tanks. Probably the worst news for the Germans was that two thirds of their 88s were out of action.

Operation Supercharge had been planned as a breakthrough, and if a breakthrough is defined as getting troops out in the open behind the enemy's defences while he is still manning those defences, then it was a failure. However this would be taking a narrow view. The really important task was the destruction of the German armour and this had been largely accomplished, and Montgomery knew it. The unsustainable attrition of his armour meant that Rommel's capacity for counter-attacks had been reduced to almost nothing. Also the infantry positions were becoming dislocated and this had already resulted in some armoured cars penetrating his front and rampaging around the supply echelons. The location of 1st Armoured Division and the armoured cars was an implicit threat to his communications on the coast road even if the immediate problem had been solved. The infantry brigade of 1st Armoured Division launched an attack overnight to try to capture the heavy AT guns. They failed, but it was a close thing.

On the next day the armoured division kept on trying to advance, the Crusader squadrons edging forward, the heavy squadrons giving them fire support. This forward movement was just held by the German AT guns, but Rommel could see that the end was in sight. His AT defence was stretched to the limit and he could not counter-attack so, early in the morning, he gave the order to retreat. Unfortunately for the fighting troops he countermanded it in the afternoon after receiving a direct order from the Fuehrer to that effect, but that only delayed the inevitable.

On 1st November Montgomery had moved the 7th Armoured Division north, he now ordered several limited infantry actions on the south flank of the salient to open up the front. As this was achieved, on the 4th November, the 7th Armoured Division broke through the front into the open desert. Operation Supercharge had finished and the pursuit had begun.

Chapter 9

Cruisers in the Pursuit

The concept of a pursuit as a means of destroying a defeated enemy is a very appealing one. It dates back to Napoleonic times, but even then it was a concept surprisingly difficult to apply. A pursuit would be carried out by light cavalry which could be expected to be far more mobile than retreating infantry, particularly if the infantry were mixed with artillery units. Even so sustained, effective, pursuits were rare, in fact apart from after Jena and Waterloo, they hardly occurred. The reason was the pure difficulty of getting started after the chaos of a battle.

In modern times the increasing complexity of battle has made pursuit more difficult. Even so when the pursuers are much more sophisticated than the pursued, a pursuit can still be effective, as several campaigns in the Middle East have demonstrated. During the Second World War, when the two sides were more evenly matched, pursuits tended to become merely a matter of following up the retreating enemy. Naturally if the two sides were not evenly matched and the defeated side was not motorised, then its troops, who would be becoming progressively disorganised, could be rounded up fairly easily.

After Alamein and until the end of the war the British armoured divisions operated well in pursuit, but did not manage, during a pursuit, to win any significant action against fighting, as opposed retreating, units. There were three main reasons for this, difficulty in getting started, the results of the issue of the Sherman tank, and the greater speed of the pursued compared to that of the pursuers.

The lack of flexibility caused by the division of British tanks into either the Cruiser or Infantry types complicated the start of the breakout. The troops making the breakthrough would have employed Infantry tanks, but the forces following on would be on Cruisers. This split was basic to Cruiser Tank Warfare, 'Modern Formations' prescribed it. '*Troops detailed for exploitation should be distinct from those taking part in the initial battle.*' It tended to result in a lapse of activity while the one force took over from the other, and this short lapse gave the defenders their change to escape. This trend was not obvious in the desert where, before Alamein, there was always an open flank and no break-in battle was required.

The difficulty in starting the pursuit was particularly unfortunate as the defenders should have been at their most vulnerable at the start of their retreat, and this vulnerability was never taken advantage of. The worst example of this was Montgomery's attempt to pass his '*corps-de-chasse*' of two armoured divisions through the minefields of Alamein. He sacked the corps commander possibly to cover for the lack of realism of his plan, but it is at least as possible that this was a personal reaction. The same corps failed to get a pursuit going after Wadi Akarit, but this time its commander, General Horrocks, was not sacked. The pursuit after Alamein will be considered in the second part of this chapter.

The defenders took advantage of the chance to escape in all the actions from Alamein through to Normandy. It is true that large numbers of Italians were caught at Alamein, but only because the Germans stole their transport.

The contribution that having two types of tank made to the difficulties of initiating the mobile stage can be assumed to be the major reason why Field Marshal Montgomery persistently called for one type of tank, what he called the 'Capital' tank, to replace the Cruisers and Infantry Tanks.

Once the armoured divisions were on their way they were good at engaging mobile forces. If they came across a column on the road they could destroy it quite efficiently, the same was true if they struck recently halted troops. This was shown by the Japanese at a critical stage of the Malayan campaign. The campaign had been an amazing success for the Japanese, they had advanced over 200 miles as the crow flies in less than a month and any other troops would be starting to slow down, but not the Japanese. The British were taking up what should have been a strong position on the Slim River, with two brigade positions, one behind the other, on the road leading to the river bridge, which was itself well defended.

To maintain momentum and deny the British the time to develop strong defences the Japanese decided to send in their tanks as soon as possible and at night. At this point the Japanese force had only about 12 tanks, and not very impressive ones at that, but they had proven very useful earlier in the campaign and had had a disproportionately great effect on the British forces some units of which were composed of poorly trained Indian troops who had never seen a tank, and who had no AT weapons. Some idea of the demoralising effect achieved by the Japanese tanks is given by the way the sound of their infantrymen advancing on bicycles was often mistaken by the British troops for that of tanks. The bicycles were running on their wheel rims, their tyres having worn away, and they rumbled on the poorly surfaced roads. This misapprehension tended to be very unsettling.

Once the Japanese engineers had cleared the rather thin obstacles on the main road, the tanks blasted through. They advanced 19 miles, largely destroyed two brigades, and crossed the Slim River. They captured a large number of guns and quantities of stores, and they sealed the fate of Singapore. An effective AT defence, unless it is based on tanks or self-propelled AT guns, takes time to set up and denying the enemy this time is Cruiser Tank Warfare at its best.

In a European context, among the best examples of this maintaining momentum was the capture of the Somme bridges by the Guards and 11th Armoured Divisions of the 30th Corps on 31st August 1944. By driving through the night and covering unheard of distances they captured not only the bridges but also General Eberbach, the German army commander, and only just missed SS General 'Sepp' Dietrich, who had arrived to organise the defence of the line of the Somme. This *coup* was only possible because of the total breakdown of German communications.

If, on the other hand, the Cruisers stumbled on a battery of AT guns, dug in and camouflaged, then the advance stopped. In the desert they could try to outflank it, but this was not so easy in Europe, and it was a matter of maintaining a long range fire with HE, which they could do with their Shermans, while the motor battalion came up and put in an infantry assault. All that took time. There was a certain irony in that the issue of better tanks able to provide indirect fire, would be a major cause of the loss of that dash which was such a requisite of Cruiser Tank Warfare.

The fact is that retreating troops, providing they are motorised to a similar extent as are their pursuers, can always move faster than the pursuers. This is obvious considering demolitions. A broken bridge would naturally stop tanks, then infantry would have to come forward, cross the obstacle and drive the enemy back far enough to allow Engineers to work at repairing the bridge or building a new one, all of which took time. The situation was similar for minefields, and other obstacles, particularly if they could be covered by long-range fire from units that could slip away before an assault could be launched to destroy them.

In the more open and fluid operations on the Eastern front obstacles could be used against the defenders. As a British manual [1] had it: '*Every effort is made to cut off the enemy retreat.... When possible, enemy rearguards are by-passed, and then their way of retreat is blocked by obstacles and demolitions arranged by engineers accompanying the leading elements of the pursuit'*. This was a technique that should have been presaged by the 'Battle of Hungerford Bridge' in 1934.

There was little opportunity for such tactics in Europe. The retreating troops will usually have better maps and better local knowledge, so can more easily move at night. In the retreat after Normandy this was to an extent counter-balanced by the information provided to the pursuing tanks by members of the French Resistance. The retreating troops will probably have the use of the local telephone network.

It is interesting to note that in Germany the US armoured troops, whose achievements in terms of armoured warfare seldom receive the credit they should, found that autobahns were not as useful as expected. The autobahns, having been built later, had large numbers of bridges over the secondary roads they crossed. These were easily demolished by the retreating Germans, and the US troops came to prefer to use the secondary roads for this reason. Once repaired the autobahns were excellent supply routes. As General Patton commented, 'the greatest study of war is the road net.'

An aspect of General Patton's 'greatest study' was to select locations for capture that had a large number of big roads leading from them, then, true to his motto of 'Audacity, audacity, always audacity' (probably copied from Danton), to drive hard for them, ignoring flanks, and continue until shortage of supplies forced a halt, then dig in. This philosophy, of course, assumed that the enemy is entirely broken and that, as Operation Market-Garden showed, can be a rash assumption. The Americans could also find it to be a little rash. When one of General Patton's armoured divisions captured Troyes with a small task force, the Germans closed in behind it, forcing a second attack to get it out.

Chances could be taken during the early part of the pursuit after Normandy as, because of their policy of committing all their armoured forces there where they were destroyed, the Germans had little in the way of mobile forces to fight back with. However the pursuit did illustrate the potential danger of by-passing a large force on a flank. As has been seen Rommel would not advance further to the east while Tobruk was still holding out, and there were similar worries for Montgomery as his troops pounded towards the Netherlands. There were large German forces in and around the channel ports to the west. Fortunately these troops were in no condition to make a serious assault on the British forces, but because of the vulnerability of supply units the 12th Corps was deployed as a flank guard to protect the pursuing divisions. This, of course, reduced the number of troops in the direct pursuit. It is interesting to consider what General Patton would have made of this defensive deployment.

To keep a pursuit moving the problem of overcoming static defensive positions with units containing mostly Cruiser tanks must be solved. The answer is with flexible infantry/tank cooperation, but this is difficult to obtain unless the infantry are carried in APCs that can keep up with the tanks. During the North-Western Europe campaign in British armoured divisions only one of the four infantry battalions, the original motor battalion, was mounted on lightly-armoured half-tracks. In the pursuit it was usual in mixed brigades, or smaller units, when the infantry was mounted on TCVs (Troop Carrying Vehicles, ie lorries) for the leading one or two squadrons to carry infantry on their tanks, then more infantry to follow in TCVs. Even American armoured units, which were plentifully supplied with half-tracks, would sometimes advance with infantry riding on their tanks.

Because the TCVs were not as mobile as the tanks, and the mounted infantry dismounted when action was imminent, it can be seen that the different arms in an armoured brigade had a tendency to become widely separated. Consequently restructuring armoured brigades would seldom be as easy as just altering the radio net. This was what the 11th Armoured Division did on approaching the Dortmund-Ems Canal at the end of March 1945. They had been in full pursuit mode with a tank-heavy brigade leading, and the infantry brigade following. Realising that they could expect some heavy fighting they reorganised into two mixed brigades. The divisional history says the process took half-an-hour. The division was lucky to have a halt in open country, but even so this flexibility was impressive. It certainly saved the lengthy process of regrouping which General Patton referred to, probably a little unkindly, as seeming to be 'the chief form of amusement in the British armies'. However even when the infantry/tank mix was right it would commonly take a few days for them to settle down to working together. This was a problem that was not overcome during the war, and would not be until reliable radios were more widely issued to the infantry.

Naturally once the infantry and armour has been reorganised into mixed brigades the action is lifted out of the realms of Cruiser Tank Warfare.

It should have been possible for the attackers' air force to block the retreating troops' route by bombing, but this was not achieved during the Second World War unless the example of the Po is accepted. A retreat can continue overnight but it is difficult for the attackers to continue their pursuit at night, and their air force becomes ineffective. In fact the RAF became a part of the problem. It considered that it could most effectively aid the land forces by isolating the battlefield so that the opposing troops would run out of ammunition and other supplies. This involved extensive destruction of bridges, railways and anything relating to roads. How successful a tactic against enemy troops this was is difficult to gauge, but it certainly made pursuit more difficult, and made supplying the pursuing troops much more difficult.

General Patton has been mentioned and quoted several times in this chapter because of the great success he and his army had in pursuit. However it must be noted that his troops performed much less well when they were involved in positional warfare around Metz, causing him to comment that 'the ability of American troops to manoeuvre when properly led is wonderful. Their ability to fight is not so good.' He might have been hinting by this that leadership at his, army, level is less important during static operations.

Pursuits, like everything else, must come to an end. The first and greatest reason for this is logistics. There had always been a theoretical understanding of this, the fact that pursuing troops move further away from their base of supplies and reinforcements; the retreating troops move closer to theirs. Sooner or later comes the point when the retreating troops are better placed than the attackers. Clausewitz called this the 'Culminating Point'. Clausewitz was thinking in terms of armies moving by muscle-power, but the difficulties facing armoured units in the final stages of a pursuit may be greater, as the situation at the end of that after Normandy was to demonstrate.

The pursuit was exhilarating, the Germans were swept out of France but there were problems. The German collapse had been more complete than had been expected and the transport services were having trouble supplying the front line troops. Worse, Paris was liberated, an event neither wanted nor planned for. Once free it had to be supplied. That put an extra load on the supply services, effectively halting Patton.

Unfortunately the strategic direction of the pursuit was poor. British tanks pounded into Antwerp but they did not go the extra 50 miles through Breda to the Maas that would have prevented the escape of the German 15th Army which should have been penned up in the coastal regions. The low priority allocated to this area resulted in the Scheldt estuary taking a long time to clear so that the port of Antwerp could be used, causing endless supply difficulties and, ultimately Operation Market-Garden. For a few days, it seems, Field Marshal Montgomery's control of the campaign was a little less clear sighted than usual.

The situation facing Patton's Third Army was no better. It halted, rather abruptly, in front of the Moselle. There were several factors relevant to armoured warfare contributing to this halt. One was that the 'road net study' no longer worked so well when the enemy had to be taken into account. The pursuing troops were scattered on a wide front for the sake of mobility and were not able to concentrate for fighting.

Secondly there was a shortage of fuel. Patton had captured significant quantities from the Germans and was hoping to reach the Rhine but the liberation of Paris had a disastrous effect on operations and evoked his outburst, 'My men can eat their belts, but my tanks have gotta have gas.' The arguments over fuel allocation will rage forever, but Patton's policy of driving his tanks until they ran out of fuel was potentially suicidal in the face of a determined and aggressive enemy.

Thirdly, similarly there was an ammunition shortage, resulting partly from logistic difficulties but also because the requirements of pursuing troops were different from those of troops assaulting a dug-in enemy. The latter want more large calibre howitzer ammunition, the former, smaller calibre ammunition for direct fire.

Add to these points the psychological shock of the change from the exhilaration of the pursuit to the toils of static warfare, and the pure exhaustion of it all. It is not surprising that the change from pursuit to static operations was badly managed.

On top of all the factors listed above must be added Enemy Action. The defence against Cruiser Tank Warfare will be considered in the next chapter.

Note 1,
'The Soviet Army, Tactics and Organization, 1949'. Reprinted by Naval and Military Press in association with the Royal Armouries.

The Pursuit after Alamein

The morning of 3rd November 1942 saw the Germans repulse two assaults by 1st Armoured Division on the Rahman track position, so when Rommel decided to retreat from El Alamein the Axis troops still had a chance, if a slim one, of pulling back in good order. This chance was lost on the receipt of Hitler's order demanding that they stay. However by the end of the day, even the though the Afrika Korps had pulled back around six miles there was still a coherent front, covered by the Italian 20th Corps, stretching about four miles to the south of Tel el Aqqaqir. South of that the Italians had been effectively abandoned.

General Montgomery ordered a slight shuffling of units for the start of the pursuit. The 7th Armoured Division joined 10th Corps on 2nd November, and on 4th November its 4th Light Armoured Brigade [1] joined the 2nd New Zealand Division. On the same day 8th Armoured Brigade returned to 10th Armoured Division.

Consequently the major armoured units involved in the pursuit were:

- 10th Corps – Lieutenant General H Lumsden
  - 1st Armoured Division (Maj-Gen R Briggs)
    - - 2nd Armoured Brigade
  - 7th Armoured Division (Maj-Gen AF Harding)
    - - 22nd Armoured Brigade
  - 10th Armoured Division (Maj-Gen AH Gatehouse)
    - - 8th Armoured Brigade
- 30th Corps – Lieutenant General Sir Oliver Leese, Bt
  - 2nd New Zealand Division (Maj-Gen BC Freyberg, VC)
    - - 9th Armoured Brigade
    - - 4th Light Armoured Brigade

General Montgomery concluded that the Axis forces were withdrawing overnight 3rd/4th November and around midnight he issued orders for the pursuit. Broadly speaking the NZ Division, with its two armoured brigades, was to drive across the open desert, going round the south of the Operation Supercharge salient, and make for the passage of the coast road through the escarpment above Fuka, while the divisions of 10th Corps were to stage a series of 'short hooks' against the coast road to the east of Fuka. These orders came as something of a surprise to General Lumsden who had planned, acting as commander of the *Corps-de-Chasse*, to send the 7th Armoured Division westwards in the Sollum direction, followed by the 1st and 10th Armoured Divisions. It is difficult to understand why General Montgomery made such important changes as late as this.

Accordingly next morning saw the start of the breakout. 1st Armoured Division advanced west 4,000 yards, but it was halted by the German rearguard at Tel el Mampsra and made little progress for the rest of the day. A remarkable event here was the capture of the commander of the Afrika Korps, General von Thoma. Apparently he decided that, after Hitler's order, he could no longer continue at his senior level of command. So he drove forward and took control of the rearguard and surrendered after it had been destroyed. To the south the 10th Armoured Division spent the day systematically destroying the enemy's AT screen.

Things were better for 7th Armoured Division. Its advance guard was in the open by 8.30am and it proceeded seven miles past and to the south of Tel el Aqqaqir, where its leading brigade, 22nd Armoured Brigade, was stopped by the Italian 20th Corps, which contained the surviving tanks of the Ariete and a few extra from the Littorio. This gave a total of around 100 tanks, mostly M14s. These tanks had a chance against Crusaders and Honeys, but none against Grants. As it became obvious that 22nd Armoured Brigade could not bypass the Italians, the brigade settled down to a long range artillery duel punctuated by occasional tank skirmishing. The British stood back and with their superior armament picked off the Italian tanks, which was a little pusillanimous in that the Italian tanks' guns were ineffective against the Grants, though it should be mentioned that the enemy force was believed to contain some 88s. This lasted all day despite the divisional commander's impatience. The battle was certainly a one-sided one. Next day the British counted 29 knocked out M14s and several guns, they lost one Honey. The British brigade commander rather complacently commented that the action provided 'good battle practice for the brigade', but he missed the point. The bulk of 20th Corps escaped overnight, and it cost the 7th Armoured Division a full day's worth of pursuit. It had been a magnificent stand by the Italians by any standards.

The 7th Armoured Division only moved a short distance after the battle with 20th Corps. The problems for the British were mostly in traffic control. Too many vehicles were trying to drive through the narrow lanes through the minefields and thick dust and smoke were making visibility variable. Presumably it was to control this kind of near chaos that Montgomery set up his *Corps-de-Chasse,* but it was not showing much signs of working at this stage. With three armoured divisions, two armoured brigades and an infantry division all trying to pass through the Operation Supercharge front and getting in each other's way, it seems that Montgomery's usually tight control of the battle had slipped.

The NZ Division which, having the greatest distance to travel, should have been the first away, but it got off to a slow start. The fighting had left it widely scattered and 4th Light Armoured Brigade only moved off at 10.30am, and 9th Armoured Brigade at 2pm. The bulk of the division spent the night at El Agramiya, but 9th Armoured Brigade made little progress in that direction. Following Operation Supercharge this brigade was really only a composite regiment built round the Warwickshire Yeomanry. So overall the day had been a little disappointing and well demonstrated the difficulty in getting a pursuit started.

On the next day, 5th November, the pursuit can be said to have really started. The 1st Armoured Division, being north of 7th Armoured Division and having moved overnight, delivered the first of the 'short hooks' and sent its 2nd Armoured Brigade north to El Daba, effecting large captures. Then the 8th Armoured Brigade, 10th Armoured Division, drove to Galal station and, like 22nd Armoured Brigade the previous day, had a one-sided battle with Axis tanks, mostly belonging to the Ariete but with some from workshops. The British achieved total surprise, some of the Italian tanks still had muzzle covers on their guns, and the result was a massacre, the Axis tanks being caught on the road. 14 German and 29 Italian tanks were destroyed together with 100 vehicles destroyed or captured and 1,000 personnel captured.

Some Italian tanks did deploy and attacked the British tanks in their hull down positions, but against Shermans and Grants they had no chance. The British had no casualties. This action reduced the Ariete to 14 tanks. The brigade then swept along the road west in the direction of Fuka.

As impressive as these short hooks were the fact was that the German troops were escaping, and the NZ Division was not going to get to Fuka in time to round them up. Being badly strung out it did not make a night move, not starting till 5.30am. Then, at midday, when its leading elements were in long range contact with the enemy, it was held up by a minefield. This halted it and allowed the panzer divisions, which were the German rearguard, to escape. The minefield turned out to be a dummy.

Seeing this, General Harding, the commander of 7th Armoured Division which was approaching the coast road, suggested to General Lumsden that his division should be sent off westwards on a detour round the south of the escarpment, and cut the road there. Initially this idea was turned down, but some approval must have been hinted at as General Harding turned his division round and started west. Soon after General Montgomery, realising his initial plan was failing, confirmed that this was what he wanted this division to do, and sent it off on the detour to Qasaba where there were several airfields. The division drove heroically and covered over 50 miles in the day even though it was held up for three hours by a dummy minefield, an extension of the one that had held up the NZ Division. It kept up the advance overnight but finally halted 20 miles short of its objective due to lack of fuel, just as its leading regiment was opening fire on the German rearguard at a range of 3,000 yards. It knocked out five tanks and various artillery for the loss of two Grants. But then the heavens opened and down came the rain.

The rain not only reduced visibility but made cross-desert movement difficult for tracked vehicles and all but impossible for wheels. The German rearguard was also having fuel supply problems, but having the coast road to drive on they could resupply more easily than could the British. It could be that the rain saved the Germans but that can never be known with certainty, but it was what Montgomery believed.

When the 7th Armoured Division was diverted, the 1st Armoured Division also got new orders. It was to attempt an even wider envelopment and was to go 40 miles further than the 7th Armoured Division to take up a position ready to attack Matruh. This it nearly did, driving all night. However it also had to halt short of its objective due to lack of fuel.

The fuel supply was the major problem and inevitably a controversial one. Some felt that the corps commander gave priority to the 1st Armoured Division because he was once its commander. But the essence of the matter was that General Montgomery believed in the overriding importance of freeing up the coast road because of RAF demands to open forward airfields as soon as possible. Consequently he would have favoured the NZ division with its two armoured brigades, and that was not a part of the 10th Corps, so out of Lumsden's jurisdiction.

The morning of the 7th November saw the 9th Armoured Brigade on the coast road to the west of Fuka, the 8th Armoured Brigade approaching Fuka from the east, and the 1st and 7th Armoured Divisions out of fuel and rained on in the desert. That was the situation at the end of this stage of the pursuit.

After the rain the 7th Armoured Division, now with 4th Light Armoured Brigade restored to it, led the pursuit, though to save fuel it left its infantry brigade behind. It was followed by the 51st (Highland) Division. It really achieved nothing more than following the retreating Germans. The pursuit was certainly very fast, reaching Tobruk on the 13th, and Agedabia on the 23rd November, a total of 778 miles in 20 days. This was faster going than even the retreat to Alamein even though the Germans had developed the laying of mines and setting up of booby traps into something of an art form. When the 7th Armoured Division reached Tobruk its tanks were in such a poor state that it was doubtful if the heavy armoured brigade could proceed. So the division's light armoured brigade was sent forward on the coast road and the heavy brigade concentrated its good tanks in one regiment, 1RTR, to form one light and one heavy squadron. It put these tanks on transporters and formed a battle group round them, and set of across country following the Operation Compass route to Msus. No doubt the going had been much improved since then. Also it had been issued some new Shermans and was allocated tanks from other armoured divisions. Even so little was achieved. The Germans made a brief stand at Agedabia but were soon forced out though the broken country gave a hint of things to come. They then dug in at Mersa Brega where the pursuit can be said to have ended, and a formal assault had to be mounted.

One major factor in favour of the Germans was the lack of effectiveness of the RAF. This had two causes. One was the very speed of the retreat. Planes of the time had a short radius of action and it was difficult to get forward airfields functioning in time to be useful. The other was that in the open desert there were few vulnerable points, like defiles and bridges, that could be attacked to form bottlenecks.

The 8th Army had carried out one of the longest pursuits in history but did not succeed in destroying the German force. One interesting sidelight on Montgomery's conduct of operations was his cancellation of Operation Grapeshot. This was a plan to send a mobile, self-contained, force based on an armoured brigade direct to Tobruk. This would have involved a certain risk and probably would have slowed the pursuit, but it may well have put an end to the campaign. Perhaps Montgomery would have agreed to it if he had had greater faith in his armoured forces and their commanders. Or perhaps his personal requirement for maintaining a tight control of the battle would never have permitted anything so bold.

The remarkable fact about the pursuit is how Montgomery seems to have lost control of it. Initially he overrode General Lumsden's orders and ordered the New Zealand Division to cut off the Afrika Korps, using his *Corps-de-Chasse* only to harass it. Then the 7th Armoured Division had a try, then the 1st Armoured Division. When the rain came and this phase of the pursuit was ended the 7th Armoured Division had been warned to be ready to make a 170 mile march across the desert to Sollum. The result was five armoured brigades achieving very little. All this was inevitable in view of the traffic congestion and insufficient fuel supply. Perhaps the *Corps-de-Chasse* idea could have worked if no other formations were permitted to move and it had total priority for fuel. As it was the 7th Armoured Division took the lead despite being in the worst condition of the three armoured divisions. The other two had new tanks, mostly Shermans, whereas the 7th Division's tanks were worn out, far beyond their maximum track mileage. Also they had few Grant tanks with 75-mm main armament. This would have badly affected their ability to swamp any resistance with HE and pound on through. In the event, as the Germans did not make a stand, it made little difference.

An important aspect of the war in North Africa must be considered. Anglo-American forces landed in Morocco and Algeria on 8th November. From then on the bulk of the Axis forces in Africa had to face west and, even if there had been no Battle of Alamein, it is likely that Rommel's forces would have been pulled back to Tunisia. Certainly the reinforcements that flooded into Africa, which would have halted the 8th Army's pursuit, could not be deployed against it. In fact it would have made sense to have kept Rommel as far to the east as possible as long as possible. This, of course, was not discussed with the 8th Army soldiers.

Note 1,
The 4th Light Armoured Brigade was a short term manifestation of the 4th Armoured Brigade. Its purpose, as was given in the brigade history, was partly to control 'the increasing number of armoured car regiments becoming available'. Its sub-units varied wildly. The following list is representative only:

4th Light Armoured Brigade – Brigadier MG Roddick DSO

1st Household Cavalry Regiment	- Armoured Cars
The Royal Scots Greys	- Grants and Stuarts
4th/8th Hussars	- Stuarts
one motor battalion	

Chapter 10

Defence against Cruiser Tank Warfare

Cruiser Tank Warfare was developed as a new concept. At first it seemed to carry all before it but it soon became apparent that, like its tanks, it was vulnerable to various types of defence. There are four types available. They are not totally discrete and actual measures taken may take on characteristics of two or more. They have all been mentioned already on the text, but not from the defender's point of view.

The first case shows the pursuit being halted by coming up against the next prepared defensive position which will usually be on a geographic feature, such as a river. This check will be more effective the close to the culminating point it occurs. Cruiser tank units cannot break through such a position so they will have to wait for the infantry to mount a set-piece assault. The previously mentioned example of the US 3rd Army on the Moselle is a case in point. Battlefield AT defence will not be extensively considered in this study.

The second case is when the defenders have enough mobile forces to force a tank battle on the pursuers. This is what the Italian forces were unable to do in the Wavell Offensive. A more modern example of this kind of failure was the Israeli campaign in the Sinai desert in 1967. The Egyptians had dug in close to the Israeli border. The Israelis attacked these positions and penetrated them after a hard fight. After that they so hopelessly outclassed the Egyptian Armoured forces that there was nothing to stop the pursuit until they reached the Suez Canal. An example of this method succeeding in the Second World War was the halting of Rommel's troops at Alamein. A series of armoured actions had been fought, both sides were exhausted, and even Rommel could push his men no further.

The Germans did not manage a tank battle to stop the British pursuit after Normandy, though, as will be seen, their counter-attacks in Operation Garden did halt this operation. They did try to stop the Americans at Arracourt, but failed.

The third defensive method is to defend urban areas where such locations are essential to the road net. Cruiser Tanks are at a great disadvantage in urban warfare, particularly with the wartime improvements of infantry AT weapons, and will usually have to wait for infantry units to move forward and drive the defenders out. The concept of such 'Anti-Tank Islands' was basic to the preparations for the defence of England against the expected invasion of 1940, when towns and villages were fortified against the anticipated rampaging German armoured columns. Many pillboxes and concrete AT obstacles remain as witnesses of this activity.

However regardless of preparations defending an AT island was not likely to be easy if the defenders had few AT weapons and were not familiar with tanks. On 16th June 1941 the bulk of a British regular infantry battalion defending Kuneitra in the Syrian campaign surrendered when attacked by a French force spearheaded by five light tanks. With just a few 2-pdrs their position would have been unassailable.

Three years later the vigorous defence of Nijmegen was one of the reasons for the failure of Operation Garden, but probably the most well known example of an AT island held against an armoured assault was the defence of Bastogne by American troops during the Ardennes campaign. Even after an AT island has been destroyed the rubble left by the fighting can be, for a while, a barrier against movement, as was the case at Cassino and Villers-Bocage.

The fourth defensive method takes advantage of the vulnerability of an armoured unit to interruption of its supplies. The importance of this method was emphasised by General von

Thoma, who was captured at Alamein, when he commented to Captain Liddell Hart that "In modern mobile warfare the tactics are not the main thing. The decisive factor is the organisation of one's resources – to maintain the momentum."

The problem for the attackers is that as the defenders become stronger so any troops that the armoured spearhead had bypassed become more dangerous via threats to the lines of communication. It has been shown in the opening phase of the Gazala battle how the German supply columns were attacked by fragments of British units roaming the desert. In Europe, with supply routes being much more constricted than they were in North Africa they were vulnerable to counter-attack if flanking units fell too far behind the armour. Conversely, in general, the defenders will find great difficulty in putting in a counter-attack quickly enough and strongly enough to achieve its purpose. This is because the reserves will not be conveniently located and their move forwards will be slowed by air attack. Secondly the situation, and objectives, will be in a state of flux so orders will quickly be out of date and confusion result.

Consequently any units under attack by armoured forces would try to hold the shoulders of the break-in. At one time these were picturesquely termed the 'Haunches'. Field fortifications here would prevent the front being rolled up, and would allow the armour's supplies to be threatened. The Germans understood the requirement for rolling back the enemy's front laterally, they had a name for it, '*aufrollen*'.

The requirement for making a wide enough breach was appreciated in 'Modern Formations'. '*The object of the initial attacks is to make a breach of such width in the defence as will enable their supplies to reach exploiting troops. This will not be satisfactorily done unless this avenue is free from fire from the flanks.*' There was no appreciation of any threat to lines of communication in the mobile phase.

The most sensitive place for such attacks was at the junction between the armoured, and mobile, forces and their infantry supports which constituted a potential weak point. This was why the Arras counter-attack, which was a tactical failure, made such an impression on the Germans. Attacks on this weak point were also the main cause of the failure of the Operation Garden.

Counter-attacks can come from the air. During the Second World War ground attack was not particularly effective against tanks, but could be devastating against supply columns, specially those carrying fuel. Once a vehicle had burned the smoke would attract other planes looking for targets. In normal circumstances aerial superiority would be a precondition for the launching of Cruiser Tank operations.

Finally there are obstacles. They comprise of demolitions and mines/booby traps. The Germans were particularly adept at leaving mines and booby traps behind them. Obstacles do not form a class of defence by themselves, but if used in conjunction with one of the four types of defence listed here, and covered by fire, they will substantially improve AT effectiveness. If used by themselves they will slow down an armoured division, but nothing more. Bringing down bridges that the enemy must replace is the easiest, and a very effective, method. Every bridge can be regarded as a potential demolition, a comment that will be repeated in the next chapter.

It is worthwhile to consider the destruction, in 1940, of the 12th, 23rd and 46th Divisions in terms of the last two methods just listed. By 20th May the German breakthrough was in full cry, and five panzer divisions, with two more in immediate support, and a motorised infantry division were pounding through the gap between the British and French armies. Into this gap were sent the three British divisions. These were territorial divisions of a low level of training. They were classified as 'labour only', and were in France only to work on field fortifications. They were undermanned and had very little in the way of artillery and AT weapons. It was not expected that they would to be used in the front line, but as an act of desperation they were called on to halt the Germans.

There can be little doubt that whatever they did the result would have been a disaster for them, but they tried the wrong tactics. They tried to hold a series of defensive lines, where possible along rivers or canals. Brigade frontages were from 15 to 20 miles long. Even though the three divisions fought gallantly they were forced out of one position after another until they disintegrated, and few survivors returned to England. They may have delayed the Germans by half a day.

The alternative would have been to identify which roads the Germans must use, then to use about half the troops and all the artillery and AT weapons to set up AT islands on these roads. The other battalions should have moved away from the roads and kept quiet hoping to be by-passed by the Germans, then set up ambushes to catch the supply echelons.

The German panzer divisions, being balanced all-arms units, would not have been so vulnerable to these tactics as Cruiser Tank brigades would have been, and it is not suggested that these tactics would have been particularly successful. However they should have delayed the Germans longer than did the tactics actually used.

In the desert campaigns armoured units were naturally not as vulnerable to such tactics as their supply vehicles were not so restricted to roads. Even so Rommel would not go far to the east while Tobruk remained unconquered behind him.

An impressive awareness of the vulnerability of a large armoured force advancing without totally secure communications was shown by General Patton who, at a high level conference to discuss the response to the German attack in the Ardennes, suggested letting the Germans drive to Paris, then "we'll really cut them off and chew them up."

The Germans would not have got that far, but if Patton's plan had been taken up then the German armoured/mobile forces would have come up against all four types of defence against Cruiser Tank Warfare. They would have hit prepared defences, most importantly on the Meuse. The Allies' armour would have closed in behind them. The Germans would have had to fight for every road junction and town they passed through. Finally, and most importantly, they would have run out of fuel as the weather cleared and their lines of communications came under air attack. Had Patton's plan been adopted the cream on the German army would have been rounded up with minimal Allied casualties. The actual tactics adopted also resulted in heavy German casualties, but this was at the cost of heavy Allied casualties, and the surviving Germans were just driven backwards to fight again another day.

Chapter 11

CRUISERS IN NORTH-WEST EUROPE

There can be little doubt that, by June 1944, the golden age of Cruiser Tank Warfare had passed. The reasons for this fall into three main groups: the nature of the Sherman tank, the geography of the theatre of operations, and the determination of the Germans to fight.

The most important of these three groups was the last. The previous chapter has shown the methods to be used to counter Cruiser Tank Warfare. The Germans were aware of these methods and eager to apply them. The two operations studied in this chapter will illustrate the degree of success they achieved. The dazzling German victory in France in 1940 was only won because of the lack of initiative and general apathy of the French army in the face of a new threat. The German army would not fail as the French army did.

The issue on a large scale of the Sherman tank had far reaching effects for British tank warfare, and a rather paradoxical one. The tanks themselves, mounting the medium velocity 75-mm guns in their turrets were more effective than earlier vehicles. Most importantly the guns were provided with the Azimuth Indicator M19. It has been shown in Chapter 3 how this sometimes had the effect of making tanks little more than self-propelled howitzers. Consequently tactics changed. A squadron would be advancing and strike an AT screen. One or two tanks might be knocked out, a terrifying event which would have its effect on the minds of the surviving tank commanders. The squadron would then pull back and systematically shell each possible location for AT guns before cautiously continuing its advance. By this stage of the war there was no ammunition shortage, fresh supplies being brought up to the tanks in armoured carriers. Naturally this slowed the advance down.

This trend was well understood and measures taken to counter it on the basis that the accompanying 25-pdr artillery was better at supplying this kind of neutralising fire. This was somewhat unnecessary as the 75-mm HE round was in no way inferior to the 25-pdr round, but the priority was to keep the tanks moving. A good statement of the thinking of the time was given by General Roberts on his Notes on Armoured Division Tactics which he drew up in December 1943 shortly after taking command of the 11th Armoured Division. The many abbreviations so necessary to service lore have been expanded.

Of the 75-mm he wrote '*its great asset is that it can destroy anti-tank guns, not merely neutralise them but destroy them, and when we bear in mind that 75% of the fighting of an armoured division is against anti-tank you will realise that this is a very great asset*', but he emphasised that 75-mm gun '*is not very suitable for neutralising; certainly nothing like as good as a 25pdr and far less a medium.........So generally speaking not only is the gun indifferent as a neutralising weapon, but we do not carry enough ammunition for such a task.*'

In defining how the tanks are to keep moving he continues. '*How does the Armoured Brigade really function? Broadly it is by the application of the principle of fire and movement at all levels from brigade down to troop. Who fires and who moves is decided at the time as the enemy dispositions and the ground disclose themselves. Generally speaking the battle develops and there is no set-piece attack, but it is not easy to describe this armoured attack development. The leading regiment gets contact with the enemy on a fairly broad front and engages him with the maximum firepower, thereby making him disclose his positions. The armoured brigade commander then manoeuvres the other two armoured regiments, either round one flank or both flanks, and they in turn engage the enemy with fire. Meanwhile artillery concentrations are put down on any particularly strong centres of resistance, the armour in the area of these concentrations taking every advantage of them to manoeuvre and get forward. But there is no "charge" on a regimental or squadron basis, - such tactics may be successful but will be expensive and will only be resorted to in exceptional circumstances.'*

Returning to the worry about indirect fire he notes, '*There is a tendency, with the 75mm gun, to fire and then sit back and continue firing. That will never get us on. As soon as it seems possible that the targets have been knocked out then somebody must go forward, covered by another portion of the squadron or regiment....*

...A word about turret down shooting. Turret down shooting is the exception rather than the rule and should never be undertaken by more than one tank at a time. If turret down shooting becomes in any way emphasised, stickiness will set in.'

It can be seen that the danger to the cut-and-thrust tactics of the armoured division, posed by the potential for semi-indirect fire of the 75-mm gun, were well appreciated.

An important aspect of the General's thinking was that the 75-mm would reduce the necessity for deploying infantry and slowing the advance down. This turned out to be a vain hope. At this time the infantry brigade was transported in TCVs, but half-tracks were being procured for the motor battalion of the armoured brigade. Perhaps if the role of the armoured division's infantry had been emphasised, half-tracks could have been obtained for all the division's infantry, and mobility and speed of deployment improved.

The deployment of tanks was much more difficult in Europe than it was in the desert. In the desert tanks could travel in tactical formation so being always ready for action, whereas in Europe tanks travelled on roads and there was bound to be a delay between receiving the order to deploy and coming into action. In the desert there were, naturally, few obstacles such as rivers and streams, defiles and villages, that would slow tank movement.

Most importantly between Alamein and the Normandy landings there had been a revolution in infantry weapons. This was the issue of what are currently referred to as 'shoulder launchers', these being man-portable AT weapons. The German version was the Panzerfaust, the British the PIAT and the American the Bazooka. These were all short range, and were available in quantities. They had the result of making tank commanders reluctant to enter close country or built-up areas unless preceded by infantry. These factors would inevitably slow down the tempo of tank operations.

It was against this background of increasing difficulties for the mass deployment of armour that Cruisers were used in Europe. They were used in no small numbers. There were three British armoured divisions, one Canadian and one Polish. Also there were six American Armoured divisions and a French one. This is apart from independent armoured and tank brigades. There was a good deal of faith in the capabilities of armoured divisions, and yet the achievements of the British ones must be allowed to have been disappointing.

There was no repetition for the British tanks, in North West Europe, of the great tank battles of the desert war. There were tank battles, the Germans forced them on the Americans at Mortain, the Ardennes and Arracourt. In each case the Americans were the victors. The British tanks saw plenty of individual action, but no tank battles.

The Training Instructions quoted in chapter 5 made the obvious point that armoured divisions could not fight their way through prepared infantry positions. However in the Normandy campaign this is what they were called on to do. Less ground was captured on 'D' Day than was anticipated so the armoured divisions had to be employed in the *bocage* against deep infantry defences. No doubt had more ground been made on 'D' Day the armoured divisions would have been deployed more suitably.

German armour found attacking in the bocage just as difficult as did the British, but the Germans had the advantage in tank against tank actions as their tanks usually carried better main armaments.

The British armoured divisions took part in the pursuit after Normandy, but that was really an exercise in logistics and there was little to learn about it from the Cruiser Tank Warfare point of view. There were, though, two operations in which British armoured divisions were used in that are of great interest, but unfortunately they show up the weakness of these divisions.

The first is Operation Goodwood, an attempt to find an alternative to the *bocage* fighting of the Normandy campaign. It has already been shown that armoured divisions were not expected to be used for breakthroughs and that was what Goodwood was expected to be. However heavy bombing was expected to make a significant difference. The operation will be considered in the second section of this chapter.

The second operation to be considered, Operation Garden, is by far the more significant of the two in terms of their importance for Cruiser Tank Warfare. It may be considered as an example of an opposed advance. Although it was always appreciated that Cruiser tank units should not be used to break through prepared positions, they should be able to force a way forward through a reasonable degree of resistance. These operations existed on a theoretical sliding scale somewhere between a pursuit and a break-through operation.

In such operations the retreating force will try to slow down their pursuers initially by demolitions, mines and occasionally, ambushes. As soon as their organisation and strength will allow they will start to set up Anti-Tank Islands. These will be towns and villages on important road junctions. In such locations the defenders could deploy their AT weapons at short range, and they would find plenty of petrol to make 'Molotov Cocktails'. They would also find rations and accommodation. The attackers would be reluctant to risk their tanks in these places which would be difficult to by-pass, so they would have to wait for them to be cleared by an infantry assault. This delay should give the defenders' armour a chance.

How this could work out in practice, as shown in Operation Garden, is the subject of the third section of this chapter.

Operation Goodwood
The First Day

The allied landing in Normandy in June 1944 was followed by weeks of slow-moving and bitter fighting in the *bocage*. When it was judged that German resistance was starting to weaken two breakthrough operations were planned. The first would be undertaken by the British forces just to the east of Caen, the second by the Americans. The British operation was codenamed 'Goodwood'.*(see Sketch 5)*

There is some controversy as to the objective of Operation Goodwood. Field Marshal Montgomery wrote afterwards that there was never any intention of making a breakthrough but rather it was to be a holding attack designed to keep German armour to the east to assist the American operations at the western end of the front. This is confirmed by paragraph 1 of his instructions to General Dempsey, commanding British Second Army:

1. Object of this operation

To engage the German armour in battle and "write it down" to such an extent that it is of no further value to the Germans as a basis of the battle.

To gain a good bridgehead over the Orne through Caen and thus to improve our positions on the eastern flank

Generally to destroy German equipment and personnel, as a preliminary to a possible wide exploitation of success.

However there can also be no doubt that he deliberately let everyone on a lower level of command than his believe that Operation Goodwood was an attempt to break through to Falaise.

The basis of the tactical plan for the armoured divisions was spelt out in paragraphs 5 and 7 of Montgomery's instructions. Paragraph 5 states:

5. Initial operations of VIII Corps [on 18th]

The three armoured divisions will be required to dominate the area Bourguebus-Vimont-Bretteville [sur Laize], and to fight and destroy the enemy, but armoured cars should push far to the south towards Falaise, spread alarm and despondency, and discover the "form".

Paragraph 7 continued:
7. Later operations VIII Corps

When 6 is done (Canadian operations around Caen), *the VIII Corps can "crack about" as the situation demands.*

But not before 6 is done.

The 8th Corps, the reserve corps of the British Second Army, was to play the major role in Goodwood. For this operation it was to command three armoured divisions. The major formations being:

8th Corps, Lieutenant General N O'Connor
- Guards Armoured Division, Maj Gen AHS Adair
- 7th Armoured Division, Maj Gen GWEJ Erskine
- 11th Armoured Division, Maj Gen GPB Roberts
  - 2nd Northamptonshire Yeomanry (reconnaissance regiment)
  - 29th Armoured Brigade
    - 23rd Hussars
    - 2nd Fife and Forfar Yeomanry
    - 3rd Royal Tank Regiment
    - 8th Battalion, The Rifle Brigade (Motor)
  - 159th Infantry Brigade
    - Three battalions

Two factors came together to define the basic tactical concept of Operation Goodwood. The first was the forces available. The fighting so far had been infantry based and the infantry was now facing a replacement problem, whereas the armoured divisions had seen little fighting. The second was that the land to the east of Caen was much more open than the *bocage* and judged to be 'good tank country'. Experience so far in the war had shown what was obvious, that tank battles caused far fewer casualties than did infantry battles. As a rule of thumb it was expected that the knocking out of a tank would cause an average of one and a half casualties. This figure was a little optimistic but the principle was a good one. Also any attrition of armour must work out in favour of the British. Not only did the Allies have many more tanks than did the Germans, but their tank casualties could be replaced much more quickly.

In essence the plan was a simple one. The way would be prepared by heavy bombers, then the tanks of three armoured divisions would drive through towards the area specified by Montgomery. There was some similarity between Operations Goodwood and Supercharge, the last phase of Alamein. Both operations were massed tank assaults on battered AT screens. Supercharge had very heavy tank casualties and did not burst through the German lines as hoped, but it was effective enough to convince Rommel to order a retreat. This might seem to bode ill for Goodwood, particularly because by this stage of the war German anti-tank tactics had become very sophisticated. The bombing was expected to give Goodwood that extra edge.

The Germans were fully expecting the attack. Actually it could hardly be otherwise, they had excellent observation of the British forming up area. The direction of the attack was obviously Falaise, and the nature of the countryside ensured that that attack would be made by tanks. But the Germans did not expect the liberal use of heavy bombers.

The 8th Corps plan of attack had some weak points. The difficulties in moving three divisions forward were huge. There was a total of 877 tanks, and an overall total of around 8,000 vehicles. They had to cross the Caen canal and the Orne river, each of which had only three bridges, then wend their way through a thick defensive minefield, which was heavily overgrown with corn and not properly charted, the lanes through which had been cleared as late as possible because of German observation. All this was a sure recipe for chaos.

Once the tanks were through the minefield there was only enough space for one division, so the other two divisions must follow through the obstacles as quickly as possible after the first division had moved off. Then the tanks would have to fight their way through a corridor only 3,000 yards wide between the 3rd Canadian Corps on the western flank and the 1st British Corps to the east. After an advance of 5,000 yards the front would widen dramatically. The plan was for 11th Armoured Division, leading, to swing to the south-west; the Guards Armoured Division, coming next, to swing to the south-east; and the 7th Armoured Division to be available to exploit to the south.

The front facing the Goodwood attack was defended by the LXXXVI corps. This had three divisions in the line. The 346th Infantry Division held the German right flank, from the sea to Touffreville, and was only involved to a small extent in Goodwood. The 16th Luftwaffe Field Division held from Touffreville to Caen, and 21st Panzer Division held the front round Caen. To the west of Caen was the 1st SS Panzer Corps which was involved in fighting off Canadian attacks.

The plan of defence should have been fairly predictable. It is sometimes written that Rommel was responsible for it, but that is unlikely. No doubt he approved the Corp's plans. Perhaps they reminded him of his defences against the 'Battleaxe' attacks.

The narrow corridor approximated in depth to the infantry zone, stretching as far as the Caen-Vimont railway. Then there was a zone of defended villages, another 5,000 yards deep, these two zones making a plain bounded to the south by the Bourguebus Ridge. After that the tanks should be in the open. The bombing was expected to neutralise these two zones and, in the south-western corner of the battlefield, extended as far as the village of Bourguebus village, but not the ridge.

The ridge was not an imposing geographical feature, rising less than 100 feet above the plain, but it dominated the plain south of the Caen-Vimont railway. On it were located the 88-mm AT and AA guns of the 21st Panzer Division's artillery, seventeen of the former and eight of the latter, the latter were behind the crest and not able to fire on the attacking tanks. Behind them was a large number of AA guns defending the road to Falaise, and the land was prepared for defence, to one degree or another, for several miles.

The plain was dissected by three railway lines. One ran east from Caen to Troarn, and one ran south-east across the middle of the battlefield from Caen to Vimont. These were obstacles, but not great ones to tanks, but significant ones to wheeled vehicles. As such things are always welcomed by anyone trying to read a map and look for reference points on the ground, they were used as reporting lines and are often mentioned in accounts of the operation. The other line, Caen to Falaise, ran due south and divided the battlefield in two. For some of its length it ran along an embankment and there it was an obstacle both to tank movement and vision.

The strength of any German defence lay in the counter-attack, and the Germans opposing Operation Goodwood had several armoured units in the immediate area. They, and other troops, came under 'Battle Group von Luck'. It was normal to name a battle group, which was an ad-hoc grouping, after its commander. The armoured units were:

> The 22nd Panzer Regiment. This was the tank regiment of the 21st Panzer Division. It would normally have had two battalions, but only one was in Normandy at this time. It contained upwards of 50 tanks. A company of ten tanks was posted close to Colombelles and the remainder were at Emieville.

> The 503rd Heavy Tank Battalion. This consisted of 45 Tiger tanks, six of which needed some repairs. The unit was at Manneville. Remarkably its presence was unknown to the British. It was unusual to station Tigers this far forward. Normally they would have been held back, ready for counter-attacks. In this case it was judged that the front was very weak and needed this immediate support.
>
> The 200th Assault Gun Battalion. This remarkable unit contained 50 self-propelled guns, being modern guns mounted on the hulls of captured French tanks. 30 were 75-mm AT guns, 20 were 105-mm howitzers which could be used in the anti-tank role. This battalion was divided into five batteries which, numbered 1 to 5, were posted at Demouville, Giberville, Grentheville, Le Mesnil Frementel and Le Prieure.

It must be emphasised that although the Germans might defend villages as AT strongpoints, the guns, whether towed or self-propelled, would usually not be actually in the villages, but camouflaged and scattered round them. There would be infantry and radio equipment in the villages, making use of cellars and building materials.

A further and probably deadlier counter-attack could come from the 1st SS Panzer Corps to the west, but naturally there would be a delay while its units were moved across from their positions covering the Canadians.

The battle started at 5.25am on 18th July 1944 with an artillery barrage and a bombardment delivered by 1,100 heavy bombers. This was followed at 7.00am by 500 medium bombers, and they, in turn, were followed by 300 fighter-bombers. The heavies struck the flanks of the break in, and the deep bomb craters were acceptable as these areas were to be attacked by infantry. The bombs hit the eastern parts of Caen and, on the other flank, the Touffreville/Emieville area. They also hit Cagny which appears to have been unoccupied at the time. The mediums dropped lighter fragmentation bombs along the axes of the attack so as not to crater the ground too much. The fighter-bombers attacked known German positions. The aircraft involved in these attacks were British. At 8.00am around 500 heavy US bombers turned up and dropped more fragmentation bombs on the attack axes. By this stage the smoke and dust were making target identification difficult. Unfortunately few bombs were dropped south of Cagny, and no attack was made on Bourguebus ridge. It was not believed that the defences stretched back this far.

All this was a terrible experience for the defenders. The outposts in front of the Caen-Troarn railway were afterwards not capable of any real defence, and the assault gun battery in Demouville was hit, its six guns being destroyed. However the bulk of the 21st Panzer Division's infantry in and near Caen survived, as did the 22nd Panzer Regiment's company at Colombelles, but the rest of the regiment was badly hit, losing all but approximately six of its tanks. Of the Tiger unit four tanks were destroyed, a bomb turned one entirely over, but the rest survived, though most were damaged to one degree of another and this potentially very powerful unit played little part in the rest of the battle, certainly not as a complete unit. This was a piece of amazingly good fortune for the British.

The attacking force was led by 11th Armoured Division's armoured brigade (29th) which moved off at 7.45am. It was led by 3RTR, then came the F&F Yeomanry, the 23rd Hussars followed in reserve. Each regiment had two squadrons forward, each with two troops forward. Each troop had its four tanks in a diamond formation, the Firefly being the rear tank. The squadron frontage had to be kept to a maximum of 600 yards for the two regiments to fit in the narrow corridor. The tanks arrived, unopposed, at the Caen-Troarn railway at around 8.30, meanwhile, in compliance with the Corps Commander's orders, the infantry brigade, supported by the Northamptonshire Yeomanry, settled down to its own battle clearing Cuverville and Demouville, leaving the armoured brigade very short of infantry.

Up to this point the tanks had been following a creeping barrage, though in fact due to the difficulties of traffic control, smoke, dust and cratering they had been getting very disordered and failed to keep up with the barrage, which was moving at 5mph. Unfortunately the railway, which had not seemed much of an obstacle when studied on aerial photographs, turned out to be a considerable one. Most of this line was on an embankment between three and six feet high. Tanks could negotiate it but the half-tracks of the motor companies found it nearly impossible, and wheeled vehicles found it totally so. This caused a major delay. The barrage was stationary for 20 minutes to allow for the F&F Yeomanry to come up on the left of 3RTR, and it started forward again at 8.45am leaving the tanks behind. It ended at 9.20. The greatest disadvantage of the plan of attack was that the field artillery batteries supporting it were still to the west of the Caen canal, so the point of the attack was soon beyond their reach. However medium artillery could still reach targets across the battlefield, and the regiments were supported by their accompanying self-propelled artillery.

The leading two regiments moved forward as planned but the third, the 23H, fell behind due to the traffic hold ups and was soon a mile behind. They drove towards the Caen-Vimont railway line. Up to this point the bombing had been very effective. German soldiers were sometimes found still sheltering, probably stunned, in trenches and some were killed there by hand grenades thrown by the tank commanders, but mostly they were waved to the rear. However there were no wrecked AT guns to be seen except three destroyed by the tanks.

Up to the Caen-Vimont railway the land had been rolling enough for the tanks to advance by fire and movement. That is one troop taking up a hull down position and covering the advance of a second troop, then vice-versa. But after the railway the land was flat right up to the Bourguebus ridge.

The two forward units advanced roughly in line. The left unit, the F&F Yeomanry, was a little behind 3RTR. It swept towards the Caen-Vimont railway having passed east of Le Mesnil Frementel. Unfortunately one of the self-propelled batteries, No 5, was posted around Le Prieure and the battery, No 4, that had been at Le Mesnil Frementel had moved east and taken up position in and around Cagny. Guns of one of these batteries let the tanks pass, then opened up and destroyed the Yeomanry's rear squadron which was followed by the motor company and artillery battery. This was the time the infantry brigade was really missed. The Colonel, assuming that Cagny was the problem, ordered his motor company to dismount and clear it. The divisional commander countermanded this order and told him to keep moving south.

The right hand unit, 3 RTR, may also have suffered some casualties from these SP guns, but was certainly taking casualties from guns of the battery that had been posted in Grentheville. These guns had pulled back to the south-east, but the 3RTR tanks were easily in range. It halted along the Caen-Vimont railway, which gave it a little shelter. To get moving again it moved to the right, and crossed the Caen-Falaise railway. The leading squadron leader went through the tunnel where the railway ran over the Caen-Vimont track, most of the remaining tanks went over the tracks. The regiment, now being largely out of visual contact with the rest of the brigade, attempted to rush the villages of Bras and Hubert-Folie. A quick reconnaissance, which involved a bren gun carrier driving as fast as possible through Hubert-Folie, had failed to locate any Germans in the village, so a risk was taken. Unfortunately, although there may well have been few German infantrymen in the villages there were several AT guns on the rising ground behind them. The regiment came under heavy fire from these AT guns, and also from the 2nd Assault Gun Battery which had fallen back from Giberville, from the 88-mm AT guns on Bourguebus Ridge, and possibly from the tank company of the 22nd Panzer Regiment that had been posted at Colombelles. The survivors of 3RTR pulled back to the tunnel for the Caen-Vimont railway. It was midday.

After 3RTR had crossed the Caen-Falaise railway the brigade was fighting two entirely separate battles, divided one from the other by the embankment of the Caen-Falaise railway. Both battles were based on tanks attacking an AT screen, and the results were similar. At roughly the same time as 3RTR launched itself at Bras and Hubert-Folie the F&F Yeomanry attacked the ridge. They came under heavy fire from the assault guns of the 3rd Battery which had taken up position in Soliers and the 4th Battery which was around Four, then from 88s and other artillery dug in on the ridge. They were all but annihilated, losing 29 tanks. The third armoured regiment, the 23rd Hussars, came up just as the Yeomanry had been halted. The Brigadier, as he became aware of the disaster, ordered them not to go south of Soliers, but that was of little help. As soon as they had passed Grentheville the 23rd Hussars were in the killing zone, and, making things worse, the balance of power had decisively shifted.

The German commander, General Eberbach, quickly realised the scale of the attack and ordered 1st SS Panzer Corps to provide a battle group for the counter-attack. This battle group, based on a battalion of 46 Panthers, started to arrive on Bourguebus Ridge at 12.45pm. The fire from them was crushing and the F&F Yeomanry and 23rd Hussars could make little reply, particularly as the German gunners hit their Fireflies first. There was no counter-attack in *La Grande Maniere* but some of the German tanks did creep forwards to find better fire positions. They were very circumspect in the face of British airpower.

This fire fight all but destroyed the two regiments, but Grentheville had been captured and, reinforced with some tank destroyers, was now as strong a defence for the British as it and several other villages had been for the Germans. Consequently even if 29th Armoured Brigade had been bled white the division as a whole would hold the ground it had won.

At around this time another threat started to make itself felt. German infantry, with panzerfausts and covered by smoke and dust, were infiltrating along the line of the Caen-Vimont railway towards Frenouville. The *bocage* fighting had shown that a stationary tank could quickly become a target for tank hunting parties and this was now happening in more open country. This threat was overcome only when the infantry brigade finally came up.

The division did try one last aggressive move. When the infantry brigade had, at last, cleared Demouville and Cuverville, the recce regiment, the 2nd Northamptonshire Yeomanry, which had been supporting them was freed up. This regiment, on Cromwells, was sent in the tracks of 3RTR to assault Bras. The predictable results were no progress and heavy casualties.

Throughout the afternoon, as it became increasingly apparent that the armoured brigade was halted, the divisional commander was becoming irritated by the tardy arrival of the Guards Armoured Division on the left. He was right to be irritated, his armoured brigade, such as had survived, was now spread over a much wider front than had been planned. The fact was that the Guards had made rather slow progress and were several hours behind schedule. There were two major reasons for this. One was the pure difficulty of negotiating the traffic jams and crossing the river, canal and minefields. The other was enemy action.

This took two forms. One was the defence of Cagny and the other was the building up of resistance along the eastern flank of the salient. Cagny was defended throughout most of the day by an assault gun battery [1]. The impression is that at any time the village could have been captured by an infantry company, but one was not at hand. The Guards should really have managed this. They captured it later in the afternoon when it was abandoned by the Germans.

The Germans forces to the east deployed a large number of impressive AT weapons. They were provided by Tigers, survivors of the heavy tank battalion, Panzer IVs, survivors of the 22nd Panzer Regiment, and an AT unit, armed with 88s, rushed up from reserve. These guns could reach across the salient and this, along with some minor counter-attacks, slowed the Guards down.

Even so, the Guards were getting there which is more than can be said for the 7th Armoured Division, and that leads into one of the more remarkable events of the day. General Roberts had moved his tactical HQ close to Le Mesnil Frementel, and the armoured brigade's HQ. At 11.30, while he was fuming about the Guards being late, he was visited by Brigadier Hinde, the commander of the armoured brigade of the 7th Armoured Division. He was making a personal reconnaissance. Brigadier Hinde, observing the scene said, 'There are far too many bloody tanks milling round here. I am not going to advance until you have taken Cuverville and Demouville.' Then, General Roberts states in his memoirs, Hinde stomped off before he could speak to him.

It is difficult to know what to make of this short exchange. General Roberts had not achieved his position as an armoured division commander without having a forceful character, and it is hard to imagine his just allowing a brigadier to walk away after such an outburst. Further, Roberts states that Hinde mistook a large number of knocked out tanks for runners. However, at least half of knocked out Shermans burned, the Germans would sometimes keep firing at a knocked out tank till it burned, and of the rest a large percentage would have been obviously out of action with tracks broken, turrets and guns at odd angles, and so on, and Hinde was a very experienced tank soldier so he is unlikely to have made such a mistake. Perhaps the brigadier was giving vent to his feelings that his Cromwells, the classic Cruisers with which 7th Armoured Division was equipped, should not be used to make a breakthrough. It is, though, a pity that there seem to have been no witnesses to this conversation.

As soon at it was apparent that things were not going to plan the RAF offered to bomb Bourguebus ridge. This offer was turned down by the army staff as it was thought that the ridge was in British hands. Later in the afternoon when a desperate final assault on Bourguebus ridge was being planned the corps commander requested another bombing attack but was turned down by the RAF.

At the end of the disastrous day for British armour the 11th Armoured Division had lost 125 Shermans and 16 Cromwells. The Guards Armoured Division lost 15 Shermans, and the other division that should have made the attack, 7th Armoured, was so delayed that it hardly caught up with the battle. Perhaps Brigadier Hinde could not have got his brigade forward no matter how much he tried.

Operation Goodwood lasted a further three days, it was said to have been rained off, but really it had run its course. The initial break through had failed and after that it degenerated into a slogging match. The operation certainly achieved its aim in assisting the Americans, but Montgomery's stated aim of 'writing down' the German armour was not achieved. The whole operation destroyed 75 German tanks and self-propelled guns. Total British tank losses were 413 tanks (47.1% of start strength) of these 104 could be repaired within 24 hours. As predicted manpower losses were comparatively low, on the 18th July the entire corps sustained only 521 casualties. Casualties for the whole operation, four days, for all four corps directly involved were 5,537, mostly infantry.

In an open area like this battlefield it would be expected that air support could have made the difference, but there was only one Air Liaison Officer with the attacking brigade and his tank was knocked out, and he wounded, early on. The Germans made a point of engaging any special tanks first. The planes, though they tried hard, failed to detect the German tanks and guns. For example the movement of the battle group from 1st SS Panzer Corps was not seen.

The hold-up on the Caen-Troarn railway showed that the armoured division was not mobile enough. There was a need for fully tracked armoured personnel carriers and self-propelled artillery to be included in the armoured division. The war would end before this need was met. If infantry could have kept up with the tanks in APCs they could have cleared out some of the AT nests in the villages, but the APCs were not yet available. There were plenty of SP guns available, in fact some were being converted to APCs, but even if the need for them had been fully appreciated, they could not have been moved forward in time. This was very unfortunate, as the only way that tanks could have rushed the Bourguebus ridge would have been with the aid of a heavy artillery barrage. This barrage should have been of HE and smoke. The use of smoke seems to have been a two-edged sword at Normandy. It certainly could be a protection against long range AT gun fire, but it could reduce an attacking tank unit to chaos, and smoke could shelter panzerfausts as well as tanks

In this battle the Germans particularly dreaded infantry night attacks, but the British preferred not to use this mode. It could be that a better method of attack would have been by taking a series of small bites: infantry at night and tanks with air and artillery support by day.

The German defence was helped by the faulty British tactics. The commander of 11th Armoured Division, General Roberts, was not happy with the corps instructions with respect to the deployment of his infantry brigade but these apparently originated with Montgomery and do seem to be unnecessarily cautious. None the less he carried out his orders with the results outlined above. In his memoirs General Roberts says that he complained to the Corps Commander, General O'Connor, but was told that if he did not like it, then he, O'Connor, would get another armoured division to lead the operation. At that time 7th Armoured Division was under something of a cloud following the Villers-Bocage disaster and would soon be purged by Montgomery, and the Guards Armoured Division had only just landed, had no combat experience, and had a commander that Montgomery was not happy with. So, if O'Connor made this threat, it is difficult to see how he would have carried it out.

Certainly Roberts did not help himself. It could be that he felt under some personal pressure. His sluggishness in the pursuit after Supercharge and in Tunisia must have been commented on and, it could be, that he felt that he had to drive his armoured brigade forward. However by locating his HQ close to that of the armoured brigade, he effectively left his infantry brigade to its own devices. Had he kept his HQ a little to the rear he might have had better control over his infantry, and better liaison with the other armoured divisions.

The corps commander, General O'Connor, was the hero of Beda Fomm, and at least one participant believed that the planning was done by minds conditioned by the desert battles. However despite the fact that General O'Connor had spent some of the time since his desert victories as a prisoner of war, out of contact with tactical realities, he was well aware of the importance of infantry keeping up with the tanks and wanted to use some of the converted SP artillery gun carriages for this purpose. Unfortunately he was not allowed this though this method was used in the next major operation, possibly instigated by a more forceful commander. The apparent failure of Operation Goodwood was certainly not held against him.

General Roberts must have been disappointed in the way that his armoured brigade could not advance *'by the application of the principle of fire and movement at all levels from brigade down to troop.'* Also that there was an inevitable tendency to *'sit back and continue firing,'* and, as he put it, *'That will never get us on.'* No doubt when he drew up his Notes seven months earlier he could not anticipate Operation Goodwood, and it could be that, coming from the Royal Tank Corps and having commanded an armoured brigade in the desert, he did not really appreciate the importance of infantry/tank cooperation. This, of course, was to change.

On the basis of the results achieved it is difficult to fault the German tactics. There are, though, two points worth making. Firstly although the Germans did lay a small number of individual mines that caused some tank casualties, they did not lay any planned minefields. The reason for this might be that, due to Allied air attack of the railways, mines could not be brought from the central store at Verdun. Minefields could certainly have hindered their counter-attacks, but there must have been certain choke points, like the bridge the 3RTR went through the embankment of the Caen-Falaise railway, where a few mines could have had a great effect, even though there were a few flail tanks available. These were used as ordinary gun tanks. Secondly the Germans used no AT obstacles. Probably all the field engineers were fully occupied as infantry. Certainly the open, rolling countryside would have made building useful obstacles difficult.

If Operation Goodwood showed how effective large calibre AT guns could be, an incident a few days later, on 14th August, showed how their effectiveness could be improved by an obstacle. During Operation Tractable a small but muddy stream, the Laison, had to be crossed. This obstacle, slowing or halting the tanks within the range of a thin AT screen, caused heavy tank casualties. Tanks were to be seen frantically circling round searching for a crossing, all the while being shot at. One squadron lost 11 of its 19 tanks. This was particularly regrettable as there were AVREs available to fill the stream with fascines.

Note 1,

It will be noticed by readers familiar with accounts of this operation that this account omits the most famous incident of the operation, this is when Von Luck forces an AA battery commander, at pistol point, to stop shooting at planes and start shooting at tanks. This incident has been left out because this writer does not believe it.

Operation Garden
The Guards Armoured Division

In September 1944 the usually cautious Field Marshal Montgomery devised an audacious scheme to cross the Rhine and bypass the Siegfried Line. The scheme became Operation Market-Garden. The 'Market' part was the capture of certain bridges by paratroops, this was referred to as the 'airborne carpet'. The intention of 'Garden' was given in Lieutenant-General Sir Brian Horrocks' orders:

'XXX Corps, consisting of:

> *Guards Armoured Division*
> *50th Infantry Division*
> *43rd Infantry Division*
> *8th Armoured Brigade*
> *A Dutch Brigade*

will break out of the existing bridgehead on 17 September and pass through the airborne carpet which has been aid down in front of us, in order to seize the area Nunspeet-Arnhem and exploit north to the Zuider Zee.'

The operation was to be essentially an armoured thrust based on the Guards Armoured Division, and it is the progress, and failure, of this division which is the main subject of this chapter. *(see Sketch 6)*

The division was formed early in 1941. The Brigade of Guards was selected for conversion to armour because of its general quality, but it may be suspected that the guardsmen, who were tall fellows, would have been more comfortable inside tanks if they had been a little shorter. The initial plan was for the senior battalion in each regiment to convert to armour. This did not happen with the Welsh Guards which provided the reconnaissance regiment and converted later than the rest, nor did it happen with the Grenadiers. Their first battalion should have converted, but due to disturbances, probably as close as guardsmen come to mutiny, brought on by an excess of regimentalism in the sparse days following their return from Dunkirk, the honour went to the second battalion.

The first action of the Guards Armoured Division was Operation Goodwood. It went into it with the standard organisation of one armoured brigade and one infantry brigade, but during the battle its brigades became widely separated, resulting in its armoured brigade having far too little infantry support. Consequently the division decided to make some basic changes to its organisation.

General Adair's account gives the impression that the new organisation sprang into existence fully formed. That would be a slight overstatement. It evolved, but did so quickly. By the end of the Normandy campaign the division consisted of four groups, each of one armoured and one infantry battalion. Two groups made up a brigade. The groups were permanent, but could be allocated to brigades as required. The major units, for Operation Garden, were:

The Guards Armoured Division, Maj-Gen AHS Adair, DSO, MC
- 2nd Household Cavalry Regiment (Armoured cars)
- 5th Guards Armoured Brigade, Brig NW Gwatkin, MVO
  - *Grenadiers Group*
    - 1st Battalion, (Motor bn, halftracks)
    - 2nd Battalion (Shermans)
  - *Irish Group*
    - 2nd Battalion (Shermans)
    - 3rd Battalion (TCVs)
- 32nd Guards Brigade, commander Brig GF Johnson
  - *Coldstream Group*
    - 1st Battalion (Shermans)
    - 5th Battalion (TCVs)
  - *Welsh Group*
    - 1st Battalion (TCVs)
    - 2nd Battalion (recce bn, Cromwells)

The obvious advantage of this order of battle was that the units forming each group became used to working together.

The potential disadvantage was that, except for the Grenadiers Group, each armoured battalion was grouped with a unit on TCVs (lorries). As the campaign in NW Europe ground on the division developed a general reputation for sluggishness. It is difficult to know if this was a reaction based on the 'sour grapes' of non-guardsmen, or if this grouping of units naturally slowed the division down.

The groups without half-tracks tended to advance led by a squadron of tanks followed by one of two squadrons carrying infantry, then the remaining infantry in TCVs. Naturally when the first bullet was fired the infantry would dismount. Riding on tanks was never a satisfactory tactic but was used in Operation Garden.

On the morning of 16th September the corps commander, General Horrocks, addressed the bulk of the officers of the units involved and explained the details of the operation. Prior to this only a very few senior officers were in on the secret. The task facing the division was daunting. It held a bridge head over the Meuse-Escaut canal at Neerpelt. It would have to travel 64 miles to get to Arnhem. To do this it would have to cross six significant water obstacles, and some of these were major obstacles. They were:

> The Wilhelmina canal at Zon, approximate width, 80 feet,
> The Willems canal at Veghel, approximate width, 80 feet,
> The River Maas canal at Grave, approximate width, 800 feet,
> The Maas-Waal canal at Grave, approximate width, 200 feet,
> The River Waal canal at Nijmegen, approximate width, 850 feet,
> The Neder Rijn canal at Arnhem, approximate width, 300 feet,

Each bridge was, of course, a potential demolition. The essence of the plan was that bridges on the main obstacles, at Grave, Nijmegen and Arnhem, would be captured by paratroops. This very fact resulted in a very tight timescale for the operation. One paragraph of General Horrocks' orders read:

(d) Speed absolutely vital, as we must reach the lightly equipped 1st British Airborne Division (at Arnhem) *if possible in forty-eight hours.'* He emphasised this several times.

With this limitation in mind the logistics can be seen to be appalling. The 30th Corps had over 20,000 vehicles, including 2,300 carrying bulky bridging materials, all of which had to use the one road. The organisation of the transport given such a short time was a triumph, the result of many cold and boring exercises in England before Normandy.

The operation started on the 17th September. A remarkable fact about the planning of Operation Garden was that the Guards Armoured Division had been stationary at a bridgehead formed over the Meuse-Escaut canal (this being in Belgium the Maas was in French) close to Neerpelt since 10th September. The bridge had been captured by a surprise charge of tanks of the Irish Guards commanded by Col J.O.E. Vandeleur. The corps commander was so impressed that he ordered that the bridge should be called 'Joe's Bridge'. The Guards, having beaten off a counter-attack next morning, and finding that there was little in front of them wanted to exploit their success, pass a full brigade across the canal, and possibly continue the advance. However a large number of Germans had been by-passed and the corps commander considered that proceeding on that basis was too risky. A brigade, or even a division, could be cut off from its supplies and annihilated if it were operating along a single road.

This halt order may have been sensible, but if it was, the whole concept of Operation Garden would be called into question. However that may be the forward troops stayed unmoving until the 17th when the airborne assault was to start at 1.0 pm and the Guards Armoured Division attacked one and a half hours later. It is not obvious why the assault could not have gone in at dawn. It might be objected that by doing so the Germans would be alerted to the aim of the operation, but that would be very unlikely, and if they were there was little they could have done about it. Given that the plan was to be in Arnhem by dusk on 19th September, the division must have expected to reach Zon, 20 miles (32 km) away, by the end of the first day, and the sun set around 6.0 pm. The tactics used made this impossible.

The first obstacle the troops would meet after passing through the German front line was the small river Dommel, about 4.5 km away. There had been a problem in that aerial reconnaissance could not ascertain if the bridge was still usable, so on 11th September two Household Cavalry scout cars drove up the main road, through the German front line, and checked beyond doubt that it was usable, they actually saw German vehicles driving over it. They drove back again through the same German troops who seem to have been remarkably lackadaisical. This showed that the piercing of the German front should not be too difficult, and there were no mines. This was fortunate. Making a set piece assault is a task for infantry, and infantry tanks. Naturally an armoured division had none of the latter and not that many of the former so, if a hard fight to get through the German front line was expected it would be best undertaken by an infantry division.

To make up for the absence of infantry the provision of artillery and aerial support was prodigious. The artillery support consisted of eleven field and six medium batteries, and the heavy mortars of the Guards and the 50th division. The air support consisted of seven squadrons of rocket-firing Typhoons, controlled from the ground by the leader of one of the squadrons. The results showed what could be achieved when control was properly set up.

At 12.45pm the Typhoons appeared and shot up anything visible, then at 2.15 the artillery started. At 2.35 the first group, the Irish, moved off. They advanced at 8 mph, keeping up with the creeping barrage. All initially went smoothly. They passed a row of eight 75-mm AT guns along the edge of the road where they were stuck due to lack of transport. They had been destroyed by the Typhoons. Two 88s were also knocked out. The barrage was moving forward at 20 yards a minute which was quite fast.

Probably this easy passage for the tanks resulted in a lack of caution as after about 1.5 km the tanks were ambushed by infantry with panzerfausts. They let the first few tanks of the leading squadron pass, then knocked out the last three, and the first six of the following squadron. The Germans were driven off by the Typhoons, but they had plenty of time to round up the surviving crewmen.

What is really startling is that the Germans, who were a scratch unit, were confident enough to fall back a bit and repeat the ambush hitting two armoured cars. A little later a company of self-propelled guns (StuG IVs) formed a defensive line in front of Valkensward and knocked out four Shermans. The StuGs pulled back after one had been hit by the 17-pdr of a Sherman Firefly and the rest came under aerial attack.

The planes also hit two Shermans. Probably the recognition panels were not easily visible from the air. The crews identified themselves with yellow smoke, but this would only work when the tanks were stationary. This sort of accident would still be occurring during mobile operations decades later.

After this the barrage was restarted and the Dommel was crossed at 7.30 and Valkenswaard occupied. There were some disorganised Germans there, but they were quickly rounded up. The German command was also in some degree of confusion. The commander at Eindhoven phoned the post office at Valkenswaard with a message for the garrison that they should hold on at all costs as reinforcements were *en route*. If reinforcements were sent they must have been recalled.

The Guards stayed in Valkenswaard overnight, uneasily aware that there were more Germans around, and fighting harder, than expected. Obviously it would have been better if they had kept going, as officers on the spot wanted to, but Corps HQ ordered them not to. There were sound reasons for this. The Irish Guards were low on ammunition and resupply was slow due to the already impressive traffic jams on the single road. The British Army was against the use of tanks at night and in this case, when the tanks would have been on a road raised above the surrounding fields and forced to use headlights, this prejudice was justified. The tanks would have been as vulnerable as moving targets on a range.

Also the infantry battalion that should have occupied Valkenswaard was late. This seems to have been a result of excessive caution. The battalion was held back to protect a field battery overnight instead of being hurried forward to its objective and the battery told to defend itself.

When the halt order was given it was not appreciated that the Zon bridge was down, but this was to change. A patrol from the Household Cavalry (HCR) had made contact with the US paratroops at Zon and on returning gave the division a telephone number in Zon. This number was a contact with the Americans who supplied information about the bridge. Once it was known that the bridge was down it may have been judged that there would have been few German armoured vehicles or mobile artillery to the south of the Wilhelmina Canal and no reinforcements coming from the north, had it been known earlier a risk may have been taken and the advance continued.

The advance was planned to begin again at dawn, 5.30 18th September. The Irish group was to continue north up the main road to Eindhoven. The 32nd Brigade, led by the Welsh group, with Cromwell tanks, went on a loop round to the right but had little success. Their route ran through the village of Leende and they were stopped by a StuG, and attempts to find an alternative route failed because of the many wide ditches. The bridges over these were not strong and one collapsed under a Cromwell. The group was recalled to the main road.

The morning mist was very thick, and this slowed things down considerably. The advance was led by a troop of the HCR, around one and a half miles in front of the Irish group. The leading scout car saw a Panther and two StuGs on a side road close to Aalst. The HCR troop waited for the Irish Guards, who turned out to be led by their infantry battalion, probably because of the closer nature of the country. As the HCR were explaining the situation the German AFVs trundled off to Aalst.

Aalst should have been strongly defended. Not only were there the three AFVs but also eleven 75-mm AT guns and some 20-mm guns. There was a delay of two hours while the Irish Guards tanks were brought forwards during which Aalst was shelled by two regiments of 25-pdrs. When the tanks arrived a Firefly knocked out a StuG and an infantry/tank assault swept through the village, the defenders fading away.

While the Irish group was halted before Aalst, an attempt was made to by-pass it. A HCR unit had found a road round to the west of Eindhoven by which they were in contact with the Americans. The group following the Irish, the Grenadiers, tried to follow this route but could make little progress. One of the bridges that the armoured cars of the HCR could use gave away under the weight of a Sherman, fortunately the crew was saved. A few bridging tanks would have made a vast difference. The Grenadiers rejoined the main column when Eindhoven was cleared.

With Aalst occupied the pressure was on to get to Eindhoven, but there was the obstacle of the Dommel just to the north of Aalst. The bridge was covered by a StuG and probably eight 88s, some in concrete emplacements. It is possible that these were a part of the outer ring of defences round Eindhoven. They were discovered by the HCR who directed artillery on them with the aid of a knowledgeable Dutch civilian. An infantry company was sent to outflank the defences but the artillery was enough and soon the Germans abandoned their guns and the Irish Guards were pounding up the road to Eindhoven, which had just been captured by the US Paratroops.

First a recce squadron then the Irish Guards drove as quickly as possible through Eindhoven, their only hindrance being jubilant Dutch crowds. As telephone communications had been established with the Americans and it was known that the bridge over the Wilhelmina Canal at Zon was down, it was now urgent to get to Zon, which was done by dusk, and get the bridging train there so that the bridge could be replaced overnight. This would be a major task.

The bridge at Zon was completed at 5.50 am, 19th September, a day late, and the advance resumed at ten minutes later. The lead was taken by the Grenadiers group. They crossed the Dommel, again, at St Oedenrode, the Willemsvaart Canal, the river Aa at Veghel, and some minor obstacles, all on bridges held by paratroops who cheered them on. The route was under sporadic attack from German infantry, but the advance was not slowed. The spearhead arrived at Grave and crossed the Maas at 8.30am. The airborne carpet seemed to be working well.

Unfortunately a halt was made at Grave because Lt Gen Browning, the commander of the Airborne Corps, wanted to speak to the two Colonels of the Grenadiers group. General Browning had his HQ set up five miles south of Nijmegen. He told the colonels that a bridge on the route they had planned to use was damaged beyond use and they would have to use another about three kilometres to the south. This was done and by midday the Grenadiers group was just to the south of Nijmegen.

At this point the corps, division and brigade commanders all converged on General Browning's HQ to consider the situation and the next step. The airborne carpet had not worked in Nijmegen, and the Americans were only in command of some of its outskirts, their comparative lack of success here is still a matter of some controversy. There were two bridges and it was naturally important to capture both of them before the Germans destroyed them. The road bridge to the east was the most important. As speed was essential the plan was for an armoured charge at the southern ends of both bridges.

Only one squadron of tanks was to be deployed, the bulk of it at the road bridge. This might seem a small force to be employed on such an important task, but tanks are difficult to use in built-up areas. It might be wondered if the remainder could not have been used in probing and feint attacks. The assault started at 4.0 pm and both groups set off at speed, the tanks carrying US paratroops and the guardsmen following in half-tracks.

Both these attacks failed. The main one was halted at a large roundabout about 300 yards south of the road bridge. The Germans had used old fortifications, modern buildings and fieldworks to construct a strong position including several AT guns and two self-propelled guns. The three tanks of the leading troop were knocked out and the troop leader killed. An attempt at out-flanking failed and the troops settled down for the night where they were.

The assault on the railway bridge was similar. The tanks were halted by the obstacle of the railway embankment, and two were lost when they were hit by a battery to the north of the Waal. The infantry were not strong enough to advance without them. This force was pulled back a short distance and stayed there overnight actually surrounded by German soldiers who had infiltrated round behind it.

By the end of the day's fighting it was plain that the bridges could not be captured that way. Yet the situation at Arnhem was becoming desperate. The paratroops there had been isolated for two days. Something had to be done.

On the afternoon of this day glider-borne elements of 1st Polish Brigade had landed at Oosterbeek. They had suffered heavy casualties and achieved little. If they had landed just to the north of the bridges at Nijmegen things might have been different.

If progress had been halted at Nijmegen, the situation at Zon was becoming threatening. Here the Germans were mounting a counter-attack which, with a little luck, could have defeated Operation Garden

A panzer brigade, number 107, was under orders for the eastern front when Operation Garden started. Its main units were a battalion of 40 Panthers and a battalion of armoured infantry with some supporting assault guns. The next day, unfortunately after its workshop company had already gone east, the brigade was ordered west to oppose Garden by attacking its main supply axis.

By dusk on 19th September the Panther battalion was concentrated four miles to the east of Zon. Its aim was to destroy the bridge. The Germans had the advantages of surprise and the bad weather which would prevent allied air support. They suffered from the disadvantage, which they share with the British, of the very soft going for tanks, although the wide tracks of the Panthers might have made this more manageable. The brigade structure also had the disadvantage of few infantry and no artillery.

The brigade had to act quickly, 40 tanks with associated vehicles are impossible to hide for any period of time. A troop of Cromwells of the 15th/19th The King's Royal Hussars, operating with 231st Brigade on the right flank of the Guards, had run into some of the Panthers and lost two tanks, so the brigade commander knew he had to get moving, but when it came to it his options were limited. He had to approach the bridge from the south-east, but couldn't deploy because of the obstacle of the Dommel. He anticipated crossing the canal by the secondary bridge about half a mile to the east of the main one, but his reconnaissance found that this was down. The only approach open to him was along the tow-path, and he launched an assault there as soon as possible, at last light.

The Germans attacked with a company of dismounted infantry and a platoon of tanks. The remaining tanks were to provide HE support to make up for the lack of artillery. This very nearly succeeded. The leading tanks got to within 200 yards of the bridge and they certainly stopped traffic crossing for a short time. An ammunition truck was hit while actually on the bridge and burst into flames. But the US paratroops fought back magnificently. Initially, being surprised, they had only small arms, but that was enough to drive back the German infantry and without their accompanying infantry the tanks would have great trouble defending themselves. Then the Americans wheeled up a 57-mm AT gun, the equivalent of the British 6-pdr, and, firing across the canal and hitting its thin side armour, knocked out the leading tank.

The second tank was knocked out by bazooka fire. This was enough to cause the rest to pull back which, in view of the difficulty of using tanks at night, in a built-up area in the face of determined infantry, and in such muddy conditions, was the only reasonable decision. This raid caused significant disruption to the flow of traffic.

That night the Luftwaffe bombed Eindhoven, disrupting the flow of traffic even more and next morning the Germans tried again, but this time the defenders were ready for them. Not only had they got several AT guns in position but they had been joined by a squadron of the 15/19 Hussars and a battery of 25-pdrs from 231 brigade. The attack failed with the loss of four Panthers.

The plan for the next day, 20th September, saw the Grenadier Guards and the American battalion ordered to continue clearing Nijmegen, and be ready to assault the bridges but not until the northern ends had been captured by the Americans. The bulk of the Americans were to move to the west of Nijmegen and prepare to cross the river on assault boats, which they would be totally unfamiliar with, to be brought up by the Royal Engineers. They were to be given fire support by two squadrons of the Irish Guards.

32nd Brigade was to send the Coldstream group to support US units to the east of Nijmegen where counter-attacks seemed to be developing, and the Welsh group, standing in reserve, was to be responsible for the defence of Grave.

Clearing Nijmegen started at 8.30 am and, in contrast to the previous day, was undertaken in a painstaking and deliberate way. At 3.30 pm the US troops commenced crossing the river. This was carried out in a magnificent manner even though the smoke screen was not effective, and by 6.0pm they were moving east towards the northern end of the road bridge.

The assault through Nijmegen was progressing well and by 7.0 pm was close to the south end of the bridge, when a US flag was believed to have been seen at the northern end. Actually it was at the railway bridge. As darkness was falling four tanks pounded across the bridge. The first two made it, the second two were hit, possibly by panzerfausts, and abandoned, though the driver of one got back in when he saw that it was not burning and continued across the bridge. That German infantrymen tried to resist the tanks is demonstrated by one of them being killed by the loader of the point tank shooting through a port-hole with his revolver. The leading tanks were followed by a further one commanded by the squadron 2 i/c, Captain the Lord Carrington, who was later to have an illustrious career in politics, a scout car carrying an RE officer, and a troop of 'Archers', self-propelled 17-pdr AT guns, then some infantry.

Engineers quickly set to work making safe the demolition charges. It is not clear why the bridge was not blown. It was claimed, many years ago, that a Dutchman with a grudge against the Germans broke one of the electric cables, but this has yet to be confirmed. The link-up with the Americans was almost disastrous as, before the US troops recognised the tanks as British, they made a start at attacking them with gelignite.

The rest of the tank squadron followed the leading echelon and after crossing the bridge they pulled off the road and the crews brewed up and commenced maintenance. The Americans were incensed seeing the fruits of their hard-won victory being thrown away, and discussed the matter forcibly with Lord Carrington. However the halt order came from the Corps Commander and was based on a sound appreciation of the situation.

The traffic delays and chaos caused largely by the German counter-attacks had had two unfortunate effects. One was that the leading troops were short of ammunition and artillery support. The other was that 43rd Division was delayed. The ground north of Nijmegen was particularly unsuitable for tanks being marshy with the roads built on embankments so that it was impossible for the tanks to deploy off them. Consequently it was planned that this infantry division should takeover the lead.

Adding to these problems was the fact that the German counter-attacks aimed at Nijmegen were making progress. Consequently the British tanks made no move overnight, or next morning.

Next day, the 21st September, infantry assaults at both ends captured the railway bridge. The Irish group took over the lead from the Grenadiers who were disorganised and short of ammunition following the previous day's fighting in Nijmegen. They were to lead the attack up the main road to Arnhem, moving off at 1.30 pm, but it was too late, the paratroops there had already surrendered.

This attack was bound to be difficult. There was little artillery support, only one medium battery, though a field battery would come up later. Worse there was little air support, it is not known why, but it might be due to advanced airstrips not being useable. Air support had been vital to the original break out. During the afternoon around half the Polish Paratroop Brigade was dropped to the south of the Neder Rijn. Unfortunately they could offer no assistance either to the airborne troops to the north of the Neder Rijn or to the Guards Armoured Division to the south, suffering heavy casualties pointlessly.

As tanks could not deploy off the road, the advance had to take the form of a procession with a squadron of tanks leading followed by two squadron-company groups. The result was predictable, just as the crewmen realised when they heard their orders and muttered it was 'suicide'. After about two miles all three tanks of the leading troop were knocked out. The remaining tanks halted. The countryside was too open for an infantry flanking move, and there was not enough artillery to shoot them forwards. Finally it was impossible to contact what few Typhoons there were available due to a radio fault. A second contact car was called forward, but when it arrived it was equally useless. The Irish group made no further progress. The other group, the Welsh, which had taken the place of the Grenadiers in 5th Brigade, made a little progress along a minor road to the west, and managed to assist a US paratroop unit which was under attack by tanks. It destroyed four. Even so, so little progress was made that the corps commander decided that Arnhem could not be reached by the Guards and instructed the 43rd Division to advance in the direction of Oosterbeek. This was the admission that the main armoured thrust of the Guards Armoured Division had failed.

This was not the end of Operation Garden. The 43rd Division fought its way through to the banks of the Rhine opposite Oosterbeek where it assisted in the evacuation of the airborne troops. It was not even the end of the use of armour in Operation

Garden. Not only were there tanks supporting 43rd Division but, on subsequent days when the Germans made concerted efforts to break the main supply line south of Nijmegen, tanks from 231 Brigade proved decisive. But these were secondary actions.

It would be easy, with the wisdom of hindsight, to take the view that Operation Market Garden was doomed to failure, but that would be unreasonably pessimistic. Perhaps Horrock's 48 hour target was too tight but it would have been reasonable for the Guards Armoured Division to have had a brigade in Arnhem on the 19th had there been no delay at Nijmegen.

The plan certainly involved serious risks, and involved overcoming a large degree of Clausewitzian friction, but the Guards were making fair progress. The plan failed because the airborne forces did not achieve all they should have. A recent study has shown that the Americans could have had Nijmegen bridge on the 17th but their orders made it plain that defending the Groesbeek area was more important and the opportunity was let slip.[1] Nearly as bad the British paratroop battalions which landed at Oosterbeek were so sluggish that only one, with one company of another, made it to the Arnhem bridge despite achieving total surprise. If three battalions had made it they would have been able to defend a perimeter large enough for the RAF to drop supplies of ammunition into. That would have allowed a little more flexibility into the operation.[2]

Finally the Polish Brigade, held in reserve, could have been dropped to the rear of the Germans attacking Eindhoven.

It would seem that the operation could have succeeded, but it is open to doubt how much of a war-winner it would have been. To have, say, two brigades at Arnhem and the equivalent at

Nijmegen would not change the basic fact that Allied supplies were still coming from Normandy on a vulnerable road and there was still a German army to the west. To illustrate the potential supply problems, a few weeks after the operation a daring raid by some German frogmen brought the Nijmegen bridge down. Montgomery may well have found that his forced were out of balance, and if the Germans had decided to deploy their armoured reserves on the Dutch front rather than the Ardennes then military history may have taken an interesting turn. That, of course, is pure speculation.

To return to more practical considerations, there was only one measure that the Guards Armoured Division could have taken which might have improved its effectiveness. As has been seen on two occasions an infantry/ tank group was deployed on minor roads flanking the main route. One infantry battalion, 1st Grenadiers, being the original motor battalion was mounted on half-tracks. This would have made the Grenadier Group the most mobile in the division even though half-tracks could not keep up with tanks cross-country. If this group had been designated for employment off the main road, and given a couple of bridging tanks, it might have proven highly effective and played a major part in keeping the division moving.

Such considerations underline how invalid the original concept Cruiser Tank Warfare had become.

Notes

1 RG Poulussen, Lost at Nijmegen, e-book only

2 RJ Kershaw, It Never Snows in September, Ian Allen, 1994

Chapter 12

Conclusion

It would be easy to say that Cruiser Tank Warfare was a total failure, but that would be something of an overstatement. Even so the fact is that the British armoured divisions were never as effective as they should have been

The previous pages have attempted to summarise the history of the concept, the essential points were:

The statement of the concept in Modern Formations

The design of Cruiser tanks to fit the concept, conforming to financial limitations

The meretricious success of the Wavell Offensive

The failure of the evolution of armoured divisions.

Each of these points deserves a few comments.

The Cruiser Tank Warfare concept seems to have been the output of the musings of a small circle of RTC officers, and pundits like Captain Liddell Hart. They were acting under the influence of several forces. One was to ensure the continued existence of the RTC, another was to find an alternative to the attrition of the Western Front. Also, it may be supposed, though only on the basis of the rather slender evidence of the tone of some of their writing, that they enjoyed flaunting their supposed intellectual superiority.

However these musings came about they led to the 'small armies' fallacy which, in its turn, led to the twin beliefs that, on an operational scale, movement could replace fighting, and with the design of tanks, speed could replace armour.

Tank design suffered from the financial limitations which obtained nearly to the end of the inter-war period but this difficulty should not be used as an excuse for lack of clear thinking. Imaginative exercises could have been designed which would have shown that speed could not replace armour and that tanks should be designed around the best dual-purpose gun available. The Russians managed this. Once the characteristics of the new tanks were known, even if production was very limited, then further exercises could have been held to develop tactical drills.

The Wavell Offensive was a great victory and occurred just when such a success was really needed, however a cooler assessment would have shown that it was the result of an unreasonable deployment on the part of the Italians. This is not to detract from the fine judgement and iron nerve displayed by General Wavell and his commanders, but the British Cruiser Tank formations and methods that were so successful in this offensive would not work against the Germans, or even the later Italians.

There can be no denying the steady improvements of the British armoured divisions. This process ran through many defeats in the desert and many exercises in England, but they never approached the modern ideal of balanced all-arms formations. This was for a number of reasons, most significantly because of the lack of APCs for the infantry and, one suspects, a less than whole-hearted commitment from the RAF to ground support.

These four essential points dominated the history of the Cruiser Tank Warfare concept which lasted for only a short time. It may be taken as having been born in 1929 with the publication of 'Mechanised and Armoured Formations'. It had passed its peak by June 1944 and can be said to have died, along with many soldiers, in Operation Goodwood, when the armoured division commanders realised the limitations of tank-heavy armoured brigades. The example of Operation Garden has been given to confirm this.

Despite these points Cruiser Tank Warfare could work quite well against an enemy that was not trained, organised or equipped to cope with it. This was, though, a fleeting window of opportunity. The Germans, who had put their faith in droves of fast light tanks, realised that after the fall of France the window had closed and quickly started gearing up for realistic armoured warfare. The British army was slowed to detect the trend.

As has been seen there were three defining aspects of Cruiser Tank Warfare. These being the breakthrough, then what was slightly misleadingly termed 'exploitation', and finally the pursuit.

The breakthrough was normally to be conducted by infantry, but in the desert campaigns before Alamein, when there was always an open flank, this stage could be replaced by a tank battle. In such battles history showed that British tank units were consistently out-fought by German ones. There were occasions when the German tanks carried superior main armaments, but their success was usually down to their inter-arm cooperation. That the subject of the tank battle was ignored in 'Modern Formations' and treated so superficially in the ATI must be an indication that tank tactics were not given due weight before the war. Further, the trivial comments about the deployment of artillery in the tank action, given in the ATI, seem to indicate a narrow mindset that would hinder future developments.

The exploitation stage was as important as the tank battle, however it must be agreed that the belief in this stage expressed in Modern Formations was based on pure faith. It was found in actual operations that the act of placing a Cruiser Tank unit on the enemy's flank or rear just did not cause the defence to buckle. In considering events the Wavell campaign may be ignored because of the mismatch of the forces involved. In both of the desert campaigns considered, Crusader and Gazala, the attacking armour placed itself in position where, according to Modern Formations, the defenders should have seen sense and fled. In neither case did that happed, and the battles turned into attrition slugging matches which the Germans were better at.

'Modern Formations' did recognise that the Cruiser Tanks might come up against dug-in enemy that the tanks could not handle. Its solution was for the tanks to contain the position until infantry could come up to assault it. It did not seriously consider the difficulties in keeping the armoured troops moving by launching and supporting an infantry assault. There can be little doubt that the lack of clear thinking on this subject blighted British armoured operations right up to the end of the war.

Such a situation would be similar to Rommel's assault on 150th Brigade's position in the Cauldron battle with the 90th Light Division and elements of the DAK. No British armoured division could have managed this because of its small infantry component and the lack of infantry APCs.

Actual experience of war produced something of a variation on the exploitation theme. Montgomery's preferred use of tanks was to mount a short thrust into the enemy's lines to seize some important land, then to rush infantry forward to dig in and invite a counter-attack.

It was inevitable that Cruiser Tank units would be the prime means of pursuit and pursuit was the most successful application of Cruiser Tank Warfare. However the possibility of a successful pursuit was drastically reduced by tanks being reluctant to move at night. Some of the exercises held in 1934 involved long night marches and in Operation Compass some British armoured units undertook impressive night actions. Others were reluctant. However as the war progressed the bias against employing tanks at night increased. Even so the pursuit to El Hamma, in Tunisia, and the first phase of Operation Totalize, in Normandy, were conducted at night. Perhaps more should have been made of night fighting.

Because of this, and because of the natural tendency for retreating units to be able to move faster than their pursuers, Cruisers in pursuit could manage little more than following up a defeated enemy. Montgomery's policy of defeating, and destroying, the enemy on the battlefield may very well have been forced on him by the nature of the forces he commanded, but there is no doubt that it was the correct one. It was also a policy that can be regarded as being exactly the opposite of Cruiser Tank Warfare as envisaged in 'Modern Formations'.

Montgomery's conclusion was shared by the Germans. They became less interested in deep penetration on a single axis, and preferred several more limited assaults to chop the front up into segments which could be surrounded and destroyed separately, and the enemy would be prevented from moving troops along the front laterally. Presumably this policy was forced on the Germans by circumstances, and their increasing reliance on panzer brigades.

The conclusion to all this must be that Cruiser Tank Warfare was of limited application, being little more than a means of pursuit of a broken enemy. The really disappointing aspect of Cruiser Tank Warfare was that armoured divisions did not, during the war, evolve into early versions of modern armoured divisions, that is fully mobile, highly flexible, all-arms units. It would be easy to claim that the relative poverty of the UK made it impossible to supply the vehicles required, but that would not really be true. By late 1944 everything needed for a modern armoured division was available. The essentials may be listed as:

Tanks, the Sherman and Comet were fast reliable vehicles, with dual-purpose main armaments and radios.

APCs, significant numbers of turretless tanks or disarmed self-propelled artillery hulls, known as 'Kangaroos'[1], were available, widely used and well thought of.

Air Support, ground attack aircraft, most notable the rocket firing version of the Typhoon, were available and, most importantly, a system devised to control them from AFVs.

In the last few months of the war progress was made in Italy, by the 78th Division, in bringing these elements together to form an integrated unit. But in NW Europe, despite the availability of all these elements they were not brought together on a permanent basis to form the first modern British armoured division. Perhaps if the war had lasted a few months longer they would have been. Perhaps it was the lingering image of Cruiser Tank Warfare that prevented it.

Note 1

'Kangaroo' was the code for the Canadian workshop at Normandy that first produced these vehicles.

Sketch Maps

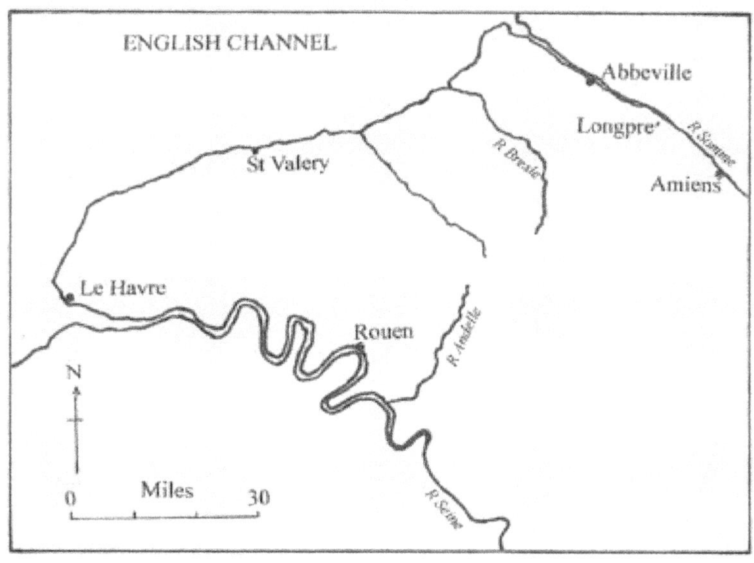

Map 1
France between the Somme and the Seine

Map 2
The Desert

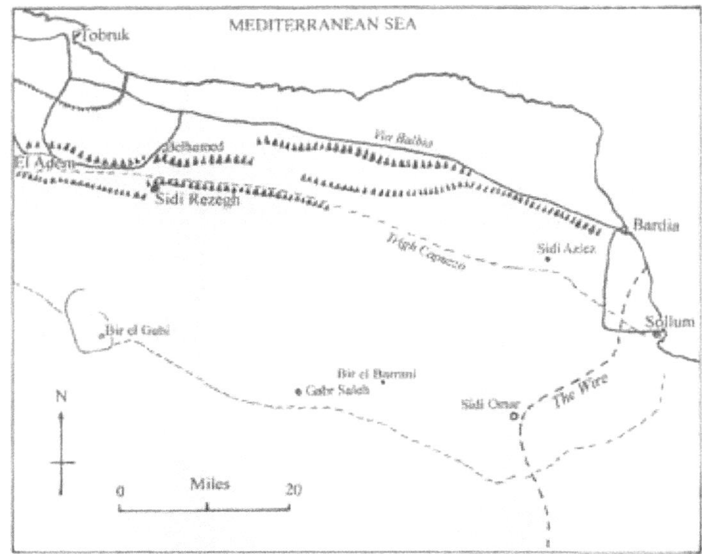

Map 3
Operation Crusader

Map 4
The Gazala Battlefield

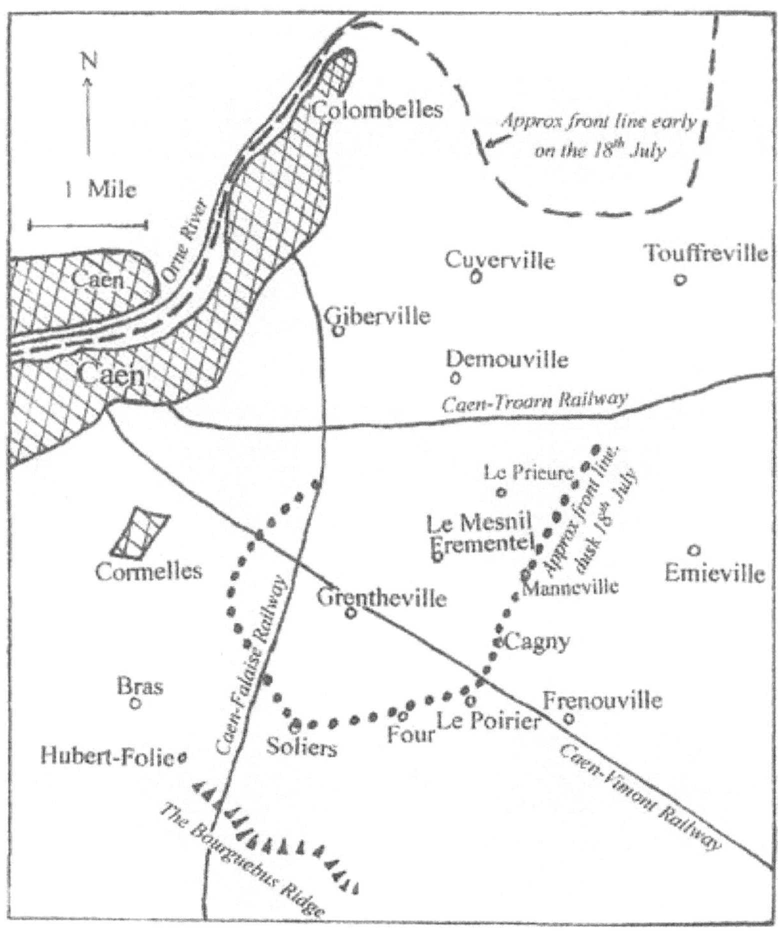

Map 5
Operation Goodwood

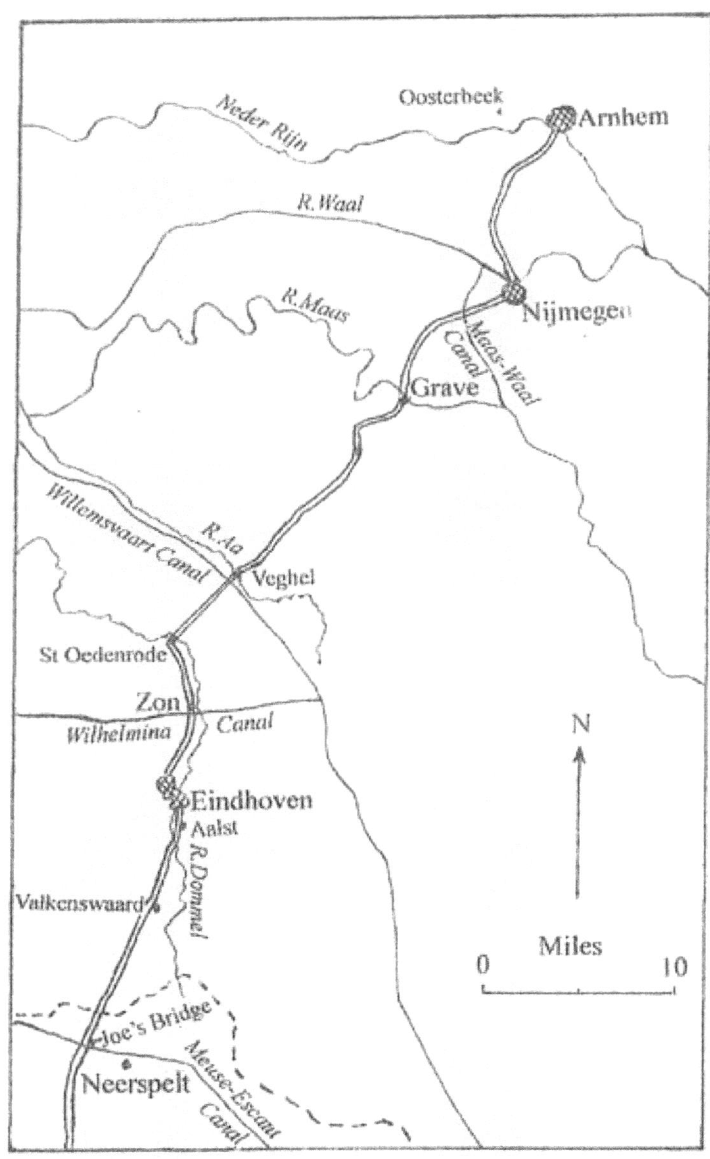

Map 6
Operation Garden

CPSIA information can be obtained
at www.ICGtesting.com
Printed in the USA
BVHW07s2126080718
521083BV00002B/157/P

9 781910 394175